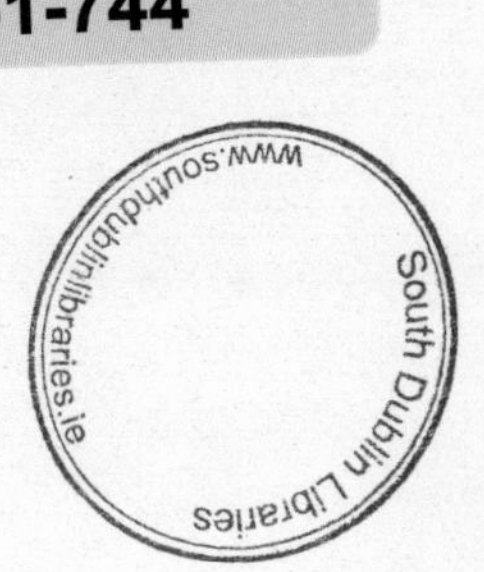


# THE NIGHT HOUSE

## ALSO BY JO NESBO

### HARRY HOLE THRILLERS

The Bat

Cockroaches

The Redbreast

Nemesis

The Devil's Star

The Redeemer

The Snowman

The Leopard

Phantom

Police

The Thirst

Knife

Killing Moon

### STANDALONE CRIME

Headhunters

The Son

Blood on Snow

Midnight Sun

Macbeth

The Kingdom

### STORIES

The Jealousy Man

# THE NIGHT HOUSE

JO NESBO

*Translated from the Norwegian by Neil Smith*

Harvill
*Secker*

1 3 5 7 9 10 8 6 4 2

Harvill Secker, an imprint of Vintage, is part of the Penguin Random House group of companies
whose addresses can be found at global.penguinrandomhouse.com

First published by Harvill Secker in 2023

First published in Norway by H. Aschehoug & Co (W. Nygaard), Oslo, as *Natthuset* in 2023



penguin.co.uk/vintage

A CIP catalogue record for this book is available from the British Library

HB ISBN 9781787303744
TPB ISBN 9781787303751

Typeset in 12/16pt Adobe Scala Pro by Jouve UK, Milton Keynes
Printed and bound in Great Britain by Clays Ltd, Elcograf S.p.A.

The authorised representative in the EEA is Penguin Random House Ireland,
Morrison Chambers, 32 Nassau Street, Dublin D02 YH68

Penguin Random House is committed to a sustainable
future for our business, our readers and our planet. This book
is made from Forest Stewardship Council® certified paper.

# THE NIGHT HOUSE

# PART ONE

# 1

'Y-Y-Y-YOU'RE CRAZY,' TOM SAID, AND I could tell he was scared, seeing as he stammered one more time than he usually does.

I was still holding the Luke Skywalker figure above my head, ready to throw it upstream, against the current. A scream echoed from within the dense forest that surrounded the river on both sides, as if in warning. It sounded like a crow. But I wasn't about to let myself be deterred, by either Toms or crows, I wanted to see if Luke Skywalker could swim. So now he was flying through the air. The spring sun had sunk towards the tops of the trees that had just come into leaf, and every now and then the light glinted off the slowly rotating figure.

Luke hit the water with a small *plop*, so he definitely couldn't fly. We couldn't see him, just the rippling circles on the surface of the river, which was running high with meltwater and made me think of a thick boa constrictor, an anaconda, slithering towards us.

I had moved to live with my relatives in this little shithole last year, just after my fourteenth birthday, and I had no idea what shitty little kids in shitholes like Ballantyne did to stop themselves from being bored to death. But seeing as Tom had told me that now, in the sp-sp-spring, the river was scary and dangerous and that he had been given strict orders at home to stay away, that gave me somewhere to start, at least. It hadn't been particularly hard to persuade Tom, because he was like me, friendless and a member of the pariah caste in class. During a break earlier today Fatso told me about castes, only he said I was in the *piranha* caste, and that made me think of those fish that look like they have sawblades for teeth and can strip the flesh from an ox in a matter of minutes, so I couldn't help thinking it sounded like a pretty cool caste. It wasn't until Fatso said that I and my caste were lower than him, the big lard-arse, that I was obliged to hit him. Unfortunately he told our teacher, Miss Birdsong, as I call her, and she gave the class a long lecture about being kind and what happened to people who weren't kind – the short version is that they end up losers – and after that there was basically no doubt that the new bully from the city belonged in the piranha caste.

After school, Tom and I had gone down to the river and out onto the little wooden bridge in the forest. When I got Luke Skywalker out of my bag, Tom's eyes opened wide.

'W-w-where did you get that?'

'Where do think, meathead?'

'Y-y-you didn't buy it at Oscar's. They've sold out.'

'Oscar's? That little rathole?' I laughed. 'Maybe I bought it in the city before I moved here, from a *proper* toyshop.'

'No, because that one's this year's model.'

I looked at Luke more closely. Was it true that the same figure had been issued in a new version? Wasn't Luke Skywalker the same stupid hero Luke Skywalker the whole time, forever and ever, amen? I'd never thought about that. That things could change. That Darth and Luke could change places, for instance.

'Maybe I got hold of a p-p-prototype,' I said.

Tom looked like I'd hit him; I guess he didn't like me imitating his stammer. I didn't like it either, I just couldn't help it. It's always been like that. If people didn't already dislike me, I soon made sure that they did, it's the same sort of reflex that made people like Karen and Oscar Jr smile and be nice so that everyone liked them, only the opposite. It wasn't that I didn't *want* to be liked, it was just that I knew they weren't going to like me anyway. So I kind of pre-empted them: I got them to dislike me on *my* terms. So they hated me, but at the same time they were a bit scared of me and didn't dare mess with me. Like now, when I could see that Tom knew I'd stolen the Luke figure, but didn't actually dare say so out loud. I had taken it during the class party at Oscar Jr's house, where everyone – even those of us in the piranha caste – was invited. The house was OK, it wasn't so big and fancy that it was a problem, but the most irritating thing was that Oscar's parents were so overbearing and the whole place was full of the very coolest toys, the best toyshop a father could ever provide, basically. Transformers figures, Atari games, Magic 8-Ball, even a Nintendo Game Boy, although that wasn't actually on the market yet. What would Oscar care if he lost one of those toys? – he'd hardly even notice. OK, maybe he would care if he lost the Luke Skywalker figure I had spotted tucked up in his bed like a stuffed toy. I mean, how childish can you get?

'Th-th-there it is!' Tom was pointing.

Luke's head was above water, and he was drifting towards us at great speed, as if he was doing the backstroke in the river.

'Good for Luke,' I said.

The figure disappeared under the bridge. We moved to the other side, and he reappeared. Looking up at us with that stupid half-smile. Stupid, because heroes aren't supposed to smile, they're supposed to fight, they're supposed to have tough fighters' faces, they're supposed to show that they hate their enemies as much as they hate . . . whatever.

We stood and watched as Luke drifted away from us. Towards the world out there, towards the unknown. Towards the darkness, I thought.

'What do we do now?' I asked. I already had ants in my pants, and I needed to get rid of them, and the only way for that to happen was if something *happened*, something that made me think about something else.

'I-I-I have to go home,' Tom said.

'Not yet,' I said. 'Follow me.'

I don't know why I found myself thinking about the telephone box that stood on the hill next to the main road at the edge of the forest. It was a strange place to put a phone box in somewhere as small as Ballantyne, and I had never seen anyone use it, I'd hardly ever seen anyone near it, just the occasional car. By the time we reached the red telephone box, the sun had sunk even lower, it was so early in the spring that it still got dark early. Tom was trudging reluctantly after me, he probably didn't dare contradict me. And, as I said, neither of us was exactly drowning in friends.

We squeezed into the phone box, and the sound of the world outside became muffled when the door closed behind us. A truck with muddy tyres and huge logs sticking off the end of its trailer passed by. It disappeared along the main road, which ran like a straight line through the flat, monotonous arable landscape, past the town and off towards the county boundary.

There was yellow phone book on the shelf beneath the phone and coin box; it wasn't very thick, but it was evidently enough to contain the numbers of all the phones not only in Ballantyne, but the entire county. I started leafing through it. Tom looked demonstratively at his watch.

'I-I-I promised to be home by –'

'Shhh!' I said.

My finger had stopped on a Jonasson, Imu. Weird name, probably a weirdo. I lifted the receiver, which was fixed to the coin box with a metal cable, as if they were afraid someone was going to tear it to pieces and run off with the grey receiver. I tapped Jonasson, Imu's number onto the shiny metal buttons on the box. Only six digits, we used to have nine in the city, but I suppose they didn't need any more out here seeing as there were four thousand trees for every inhabitant. Then I passed the receiver to Tom.

'H-h-huh?' he simply said, staring at me in terror.

'Say "Hi, Imu, I'm the devil, and I'm inviting you to hell, because that's where you belong".'

Tom just shook his head and passed the receiver back to me.

'Do it, meathead, or I'll throw you in the river,' I said.

Tom – the smallest boy in the class – cowered and became even smaller.

'I'm kidding,' I said, laughing. My laugh sounded alien even to me in the cramped, vacuum-like phone box. 'Come on, Tom, think how funny it will be when we tell the others about it at school tomorrow.'

I saw something stir inside him. The thought of impressing people. For someone who had never impressed anyone about anything, this was obviously a serious consideration. But also the fact that I said 'we'. He and I. Two friends who played jokes together, who had made a prank phone call and stood there giddy with laughter, who had had to hold each other up to stop ourselves collapsing when we heard the poor guy at the other end of the line wonder if it really was the devil making the call.

'Hello?'

The sound came from the telephone receiver. It was impossible to tell if it was a man or a woman, a grown-up or a child.

Tom looked at me. I nodded eagerly. And he smiled. He smiled a kind of triumphant smile and raised the receiver to his ear.

I mouthed the words as Tom looked at me and repeated them without the slightest trace of a stammer.

'Hi, Imu. I'm-the-devil-and-I'm-inviting-you-to-hell. Because-that's-where-you-belong.'

I put my hand over my mouth to indicate that I could hardly contain my laughter, then gestured with the other hand for him to hang up.

But Tom didn't hang up.

Instead he stood there with the receiver pressed to his ear, but I could hear the low hum of the voice at the other end.

'B-b-b-b-but . . .' Tom stuttered, suddenly deathly pale. He held his breath, and his pale face had frozen in a stunned expression.

'No,' he whispered, then raised his elbow and looked like he was trying to pull the receiver away from his ear. Then he repeated, getting gradually louder: 'No. No. No!' He put his free hand against the glass of the phone box, as if he was trying to use it as leverage. Then – with a wet, ragged sigh – the receiver came free, but I saw something go with it. Blood was running down the side of his head, under his shirt collar. Then I noticed the telephone receiver. I couldn't believe my eyes. Half his ear was stuck to the bloody, perforated listening end, and what happened next was beyond comprehension. First the blood was sort of sucked up by the tiny black holes, then – little by little – the chunk of ear disappeared, like when you rinse leftover food down the plughole in a sink.

'Richard,' Tom whispered in a trembling voice, his cheeks wet with tears, apparently not realising that half his ear was gone. 'H-h-h-he said that you and I . . .' He cupped his hand over the speaking end of the receiver to stop the person at the other end from hearing. 'W-w-w-we're going to –'

'Tom!' I cried. 'Your hand! Drop the phone!'

Tom looked down and only now realised that his fingers were halfway through the holes in the receiver.

He grabbed hold of the listening end and tried to free his trapped hand. But it was no use, instead the phone started to make a slurping sound, like when my uncle Frank eats soup, and more of his hand disappeared inside the receiver. I grabbed hold of the receiver too, and tried to pull it away from Tom, but to no avail, the receiver had now eaten his lower arm almost all the way to his elbow, it was as if he and the phone were one and the same thing. As I screamed, something strange was happening to Tom. He looked up at me and laughed, as if it didn't hurt that much, and was so ridiculous that he couldn't help smiling. There was no blood either, it was as if the receiver did what I had read some insects do with their prey: they inject something that turns the flesh to jelly which they can then slurp up. But then the telephone receiver reached his elbow, and it sounded like when you put something in a blender that shouldn't be there, a brutal crunching, grinding sound, and now Tom was screaming too. His elbow buckled, as if there was something under the skin that wanted to get out. I kicked the door open behind us, stood behind Tom, grabbed his chest with both arms and tried to back out. I only managed to pull Tom halfway out, the metal cable was stretched out of the box, and the receiver was still gnawing at his upper arm. I slammed the door shut again in the hope that it might smash the telephone receiver, but the cable was too short and I just kept hitting Tom's shoulder. He howled as I dug my heels into the ground and pulled as hard as I could, but, centimetre by centimetre, my shoes were slipping on the wet soil, towards the phone box and the disgusting crunching sound that Tom's howling couldn't drown out. Tom was slowly dragged back into the phone box by unknown forces – I had no idea where they came from or what they were. I couldn't hold on, I had to let go of my grip around his chest, and soon I was standing outside pulling on the arm that was still sticking out through the gap in the door. The telephone receiver was about to consume Tom's shoulder when I heard a vehicle approaching. I let go of Tom's arm and ran towards the road, screaming and waving. It was another truck loaded with logs. But I was too late, all I saw were the rear lights disappearing into the dusk.

I ran back. It was quiet, Tom had stopped screaming. The door had swung closed. There was condensation on the inside of the small panes of glass as I pressed my face against them. But I could see Tom. And he saw me. Silent, with the resigned look of prey that has stopped struggling and accepted its fate. The telephone receiver had reached his head, it had taken one cheek, and there was a cracking sound when it made a start on Tom's exposed dental brace.

I turned round, leaned my back against the phone box and slid down until I felt the ground beneath me and saw the wetness seeping through my trousers.

# 2

I WAS SITTING ON A chair in the hallway of the police station. It was late, past bedtime, so to speak. At the other end of the passageway I saw the sheriff. He had small eyes and a turned-up nose – I could see his nostrils, which automatically made me think of a pig. He was stroking the moustache that hung down from the sides of his mouth with his thumb and forefinger. He was talking to Frank and Jenny. That's what I call them, it would have felt odd to call them Uncle and Aunt when you'd never seen them before the day they came to pick you up and told you you're going to be living with them from now on. They had just stared at me when I burst in and told them what had happened to Tom. Then Frank had called the sheriff, and the sheriff had called Tom's parents, then asked us to come in. I had answered a load of questions, then sat and waited while the sheriff sent his people out to the telephone box and started the search. Then I had to answer even more questions.

It looked like Frank and Jenny were discussing something with the sheriff, occasionally glancing in my direction. But evidently they had reached some sort of agreement, because Frank and Jenny came over to me, both with serious expressions on their faces.

'We can go,' Frank said, and set off towards the exit while Jenny put a comforting hand on my shoulder.

We got in their small Japanese car, me in the back seat, and drove in silence. But I knew it wouldn't be long before it started: the questions. Frank cleared his throat. First once, then again.

Frank and Jenny were kind. Too kind, some would say. Like last summer, when I had just got here, and set fire to the long, dry grass in front of the abandoned sawmill. If my uncle and five neighbours hadn't got there so quickly, there's no way of knowing what might have happened. Obviously it was extra embarrassing for Frank, seeing as he was in charge of the fire station. All the same, I didn't get told off or punished, but comforted instead, they probably thought I was beside myself because of what had happened. And then, after supper, the same throat-clearing thing as now, followed by some vague remarks about not playing with matches. Like I said, Frank was the fire chief, and Jenny was a junior-school teacher, and I have no idea how they managed to maintain discipline. Assuming that they did, of course. Frank cleared his throat again, he clearly wasn't sure where to start. So I decided to make it easier for him.

'I'm not lying,' I said. 'Tom got eaten by the phone.'

Silence. Frank shot Jenny a resigned look, kind of playing the ball to her.

'Sweetie,' Jenny said in a low, gentle voice. 'There was no evidence there.'

'Yes there was! They found the skid marks from my heels on the ground.'

'Not from Tom,' Frank said. 'Nothing.'

'The telephone swallowed everything.' Obviously I could hear how crazy it sounded. But what was I supposed to say? That the telephone *hadn't* eaten Tom?

'What did the sheriff say?' I asked.

Jenny and Frank exchanged another glance.

'He thinks you're in shock,' Frank said.

I couldn't say anything to that. I guess I *was* in shock; my body felt numb, my mouth dry and my throat sore. As if I felt like crying, but there was some sort of blockage stopping the tears from getting out.

We reached the hill where the telephone box was. I was expecting to see loads of lights and search parties, but it just stood there, dark and deserted, as usual.

'But the sheriff promised they were going to look for Tom!' I exclaimed.

'They are,' Frank said. 'Down by the river.'

'The river? Why?'

'Because someone saw you and Tom heading into the forest towards the bridge. The sheriff said that when he asked if you'd been down by the river, you said no. Why did you say that?'

I gritted my teeth and stared out of the window. I watched the phone box disappear into the darkness behind us. The sheriff hadn't told me someone had seen us. Perhaps he only found out about that after he'd spoken to me. And the talk hadn't been a formal interview, he kept stressing that. So I thought I didn't have to tell him absolutely everything, at least not the stuff that had nothing to do with what had happened, like the stolen Luke Skywalker figure or Tom doing something his parents had told him not to. You never grass on friends. But now we had been found out anyway.

'We just stood on the bridge for a while,' I said.

Frank flicked the indicator and pulled over at the side of the road. He turned towards me. I could hardly see his face in the darkness, but I knew it was serious now. For me, anyway, because Tom had already been eaten up.

'Richard?'

'Yes, Frank?'

He hated it when I used his name, but sometimes, like now, I couldn't help it.

'We had to remind Sheriff McClelland that you're a minor, and threaten him with a lawyer to get him to let you go. He wanted to hold you overnight for questioning. He thinks something happened down by the river. And that that's why you're lying.'

I was about to deny that and say I wasn't lying, then I realised that they had already found out that I had been.

'So, what happened by the river?' Frank asked.

'Nothing,' I said. 'We looked at the water.'

'From the bridge?'

'Yes.'

'I've heard that youngsters like trying to balance on the railing.'

'Really?' I said. 'Well, it's not like there's much else to do around here.'

I carried on looking into the darkness. That was what had struck me when autumn arrived, just how dark it got here. In the city it was always light, but here you could stare into black night where there was absolutely nothing. I mean, obviously there was something there, but you couldn't help thinking it was hidden by all this strange dark stuff.

'Richard,' Jenny said, very, very softly. 'Did Tom fall in the water?'

'No, Jenny,' I replied, mimicking her gentle tone. 'Tom didn't fall in the water. Can we go home now? I've got school tomorrow.'

Frank's shoulders rose up, then relaxed, I could see he was getting ready to say something.

'Sheriff McClelland thinks it might have been an accident, that you pushed Tom and feel that it's your fault, and that that's why you're lying.'

I sighed deeply, hit my head against the back of the seat and closed my eyes. But all I could see was the telephone eating Tom's cheek, so I opened them again.

'I'm not lying,' I said. 'I lied about the river because Tom wasn't supposed to go there.'

'According to McClelland, there's proof that you're lying about something else as well.'

'Huh? What?'

Frank told me.

'He's the one lying!' I said. 'Drive back, I can prove it!'

When Frank pulled off the road, the headlights lit up the phone box and the trees on the edge of the forest, making it look like huge, shadowy ghosts were running past them. The car had barely stopped before I jumped out and ran to the phone box.

'Careful!' Jenny called. Not that I think she believed me, but her motto in life seemed to be that you could never be too careful.

I opened the door and stared at the telephone receiver, which was hung up next to the metal box. Someone – one of the sheriff's people, presumably – must have put it back, because when I left it was hanging down towards the floor and Tom was gone, leaving not so much as a shoelace behind.

I took a cautious step inside, grabbed the yellow telephone directory and backed out again. In the light from the car headlights I looked up Ballantyne, then found the entries for J and ran my finger down the same page I had opened that afternoon.

*Johansen. Johnsen. Jones. Juvik.*

I felt an icy chill in my chest, and started again. With the same result. Was I on the wrong page?

No, I recognised the other names and the advert for lawnmowers.

But Frank was right about what the sheriff had said.

I peered closer to see if someone could have removed the name, but there still wasn't enough space between *Johnsen* and *Jones.*

There was no longer a Jonasson, Imu in the phone book.

# 3

'SOMEONE SWITCHED THE PHONE BOOK,' I said. 'That's the only explanation I can come up with.'

Karen was sitting with her back against the oak tree, looking at me.

It was break time, and in front of us the boys were playing football and the girls were playing hopscotch. Next year we would be starting high school, but that just meant we would be moving to the building on the other side of the schoolyard, where there was a smoking area I was fairly confident I was going to end up in. Among the rebels. Among the losers. Karen was a bit of an exception. A rebel, but definitely not a loser.

'How does it feel that no one believes you?' she asked, brushing her boyish blonde fringe away from her freckled face. Karen was the crazy girl in class. And the smartest. She was always full of energy, laughter and mischief. She couldn't help dancing when she walked, she wore strange, home-made clothes that anyone else would have been teased about. She answered rude teachers back just as rudely, and laughed when they couldn't keep up with her. Because Karen had always done her homework and a bit more, so you sometimes got the feeling that she knew more than the teachers. She was top in English and top in PE, and top in everything in between. And she was tough. I noticed that on my very first day at the school: she wasn't afraid of me, just inquisitive. She talked to everyone, even those of us in the piranha caste. I could see Oscar Rossi Jr – who I'm pretty sure had a crush on Karen – casting long and rather curious glances at her during breaks when she stalked over to us on her long, thin legs rather than hang out with Oscar and the other popular kids. During the first break on my first day, she had just stood in front of me with her hands on her sides, titled her head with a wry smile and said: 'Being new sucks, huh?'

She was like that with all of us in the bottom layer. Asked questions. Listened. And I think she was genuinely interested, because otherwise I couldn't see the point in expending energy to be liked by kids like us. All she got in return was us getting used to it and wanting even more of her attention. But she was fine with that too, and said things bluntly in such a Karen-way that no one got offended: 'We've talked enough for today now, Tom – bye!'

Obviously I made a real effort to make sure she wouldn't suspect me of wanting her attention.

The problem was that I suspected she had already figured that out.

She never said it, just looked at me with a half-smile of

recognition whenever we had exchanged a few words and I took care to walk away from her before she walked away from me. It wasn't easy, because – unlike her – I didn't have anywhere else to go. But perhaps it still worked, perhaps she got curious about the city boy who was trying to resist her charms, because she came over to me more and more often.

'You know what?' I said. 'I don't give a damn what they think, they can go to hell. I was there, I saw what happened. Tom got eaten, and the name Imu Jonasson was in that damn phone book.'

'That's a lot of swearing in three sentences,' Karen said with a smile. 'Why are you so angry, do you think?'

'I'm not angry.'

'No?'

'I'm angry because . . .'

She waited.

'Because they're all idiots,' I said.

'Hmm,' she said, and looked at the others in the schoolyard. The boys in our class were evidently trying to play football against the year below, and were calling for Oscar Rossi Jr, who, although he was only the third or fourth best player, was still captain of the team. But Oscar waved them away. He was sitting on a bench with Henrik, the maths genius of the class, who was explaining something as he pointed at Oscar's algebra book. Even so, their body language suggested that it was Oscar doing Henrik the favour rather than the other way round. Oscar was evidently trying to concentrate; he pushed his thick, dark fringe back, looked down at the book with his brown, girlishly pretty eyes that made even some of the girls in high school cross the yard in an attempt to catch his eye. But at regular intervals, Oscar Jr looked up from the algebra book towards Karen and me.

'You've never said anything about your parents,' Karen said, running a long, slender hand over some roots that were sticking out from the trunk like thick veins before diving back into the ground.

'There's not much to say,' I said without looking away from the bench where Oscar Jr and Henrik were sitting. 'They died in a fire, I can hardly remember them.'

Oscar looked up again, and his eyes met mine. My cold, blue eyes. Oscar Jr was always such a friendly, effusive and charming guy, but in a way that clearly didn't annoy anyone but me. So when I now spotted a glimpse of hostility in his eyes, at first I assumed it was an automatic response to him seeing the same hostility in mine. Because it occurred to me that he – seeing as he was third or fourth smartest in class, even if he was light-years behind Karen – must have somehow figured out that I was the one who had stolen Luke Skywalker. Then I realised that it wasn't that. He was – and the thought delighted me – jealous, pure and simple. Jealous because Karen was sitting here listening to me instead of hanging out with the alpha male. I suddenly got the urge to put my arm round Karen, just to see Oscar's face turn green. But obviously she would have pushed my arm away, and I didn't want to give him that satisfaction. I heard Karen's calm, pleasant voice: 'You mean you don't remember anything about your parents?'

'Sorry, I have a really bad memory. That's why I do so badly in tests. That and the fact that I'm stupid, obviously.'

'You're not stupid, Richard.'

'I was joking.'

'I know. But sometimes if you tell a lie enough times, it becomes a bit true anyway.'

The bell rang and I felt my heart sink. Not because we had to go in and listen to Miss Birdsong talk about geography – anything that could take my mind off Ballantyne was good – but because I would have liked this, what was happening here and now, to last a bit longer. As Karen stood up, two books slipped out of her bag.

'Hey!' I said, leaning forward to pick them up. I looked at the covers. One, with the name William Golding and the title *Lord of the Flies*, showed a severed pig's head on a spike. The other, Franz Kafka's *Metamorphosis*, had a grotesque insect, a cockroach, maybe.

'Nice. Where did you get hold of those?'

'From Mrs Zimmer in the library,' Karen said.

'Wow, I didn't know they had scary stuff like that there.'

'Oh, Mrs Zimmer has much scarier stuff than these. Have you heard about black and white word magic?'

'Yes. Well . . . er, no. What is it?'

'Magic words that can destroy people or fix them again.'

'And the lady in the library has books about that?'

'So rumour has it,' Karen said. 'Do you read?'

'No, I'm more of a cinema guy.' I handed her the books. 'What about you – do you like films?'

'I love films,' she said with a sigh. 'But I haven't seen many.'

'Why not?'

'For a start, it's an hour and a half to Hume, and everyone I know only wants to see action films and comedies.'

'If there was a cinema here, what would you go and see, then?'

She thought about it. 'Anything except action and comedies. I like old films, the ones that get shown on television. I know I sound like an old woman now, but Mum's right. If a film hasn't been forgotten, it's probably good.'

'Agreed. Like *Night of the Living Dead.*'

She shook her head. 'What sort of film is that?'

'An old zombie film. According to Dad, it was the first one. He and I went on a fishing trip when I was ten, and he talked me through the whole film, scene by scene. That same winter it got shown on TV, so I made a fuss about watching it with Dad. I had nightmares for weeks after that, even though I already knew what was going to happen in every scene. Those were probably the best ninety-six minutes of my life.'

Karen laughed. 'Did you learn anything from it, then?'

I thought about that. 'Yes. If you really want to kill someone, you have to do it twice. You have to destroy their brain, by burning it, for instance. Because if you don't, they come back.'

'That was the how the film ended?'

'It was how Dad ended.'

She carried on smiling. 'I see. Is it very scary?'

'Yes and no. It's more the atmosphere. I don't think there's an age limit on it, though.'

'Interesting. I should watch it sometime.'

'They show it at film clubs, things like that. I can –'.

I stopped myself. I pretended to cough in the hope that she hadn't realised I had come close to inviting her to the cinema. In Hume. I had neither a car nor a driving licence. And even if I had, obviously she would still have said no. Politely and with a good excuse, but that wouldn't have hurt any less.

Karen looked like she had noticed my near-miss and was now performing a diversionary manoeuvre by holding up the two books. 'But these are good cinema, too.'

I nodded and gratefully seized the life raft. 'They look like horror as well?'

'Yes and no,' she mimicked. 'They're like the films I like. Old, but not forgotten.'

'And they're good?'

'Yes. You need to read the best if you want to be an author.'

'That's what you're going to be?'

'I'm going to try. And if I'm not good enough, then I'll marry one instead.' She laughed that wild, crazy laugh of hers, then she danced away, sort of out of control, as if she might crash at any moment. But of course that was an illusion, because Karen was always in control of everything, she was like a cat. You could throw her off a roof, secure in the knowledge that she – in marked contrast to people like me – would always land safely on all fours.

# 4

AS I WAS WALKING HOME from school, just when I had turned off onto the shortcut that runs through the forest, I heard crunching on the grit behind me. I turned round and saw three boys on bikes. I had seen two of them earlier that day. They were in high school, and during one of the breaks they had come over to our side, as if to get the measure of me. Now they were with a bigger boy I hadn't seen before, he looked like someone's older brother, and like he could have been riding a moped instead of pedalling around on a kid's Apache bicycle. They pulled in a short way ahead of me, blocking the narrow gravel path. The one I hadn't seen before got off his bike, and one of the others held on to it as he walked towards me. He was wearing one of those checked lumberjack jackets that the grown-ups round here liked to wear. I had a good idea of what this was about.

'Where's Tom?' he asked, straight out.

'Gone,' I said.

'Out with it. What did you do with him?'

He stopped with his legs a little way apart, with his knees bent slightly, then leaned forward a bit, as if to show that he was ready to attack.

'I ate him,' I said. 'With salt and pepper. Mostly pepper.'

The guy looked stunned for a moment. The two younger boys stared at me, wide-eyed. He must have felt them staring behind him, because he took one broad-legged stride closer. Warily, though. And his eyes followed my hand as I put it in my pocket.

'Three against one,' I said. 'What's the problem? Scared?'

'Spit it out, you fucking city shit,' he said, his voice sounding tighter now.

I spat on the ground in front of him.

'There,' I said. 'Now, lick it up.'

I don't know if he realised that I didn't have anything in my pocket, or that the only thing that was big about me was my mouth, but he took another quick step closer, and then he struck. First once, then – when he saw that I had no response – again, then a third time. Then he grabbed me round the waist and threw me to the ground, and sat on my chest.

'You're crying,' he said.

'I'm not,' I said, feeling warm tears trickle down my temples from the corners of my eyes.

'Where's Tom?'

'Ask the phone.'

'You'll end up in prison if you lie to the police,' he said, and I realised that the whole of Ballantyne knew my story. Not what I had seen, but my *story*. There were no doubt different theories about what had actually happened, but one thing was certain: I was guilty in all of them.

The other two had dared to come closer now.

'Hurry up,' I whispered. 'There's no one looking.'

'Huh?' the guy sitting on me said.

'Carry me into the forest and torture the truth out of me,' I whispered. 'Then you can strangle me or hit me on the head with a rock. But remember to make sure I'm not breathing afterwards, because if I survive, I'll say what happened. I'm a real blabbermouth, you know.'

The guy in the lumberjack jacket looked at me as if I was dogshit on his shoe. Then he turned to the other two. 'You didn't tell me he was crazy.'

'Yes, we . . .' one of them replied hesitantly.

'Yeah, but not *totally fucking* crazy,' lumberjack-jacket said irritably, getting to his feet.

A few seconds later they and their bicycles were gone.

I went down to the river where it formed a bend below the bridge, where there was a small inlet. I rinsed the blood and ingrained grit off myself, and tried to check the state of my nose in the water. It was too murky for me to be able to get any idea of the damage, but the way one eye was throbbing told me I was going to have at least one big bump.

When I got home, I snuck past the living room where Frank was reading the paper. He had been on night duty at the fire station and was now on a break. I heard his voice as I stood in the bathroom, confirming that a large lump had indeed swollen above my left eye.

'How was school today?'

'Fine,' I called back through the open door.

'Fine?'

'Yup,' I said. 'I didn't get tested on any homework.'

I knew he wasn't asking for bad jokes, but there was precious little he could do about what he was actually asking about. Not that I wanted him to do anything either, because who wants to look like the sort of guy who gets beaten up? A real piranha beats *other* people up.

The front door opened. It was Jenny, and suddenly she was standing outside the bathroom with bags of shopping in her hands.

'Hi,' she said. 'How are you?'

'Great,' I muttered, holding my face really close to the mirror so she couldn't see anything, trying to look like I was squeezing a spot.

'It's lasagne for dinner,' she said with anticipation in her voice, because at some point – probably to please her – I had said that her lasagne was the best.

'Looking forward to it,' I said in a flat voice.

When I heard her making a noise in the kitchen, I snuck back to the hall the same way I had come and pulled my shoes on again.

'Where are you going?' Frank asked, evidently keeping a closer eye on things behind that newspaper than it seemed.

'To the cinema,' I said, and closed the front door behind me.

# 5

THE LIBRARY WAS AT THE end of the main street. While most of the other buildings in Ballantyne's 200-metre-long centre were joined together in two-storey blocks, the library was a narrow, four-storey wooden building separated from the brick buildings by narrow alleyways on either side. It was as if Ballantyne's public library didn't want anything to do with its lower-class neighbours.

I had never been inside the library before. Jenny and Frank had got them to issue me with a library card, but of course I had never used it.

As the door closed behind me and I was left standing there in the semi-darkness, at first I wondered if it was closed. Maybe it wasn't unusual for a library to be quiet, but there was no sound and no people there, just book spines filling shelves that stretched all the way up to the ceiling. Some of the books had protective covers, others didn't, some were shiny and new, others so old that they looked like they were about to fall apart. A plaque said that the building and books had been donated to the town of Ballantyne in 1920 by Robert Willingstad. That was more than half a century ago, so it was hardly surprising that some of the books were showing their age.

I heard a sneeze from further in the building. Then another one. So at least there was someone here. I saw that the books were arranged alphabetically, and started looking for K. I had to fetch one of the little ladders to reach the top shelves. It took a bit of time, but in the end I found what I wanted, I was fairly sure of that. I walked further in, past more rows of bookcases to where I seemed to remember the counter was.

And there it was.

'You've got a nosebleed, young man,' the white-haired lady behind the counter said. There was a name badge attached to the front of her dress that said 'Mrs Zimmer, librarian', even though there didn't seem much chance of anyone else ever being confused with her in there. Mrs Zimmer tore a sheet from the roll of tissues in front of her and handed it to me before I could wipe my nose on my sleeve.

Then she sneezed hard and tore off a sheet for herself.

'Book dust,' she said, wiping her nose and looking down at the two books I had placed on the counter. 'And who are you borrowing these for, young man?'

'Who?'

'Sorry, I'm just curious, there aren't many people in Ballantyne who read proper literature.'

'They're for me.'

'You . . .' she said, peering at me over the narrow reading glasses held round her neck by a cord. 'You're going to read Franz Kafka's *Metamorphosis* and William Golding's *Lord of the Flies*?'

'I've heard they're supposed to be good,' I said.

Mrs Zimmer smiled. 'They're certainly good, young man. But they aren't easy, if I can put it like that. Not even for adults.'

'I guess not everything has to be easy,' I said.

Her smile reached her eyes, she looked like she was about to laugh. 'You'll go far, because that's certainly true.'

I liked her. I think. Maybe just because she had said something nice to me.

She opened a drawer in front of her, and I saw rows of cards in oblong wooden boxes. 'What's your name, young man?'

'Richard Elauved.'

Even though she had her head bowed and was leafing through the cards, I saw her face stiffen. Clearly it didn't take much to become a celebrity in Ballantyne. Just a flesh-eating telephone.

She stamped two cards for each book, one that she placed in a wooden box and one that she slipped into a paper sleeve inside the books. 'Yes, well,' she sighed. 'It's a sorry business when children go missing.'

I looked at her quizzically. She pointed at *Lord of the Flies*, and I realised she was talking about the plot of the book. I think she was, anyway.

It was just as quiet among the bookshelves when I left as when I arrived. But as I passed the plaque with Willingstad's name, I noticed a ladder leaning against the wall. Why hadn't I seen it when I arrived? It wasn't like an ordinary ladder, it was made of metal and had a handrail on each side, like a fireman's ladder. Yes, that was what it was, I had seen one just like it when Frank showed me round the fire station. I looked up beyond the ladder and bookshelves to the lights hanging from the ceiling. Beyond the lights it was so dark that the top of the ladder and bookshelves almost disappeared.

Only a row of glinting yellow book spines was visible.

I hesitated. Was I mistaken, or had I recently seen a book spine that looked a lot like that?

I felt the ladder to see it was secure.

Safe enough. I heard a distant sneeze. What harm would it do to check?

I put my foot on the bottom rung, took a deep breath and began to climb.

I'm scared of heights. I'm scared of darkness. I'm scared of water. I'm scared of fire. And I'm scared of telephones. But most of all, I'm scared of being scared. Well, I'm not scared of being scared the way I am when I'm huddled up next to my dad watching a zombie film. But I'm scared of being so scared of something going badly wrong, like a key breaking in a lock, or the passageway between the bedroom and the front door bursting into flames, I'm scared of being so trapped in being scared that I can never find my way out again.

But I kept climbing up, step by step, without looking down. When I got past the lights to the yellow book spines, I saw that my suspicions had been correct.

Phone books.

There was one book for every year, from left to right, twelve in total. I pulled out the oldest one and quickly climbed down, and now I didn't even think it was that high. I sat down on the dark parquet floor with my legs crossed, and looked up J. I ran my finger down the page.

*Johansen. Johnsen. Jonasson . . .*

My heart stopped. And then it started again, beating hard and fast now, as I moved my finger to the right.

*Imu. 1 Mirror Forest Road, Ballantyne. 290-3386.*

# 6

WHEN I APPROACHED THE LADY behind the desk in the police station, I was told that Sheriff McClelland was busy in the meeting room, but that I could sit and wait. While I was sitting on the chair I could hear voices and see movement behind the frosted-glass walls where I myself had talked to the sheriff the day before. I looked out of the window, over to the car park between the police station and the fire station, at a monster of a car I had noticed when I arrived, the sort of flashy, old-fashioned car there were always pictures of in Frank's car magazines. That must have been where I had seen it, because there was something strangely familiar about the car. The lady behind the desk went into the meeting room, then she and Sheriff McClelland hurried out.

'There you are!' McClelland said with a broad smile, as if my visit was both welcome and not entirely unexpected. 'You beat us to it, Richard, I was just about to ask you to come in for a chat. Follow me.'

I managed to glance inside the meeting room, and saw the back of a man in a black suit with even blacker hair, who was standing looking out of the window. Then I followed after McClelland into his office.

He moved a chair from the wall over to his desk, which was overflowing with tall stacks of papers, then asked me to sit down.

'Cocoa, Richard?'

I shook my head.

'Sure? Margareth makes really –'

'Sure,' I said.

'Great.' McClelland looked intently at me. 'Let's get straight to the point then, and get this done.' He sat down behind the desk. I was sitting much lower than him, and we couldn't make eye contact over the piles of paper.

'What's on your mind, Richard?' His voice was as soft as butter.

I pulled out the phone book I was carrying inside my jacket and put it down in front of him.

McClelland was still looking at me rather than the phone book. He seemed disappointed.

'Where the corner is turned down,' I said, pointing. 'Jonasson.'

He opened the book.

'Imu Jonasson,' he read.

'You see?'

McClelland looked at me. 'So what? Imu Jonasson is town history, as old as this phone book, and nothing to do with Tom's disappearance.' The buttery softness was gone, his voice was made of metal now.

'Yes, he does. I told you –'

'I remember what you said, Richard. But telephone receivers don't eat people, OK?' He pointed out of the window. 'We've had search parties out looking all night, and what I and Tom's parents and everyone in Ballantyne need right now is for you to tell us everything you know about what happened to Tom.'

'I've already told you, you're not listening.'

McClelland took a deep breath and looked out of the window. 'I was hoping you'd come here to tell us the truth, but seeing as you're not doing that, I can only assume that – one way or another – you're guilty. Because you're fourteen years old, you're protected by the law, and obviously you're aware of that. We can't even question you again, even if we wanted to. But . . .' McClelland leaned towards me over the piles of paper. His round face had turned so red that his blond moustache stood out even more clearly and made me think of Santa Claus. His voice dropped to a hoarse whisper: 'I'm the sheriff here in Ballantyne, I'm friends with Tom's family, and I will personally make sure that you, Richard Elauved, are locked away in a very dark, very remote place where no one will ever find you if we don't find Tom. If you think there's a single soul in Ballantyne who would care what happened to the snotty city kid who took Tom from us, you're wrong. And that includes Frank and Jenny.'

McClelland leaned back in his chair.

I stared at him.

Then I got to my feet, picked up the phone book and walked out.

On the way home I stopped in front of the display window of Oscar's toyshop. There were loads of toys, but the one that caught my attention was the Frankenstein figure. Well, obviously the figure was of the monster. Dad had explained that Frankenstein was the doctor who brought the monster to life with electricity. While I was looking at it, I noticed something in the reflection in the window: a red car on the other side of the street. I probably wouldn't have noticed it if it hadn't been the same car that had been parked near the police station. I carried on walking home, and when I glanced discreetly behind me when I was crossing the road, I saw – a long way off – the same car.

As I walked up to the house, Frank was reversing his car out of the garage. He stopped and wound down the window, and I could see by the way he was dressed that he was going to work the nightshift again. There was a stern expression on his face.

'Where have you been? Jenny was worried.'

'But not you?'

He frowned and looked at me uncomprehendingly. 'Go inside, she'll heat your dinner up for you.'

When I stepped into the hallway, Jenny came out, looking like she wanted to give me a hug, so I took an extra long time taking my shoes off to make sure I escaped that. I said truthfully that I had been to the library, that there had been something I needed to sort out.

The lasagne tasted like it should, and I didn't have to answer any more questions. Apart from the ones I asked myself, obviously. Who was Imu Jonasson? Who was driving the red car? And: who could I really trust?

That night I slept badly, and had nightmares about being locked up in a dark, desolate place. About Frankenstein and zombies.

# 7

'SO THE SHERIFF DIDN'T BELIEVE you, even when you showed him the phone book with Imu Jonasson's name in it?' Karen asked. We were on our lunch break and she and I were standing on the flat roof of the main school building while Karen swung a long, pliable fishing rod back and forth, making the artificial fly at the end of the line dance in the air. She was practising to beat her dad, who had won the local fly-fishing competition four years in a row.

'It isn't the fact that we called a guy called Imu Jonasson that he doesn't believe,' I said as I watched the fly, which now seemed to be hovering in the air right above the hole in a chimney pot ten metres away from us. 'It's the fact that the telephone receiver ate Tom.'

Karen and I used to go up there at least once a week, but she never wanted to tell me how she came to have the keys to the stairs up to the roof, just said she was going to hold on to them as long as neither the caretaker nor any of the teachers realised she had them. I don't know why she had picked me to take up there, I think maybe it was because she reckoned I was the only person who wouldn't tell anyone and who wasn't afraid of getting into trouble.

I peered cautiously over the tin-lined edge, down at the schoolyard six floors below. It was strange, but when I was up there with Karen I wasn't scared of heights. Quite the reverse, I just felt a bit of a tingle in my stomach. And from there the shitty little kids looked even smaller. I watched Fatso chase someone who had grabbed his woolly hat and was now throwing it up into the oak tree. It caught in the branches high above them. Fatso was left standing there alone, his arms hanging helplessly by his sides as he stared up at the hat, but the sun was in his eyes and he couldn't see me up on the roof.

Karen pulled a face as she let the fly drop into the hole in the chimney. 'Did it really *eat* him?'

'Well, it probably sucked more that it chewed. Like those insects that inject something into their prey to dissolve it into a kind of smoothie.'

'Yuck!' Karen shuddered as she reeled in the fly.

'The worst thing is, I keep wondering what sort of smoothie. Isn't that sick? Kind of wondering what your friend tasted like?'

'Yeah,' Karen said, blowing soot off the fly and reattaching it to the tip of the rod. 'That's pretty sick.'

I lay back with my hands behind my head and looked up at the sky. Small white clouds sailed across my field of vision.

'What do you think they look like?' Karen asked, putting the rod down and leafing through the notebook she always carried with her. She pulled out the pink hair clip she used as a bookmark and started scribbling. I assumed she was drawing something. Unless she was practising being an author. Either way, she never wanted to show me what was in those pages.

'The clouds, you mean?' I asked.

'Yes.'

'They look like clouds.'

'Don't you get any associations?'

I knew what the word meant, images that resembled something else. But unlike Karen, I couldn't say words like that as if it was the most natural thing in the world. It must be all that reading. The previous evening I had come across several words in that Kafka book of hers I didn't understand, but beyond that, it was so boring that I started the one with the pig's head on the cover instead. That one was about children who managed to reach a desert island after a plane crash, and was much more my kind of thing.

'What do you see?' I asked.

'I see Chewbacca.'

'You think the clouds look like the big furry guy in *Star Wars*?'

'He isn't a guy, he's a Wookiee. So you don't see that, or anything else?'

'Should I?'

'Maybe not should,' Karen said. 'But that's what authors do, according to my dad. They make stories out of clouds.'

'So if all I see are clouds, I can't be an author?'

'I don't know. Try to see something.'

I screwed my eyes up slightly and concentrated. The problem was that the clouds were so small and indistinct up there in the wind, and they kept moving faster than I could figure out what they looked like. The bell rang.

'We can do it next break,' Karen said, closing her notebook. We got to our feet, then made sure no one could see us as we snuck in through the door and down the stairs.

'I was going to ask you a favour,' I said when we had reached the crowded corridor.

'Oh?'

'I was going to ask if you could help me find this Imu guy.'

I wasn't looking at her, but I could hear from the way she hesitated and held her breath that she was going to say no.

'But then I realised it probably isn't a girl thing,' I quickly added.

'What do you mean, not a *girl thing*?'

'Sorry, I didn't mean –'

'Wow, I didn't know that word was in your vocabulary.'

'Which one?'

'*Sorry*. Whatever, I'd be happy to help you, Richard, you know that. But right now, I think the best way to help is to let you find out for yourself.'

We went out into the schoolyard, which was empty apart from Fatso, who was sitting alone on a bench with his head in his hands.

'See you,' Karen said, and left me. She walked over to Fatso and put a hand on his shoulder. He looked up at her but could barely see anything, because his glasses were all steamed up, he must have been crying again. But he lit up when he heard her voice. We're simple creatures, if someone speaks kindly to us, we're happy.

And, I thought, we do exactly what we're asked to do.

I went into the classroom, sat down, and looked out through the window at the schoolyard, where Karen and Fatso were standing in front of the oak tree. Karen was holding the fishing rod above her head, and the fly was approaching the hat high up in the tree, it looked like it was about to land on it. And then – with a little jerk – she pulled the hat loose, and it fell to the ground like an early-autumn leaf in the sunlight as Fatso clapped his fat little hands together in delight.

# 8

'OK,' FATSO SAID. 'I'LL COME.'

I was both surprised and not surprised. On the one hand, Fatso was a nerd who liked girly stuff, dressing up as a girl whenever a carnival or school play gave him the opportunity, and mostly hung out with girls. I had expected him to freak out as soon as he heard that this was going to require a bit more masculine courage. But on the other hand, Fatso was piranha caste, and wasn't exactly overwhelmed with offers to hang out with boys. I had seen him hovering around Oscar Rossi in vain, without ever getting any attention at all. Not that he was the only one who thought hanging with the top dog was cool, but for Fatso there seemed to be more to it. There was something desperate, almost bovine, in the way he looked at Oscar, like a well-behaved dog staring at you in silent desperation in the hope that you might spare it a morsel or two. Speaking of feeding, I had sweetened my offer by inviting Fatso home for dinner afterwards. I don't know, I guess I thought that sort of thing was more of a carrot for a fat person. And I regretted asking him when I realised that just being asked if he wanted to hang out with another boy, even one like me, was more than enough for him.

So, after the last lesson was over, Fatso and I set off along the road to Mirror Forest. It had been a warm day, a sign of what was to come. Karen had warned me that the summers here were as scorching hot as the winters were icy cold. But right now, thick white fog had suddenly crept in across the landscape, blurring the contours.

'Why are they leaving you alone?' Fatso asked as we walked through the centre of Ballantyne.

'What do you mean?'

'The sheriff and all them. Why aren't you being interrogated the whole time? I mean, everyone thinks you were with Tom and know what happened.'

'Maybe I do know.'

'Do you? Have you told the sheriff?'

'Yes, but I've been sworn to secrecy,' I said.

Fatso looked at me for a long time. He didn't seem to believe me, at least not entirely, but he didn't say anything.

I had obviously asked myself the same thing: why Sheriff McClelland was letting me go free. And I thought I had figured out why.

I didn't need to turn round to know that the red car was still there – it had been parked on the other side of the road when we got out of school. Now I knew what make it was, a Pontiac LeMans, I'd found it in one of Frank's car magazines. When I saw the picture, I also realised where I had seen one before – in *Night of the Living Dead*.

'We're going in here,' I said.

'The library?' Fatso said. 'Do we need books?'

'No, we need a shortcut.'

I pushed the door open and we went inside. I leaned against the door as it closed, and glanced out of the window alongside.

The Pontiac was parked by the edge of the sidewalk a little way up the street.

'Follow me,' I said, making my way between the bookcases. The library seemed just as deserted as last time, nothing but the books all lined up, as if waiting to be noticed. Like orphans in a children's home dreaming of being adopted.

Mrs Zimmer was sitting behind the counter, sorting what I assume were library cards.

'Back already?' she said, then sneezed. 'Well, it's all too easy to get a taste for books.'

'It is, Mrs Zimmer,' I said. 'But I was wondering something else.'

'What's that?'

'If we could go out the back way?'

'What for?'

I nodded towards the main street. 'There's a gang from school following us on Apache bikes. They like beating up bookworms like us, you know.'

Mrs Zimmer raised one eyebrow and looked at me. Then she looked at Fatso, studying him intently. Then back to me again.

'Do you know what?' she said, sneezing again and reaching for a paper handkerchief. 'I know all about that. Follow me.'

Mrs Zimmer led us behind the counter, and we followed her through a small kitchen, then a storeroom containing an assortment of office supplies, to a door that led out onto a metal staircase at the back of the library.

'Achoo!' she exclaimed. 'And good luck. Take up boxing, and read poetry.'

Fatso and I walked along a few side roads before emerging onto the main road again, not far from Mirror Forest. As I turned off onto the path that led into the forest, I glanced over my shoulder to check that Fatso was still following me and hadn't tried to escape. He was still plodding along behind me, and smiled back at me. He seemed oddly unconcerned about going into the same forest with the same guy everyone thought was deeply involved in Tom's disappearance. And he hadn't said anything about being afraid of meeting this Imu Jonasson either. But then, Fatso hadn't seen Tom being eaten.

The fog seemed to get thicker and the afternoon darker, the further we got into the forest.

Fatso was walking with short little steps, with his arms straight down by the sides of his round body, his hands splayed out, as if he needed to balance. Just like when he played Tinker Bell in the class production of *Peter Pan*. The adults in the audience did their best not to laugh as the chubby little boy skipped around the stage in a skirt and angel wings. But Fatso himself didn't seem to notice, he was completely absorbed in the role and seemed to be loving it.

We reached a clearing from where we could see the river and bridge, but carried on up a muddy slope.

'Are you sure it's here?' Fatso asked.

'Yup,' I said confidently. And why not? I had memorised the map of Ballantyne at the back of the phone book, it ought to be impossible to go wrong. When we reached the top of this slope, we just had to carry on along a dead end that went past number 1, Mirror Forest Road a couple of hundred metres further on.

I slipped on the mud a few times, but Fatso had no trouble keeping his balance.

At the top of the slope I found a path that seemed to lead in the right direction.

A deep, hollow sound came from within the misty forest, making me start. I think I may even have grabbed Fatso's hand, but if I did, I let go of it immediately.

'It's just an owl,' Fatso said.

We carried on walking, only with Fatso in front now.

'Have you seen *Swan Lake*?' he asked.

'Is there a lake called that near here?' I asked, walking straight into a branch he had ducked under.

'No,' Fatso laughed. 'But Swan Lake is in a forest like this. A lake filled with tears. It's a ballet.'

'Dancing? Sorry, but I need a storyline. You know, like films and –'

'Oh, it has a story.'

'It does?'

'A young hunter finds a lake where he sees a swan, and just as he's about to shoot it, it turns into this beautiful person, Odette.'

'A girl?'

I saw Fatso shrug. 'You see, in daylight Odette has to be a swan, and swim on a lake of tears. Odette can only be human at night.'

'That's too bad.' I almost tripped over a root. I prefer sidewalks and stairs. 'Is there a happy ending?'

'Yes and no. There are two versions. In the one I know, the hunter falls in love with Odette, and they fight everyone who's out to destroy them. In the end they can get married and Odette can be human all the time.'

'And in the other version?'

'I haven't seen that one. But my mum says it's sad.'

I heard myself scream. Something had landed on my face. It wasn't a branch, it was something alive, something crawling. I hit myself, first on the cheek, then on the nose, then on the forehead, but I obviously didn't get it, because it carried on creeping and crawling.

'Stand still,' I heard Fatso say.

I did as he said and he brushed my face with one hand while I screwed my eyes shut. When I opened them again, he was holding his hand up in front of me. On the back of his hand was an insect with red eyes and transparent wings.

'Ugh!' I shuddered. 'What is it?'

'I don't know,' Fatso said. 'But I've seen it in Mum's entomology book.'

'Ento-what?'

'Insect book. She collects insects. Dead ones, obviously.'

'Ugh,' I repeated.

'No, no, lots of them are really beautiful, you know. Like this one, don't you think?'

'No.'

Fatso laughed. He obviously felt he had the advantage now that he'd seen I wasn't quite as confident as he thought, but if he laughed too much he was going to get a slap. I considered warning him about that. The six-legged mini-monster seemed perfectly happy on Fatso's hand, and as he studied it from every angle I felt something land on my hair. I shook my head wildly, and two more red-eyed mini-monsters fell out.

'There are more of them!' I moaned. 'Let's get out of here!'

I didn't bother to wait, I just ran. I heard Fatso laughing as he followed me.

And then suddenly there we were, at the end of a gravel road that just stopped in the middle of the forest. I walked on quickly, I had a feeling it was going to get dark early that day. The bend in the road gradually opened out, the trees were less dense, and something tall and black loomed up out of the fog.

A black, wrought-iron fence, at least three metres tall.

I walked over to the gate. The curlicues in the middle formed the initials B.A., and beneath them was a sign saying *1, Mirror Forest Road*, then *Warning. This fence is electrified.*

I looked through the gate. It was as if the fog was shut out by the fence surrounding the property, there was no more than a slight haze covering the clear outline of the building. There was a taller section in the middle, with lower wings on either side. The tall part looked like it had horns, which might be what made me think of a bull or a dragon. The left wing had some sort of growth, like a giant mushroom on the roof.

'That . . .' Fatso whispered behind me. 'That's a weird house. Stop!' He grabbed my hand just as I was about to take hold of the handle of the gate. 'It says it's electrified!'

'Idiot. Those signs are just so people will stay away.'

I raised my foot and kicked the gate with the sole of my trainer. The door swung open with a plaintive, drawn-out creak.

'What did I say?' I said triumphantly.

'Rubber soles don't conduct electricity,' Fatso said.

I expressed my opinion with a well-directed snort, then walked in. 'Coming?' I called.

'No,' Fatso said.

I turned round. He was still standing outside the gate.

'Are you a coward?'

'Yes,' he said simply.

'You mean you daren't walk up to the door of a perfectly ordinary house?'

'This isn't an ordinary house, Richard.'

'It's got an address, and walls and a roof. It's as ordinary as you can get. And you know what, Fatso? If you don't go up there with me, I'll tell everyone at school what a coward you are.'

'Fine, I think they already know. And my name's Jack, not Fatso.'

I looked at him. It dawned on me that I had painted myself into a corner. If I didn't walk up to the house on my own, he'd tell the whole school, and unlike him, I actually had a reputation to lose.

'OK, you can stand here and keep watch over nothing, Fat Jack. Watch out for the fence.' I turned round and marched up the gravel path. As I got closer, I noticed a rising and falling humming sound that was coming from the house. And now I could also see that it wasn't made of wood like all the other houses in Ballantyne, but had red-brick walls covered with moss, with a few loose bricks. The two devil's horns were formed by the ridge of the roof. But the strangest part was the thing that had looked like a mushroom from a distance, which I now saw was the crown of a large oak tree. It was evidently growing out of the left wing, and had grown right through the roof. How was that possible? An oak tree like that doesn't grow up from the floor and through the roof overnight, they usually take hundreds of years to get that big.

Something hit me on the cheek. I brushed it away and looked down at a red-eyed insect crawling across the gravel path. Something crawled down my temple and tried to get inside my ear, but I shook my hair to get rid of it.

Then it dawned on me. The humming sound . . . I looked up at what I had thought was mist above the building. That was where the humming was coming from. Or rather, the buzzing. The buzzing from a living, flying swarm.

I stared.

The swarm was so large that it covered the sky, it was as if dusk had fallen early. I stopped and looked round. Was Fatso still watching, or could I turn back now and say I knocked but no one was home? Because there couldn't be anyone there, I couldn't see any lights behind the dark windows, and who lives in a house with a tree growing out of it? Even someone called Imu wouldn't do that, surely?

Something was crawling up my leg beneath my trouser leg and I looked down. More insects, they looked like they were coming straight out of the ground, like the living dead rising from the grave, crawling on skinny insect legs with eyes that glinted red. As I stood on one leg and brushed the other leg with my hand, a light came on in the large window in the middle of the building on the top, third floor. The light fell on the ground in front of the house. Sturdy tree roots emerged from the foundations and disappeared into the ground, as if the house itself were a tree. In the light it looked like the roots were moving, as if they were huge muscles, or boa constrictors. I tripped over my foot, hit my calf and fell to the ground. Onto a blanket of insects, suddenly they were everywhere, on my face, under my collar, in my mouth. I screamed. I got to my feet, spitting and slapping my neck and forehead. Something moved up by the window. I looked up. A face. Pale. The expressionless face of a man, as motionless as a painting. A face I had never seen before, yet which still gave me a strange feeling of looking in a mirror.

I felt something crunch under the palm of my hand, at last I had managed to put a stop to one of the insects! At that moment, as if on cue, all the buzzing stopped.

I looked up.

And then it struck me. That the insect I had just crushed, its innards now trickling down my neck, was the first one I had actually killed.

A starry sky of red eyes was staring down at me. A shoal of piranhas with wings. Then the buzzing started up again. Louder now. And the swarm was gathering, getting more compact, turning into a black cloud. Then it began to grow bigger. No, it wasn't growing, it had just come closer, it was heading right towards me.

I turned and started to run towards the gate. Behind me, out of the steadily increasing buzzing sound, rose a piercing, vibrating sound.

I could see the open gate now, and Fatso was standing there, as if the sky had fallen in as he stared past me.

'Run!' I yelled. 'Run!'

But Fatso didn't move. I ran past him. I ran down the road towards the river and the bridge. After a while I realised that the buzzing was quieter now, and stopped and turned round. And there, still standing by the gate, was Fatso.

He was holding his arms out from his sides, his smiling face turned up to the sky, like a farmer finally seeing rain.

Around him the swarm swirled like a tornado.

I waited for it to start, for them to devour him like the telephone had devoured Tom.

But that didn't happen.

The swirl of insects gradually rose up into the sky while Fatso reached his hands out after them, as if begging them to come back. Then his arms fell to his sides, and he padded down the road towards me with a broad smile on his face.

'What was that?' I asked.

'That,' Fatso said, 'was magicicadas.'

# 9

'THE INSECTS ARE CALLED MAGICICADAS,' Fatso repeated as he wolfed down Jenny's lasagne. 'They're completely harmless. There are just an awful lot of them at once. But you should have seen how frightened Richard was!'

Jenny, Frank and Fatso laughed, as I felt the blush burning my cheeks. I stared at Fatso, but he didn't notice and went on babbling.

'I realised they were magicicadas the moment I saw the swarm, then I remembered that it's my thirteenth birthday next week.'

'They must be what we just call cicadas,' Frank said, pouring more water in Fatso's glass. 'I've never seen them, just heard about them. But what does your birthday have to do with it?'

'My mum told me that the magicicadas were swarming when I was born. And they swarm every thirteen years.' Fatso smiled triumphantly, and looked very pleased with himself as he sat there at the dinner table, the centre of attention.

'Really?' Jenny said, shovelling more lasagne onto Fatso's plate. 'So what do they do in the meantime, then?'

'They live underground. No one knows how they figure out when it's time to emerge, but somehow they do, all of them at the same time. Millions of them. And they're so happy, because they've finally got wings!' He was beaming as he looked round the table, as if to check that everyone was keeping up. 'So they party. They make babies and lay eggs for a couple of weeks. Do you know what, Mrs Appleby? This is the best lasagne I've ever tasted.'

'Thank you, Jack.' She laughed, but I could see that his smooth flattery had hit home. 'What lovely manners!'

'I mean it!' he said with an idiotically sincere expression on his face.

'Even better manners,' Frank chuckled, and looked at me, as if to point out that I had a lot to learn.

'So you probably know what happens to the cicadas once they've finished partying, then?' Jenny said, leaning her elbow on the table and resting her chin on her hand, looking at Fatso as if the bastard could tell her anything she didn't already know.

'Then they die,' Fatso said.

'I might have guessed,' Frank said. 'Not all of them, though?'

'Yup,' Fatso said. 'All of them.'

'Phew,' I said.

The other three looked at me quizzically. But what else was I supposed to say? I didn't know anything about magicicadas, I just knew that it was pretty annoying that Frank and Jenny were prepared to swallow dull stories from a stranger seeing as they obviously didn't believe a word of it when I told them about flesh-eating telephones, for instance. Anyway, I hadn't been *that* frightened.

'Ah, well,' Jenny said, going back to the stove. 'We all have to die sometime, so it must be better if it happens while you're having fun.'

I didn't agree, it had to be better to die when you were having a bad time. But I didn't say anything.

'Anyway, what were you doing at that house?' Jenny asked.

'We were just passing,' I said, as Fatso wolfed down the last of the food. His jaw got to work, grinding the food into even smaller pieces. He looked just as hungry as when we started. He finished by scraping the plate clean with his fork, then slurping up the last remnants of sauce like a . . . well, like a telephone.

Frank said with a chuckle. 'Dessert, boys?'

I waited for a resounding 'Yes!' from Fatso, but instead he adopted a mournful expression.

'Mum doesn't let me. We put on weight easily in our family, so I'm only allowed sweet things on Saturday.'

'We understand,' Jenny said, tilting her head and looking at Fatso with her poor-dear smile. 'Well, then, you're both excused and can go and play in Richard's room.'

'Thank you very much for dinner, Mr and Mrs Appleby.'

I made fun of Fatso's fancy words behind his back, but Jenny and Frank pretended not to notice.

'What are we going to play?' Fatso asked when we got up to my room. He was sitting on one of the child-sized chairs in front of the toy box. They had been here when I arrived. Jenny and Frank had never told me why they thought a teenager needed children's furniture or liked playing with wooden building blocks, and for some reason I had never got round to asking them. And now here he was, sitting there as if he owned the room – as if it was him that Frank and Jenny had adopted, not me.

'We're going to play you going home now,' I said.

In the silence that followed, I thought I could hear the distant sound of the swarm partying somewhere outside the open window, it sounded like the low hum from an electricity substation. Unless the buzzing was just in my head, a symptom of a rage I couldn't remember feeling before. And which only grew stronger from the gawping expression on his face.

'And one more thing. You don't say a word to anyone about me being scared. Not at school, not anywhere. If you do, I'll crush you like a fucking cockroach. Because I wasn't scared. That's a lie! Understand?'

He didn't answer, but I saw him swallow, and the buzzing in my head just got louder and louder. As did my voice.

'Do you understand, Jack the Cockroach?'

Then Fatso seemed to get over the shock. He shook his head, almost indulgently, like an adult who has to deal with a brat that doesn't know how to behave. A brat who has no *manners*.

'But, Richard, it's nothing to be ashamed of. A million insects –'

'And if you do,' I said, as coldly as I could, 'I'll tell everyone that you're in love with Oscar Jr.'

At that, finally, he looked genuinely hurt.

I could have stopped there. I knew I *should* have stopped there – well, actually I should have stopped way before then. But I couldn't, my rage was like a snowball that had started rolling and that I had lost control of.

'Do you hear, Jack the Cockroach?' I went on. 'You're so fucking disgusting, that's why no one wants to play with you. Jack the Cockroach. Jack the Cockroach.'

His mouth fell open, but if he actually tried to say anything, nothing came out.

'Jack the Cockroach! Jack the Cockroach! Jack the Cockroach!'

Instead his glasses started to mist over. So I carried on chanting his new nickname as I stood over him as he sat wedged between the armrests of the tiny chair. He was holding his hands in front of his face and his glasses as if to protect himself against the words, but I leaned closer. I heard the sound of low sobbing, and big tears began to trickle past his hands and down his round cheeks.

There was something wrong with my voice too, like there was grit in the machinery. Weird, I seemed to be crying too. But my voice grew steadier as I shouted louder:

'Jack the Cockroach! Jack the Cockroach!'

Then something strange happened.

Something was growing out of Fatso's hunched back.

I can't find any other way to explain it. Something thin began to stick out from his sweater, like cling film or the stuff those see-through umbrellas are made of. It began to stretch out, like the roof of a convertible, something black and shiny started to spread out around his body, like the shell of a hazelnut. Or an insect. Because now I could see that the things growing out of his back were actually wings.

'Jack?' I said.

He removed his hands from his face and looked up at me.

I jerked back. I wanted to scream, but my mouth was too dry. His glasses were no longer glasses, but two protruding, red-shimmering, multifaceted eyes that were staring at me.

I backed away towards the door as he stiffly and rather creakily got up from the chair. I reached for the door to escape, but then I stopped. Because Fatso was getting smaller. Yes, as I watched, he was shrinking in size and was no longer quite as threatening. Apart from the pair of tentacles sticking out from his head and the extra pair of jagged black legs that were growing out from either side of his stomach. He was already so small that the chair looked like it was the right size.

'Fatso, stop,' I whispered, that was all I could manage. 'Stop that, do you hear?'

He made a noise, a sharp clicking sound, as if he was trying to reply in Morse code. He was shorter than the chair now, no bigger than the teddy bear in the toy box. The black shell was closing over his head, but there was a look of horror on what could still be seen of his face, and I realised that this wasn't something he was doing, it was something that was being done to him.

'Fatso?' I whispered. 'Jack?'

He was no bigger than an insect now. Or, to be more accurate, he *was* an insect. A magicicada that was looking up at me with red eyes.

I moistened my mouth to shout for Frank. But I didn't. Maybe I couldn't. Maybe I didn't want to. Because a thought had occurred to me. That I was the person who had done this. I don't know how, but maybe I shouldn't have said that stuff about cockroaches so many times. Actually, maybe I shouldn't have said it at all.

I stared down at the insect. Obviously I felt sorry for Fatso, because he was finished, he was going to die in a week's time anyway now, if what he had said about magicicadas over dinner was true. All my rage was gone now, replaced by a growing feeling of panic. If this was my fault and anyone found out, McClelland probably wouldn't only want to lock me away somewhere dark. He'd want to see me hanged, I'd end up dangling from the ceiling of a cell somewhere. I could imagine the rope, the lamp hook it was tied to, the chair being kicked away beneath me.

My heart was thudding hard, and there was only room for one thought in my head:

Get rid of the evidence!

I raised my foot and brought it down on the insect.

But no, it slipped away in a flash and hid under the chair. I grabbed the Kafka book from the bedside table and crept towards the chair on my knees. But as I raised the book to smear the magicicada on the floor, it spread its wings and took off. It flew straight towards the open window as I leapt to my feet, far too late. By the time I got there it was gone, swallowed up by the evening darkness. I stared out. I thought I could see a pair of red eyes glowing out there, but Fatso was gone. I listened to the low buzzing coming from Mirror Forest for a while. Perhaps Fatso had finally been invited to that party people like us never got invited to. I sat there until my heartbeat had slowed down. Then I closed the window and went downstairs to Jenny and Frank.

# 10

SHERIFF MCCLELLAND WAS STANDING BY the window of the meeting room, looking out. The board at the end of the room was covered by a map of the immediate area, with various places circled, some of them crossed off. I had figured out that these were areas they had already searched for Tom.

The sun was shining on the car park outside. On the far end, next to the fire station, was a tall lookout tower that was evidently the tallest point for miles around. Frank had taken me up there a few days after I first arrived, perhaps in the hope that I would be impressed. Like, the fire chief's tower. I didn't have the heart to tell him that the building I used to live in back in the city was twice as tall. He told me that the tower was manned day and night during the summer, to keep a lookout for forest fires. He told me they were common, and very costly to a small community that lives off its forests. And I couldn't take that away from Ballantyne, it really *did* have a lot of forest. And precious little else. People, for instance. Right now, around half of them were probably out searching for Fatso and Tom, while I was stuck here on a chair between Frank and Jenny.

'So Jack Ruud left your house at eight o'clock?' McClelland said. 'To go home?'

'Yes,' Frank said.

McClelland ran his thumb and forefinger over his moustache, then nodded to the officer who was sitting at the table taking notes.

I hadn't said much so far. It was Frank who had advised me to let him do most of the talking, and that I should stick to giving short answers to any questions directed specifically at me. And that I definitely shouldn't say anything about a drainpipe.

When I went down to the living room after Fatso – or what had once been Fatso – had flown out of the window, I had lied and told them that he had gone home, that he had climbed down the drainpipe outside my room. They were a little surprised, because Fatso hadn't exactly given the impression of being particularly acrobatic. But they believed me, seeing as they had caught me climbing down the drainpipe several times, even though I had been told sternly that this was forbidden, not just because it was dangerous, but because drainpipes weren't very strong and cost a lot of money. And when Fatso's parents phoned later that evening to ask where he was, Jenny had replied that he had set off at eight o'clock, omitting to say anything about drainpipes. Now that I had finally brought a friend home with me, she didn't want us to look like an irresponsible family. That's why she and Frank stuck to that story when the police called just after midnight. But of course, Frank and Jenny were no doubt thinking that this was the second occasion in a very short space of time that one of my playmates had disappeared without trace, so perhaps it was best not to leave any room for doubt – so they confirmed that yes, they had seen Jack Ruud walk out of the door with their own eyes.

'A very polite boy,' Jenny said. 'A thoroughly nice person.'

I had only been to two funerals, but I knew that was the sort of thing you only say about people you don't know well when they're dead. But McClelland didn't appear to react. There was no reason for Jenny to assume that Fatso was dead, was there? Because as far as anyone knew, he was just a bit . . . missing.

'OK,' McClelland said, turning back towards us and fixing his eyes on me. In spite of his little piggy eyes and wispy moustache, he actually looked quite kind. Perhaps he was, perhaps he was just trying to do his job as well as he could. And right now, that meant watching me, checking to see if he had X-ray vision and could figure out what was going on inside my head. Which, just then, was quite a lot.

'Thanks, you can go,' he said, his eyes still fixed on me: 'We'll talk again soon.'

# 11

'THAT'S EVEN WORSE THAN THE story about the phone, you know that, right?' Karen was standing at the edge of the roof, looking down at the schoolyard. I had told her everything, about the house, the swarm and Fatso's transformation.

'I know,' I mumbled. 'That's why I can't tell anyone, they'd just think I was the worst liar in the world and not believe a word.'

She turned towards me. 'And what makes you think *I* believe you?'

'Because you . . .' I hesitated. 'Don't you believe me?'

Karen shrugged. 'I think *you* believe it.'

'What's that supposed to mean?'

Karen sighed. 'No one ever goes missing in Ballantyne, Richard. This is the second disappearance in a few days, and in both cases you were the last person they were with. Which is even more weird, because everyone knows you haven't actually got any friends.'

'I've got you.'

'I said *friends*. Plural.'

'But I've got proof, I keep saying that!' I realised I had raised my voice. 'The old phone book!'

'I hear you say you found the name Imu Jonasson, but that doesn't mean –'

'Doesn't mean what, then? That I'm telling the truth? I couldn't have invented a name like that if I hadn't heard or seen it!' I rubbed my temple, I could feel a headache coming on.

'I'm just saying, the sheriff will think you came up with that name because it's well known, it's . . . how did he put it?'

'Town history. OK, have *you* heard of Imu Jonasson?'

'No.'

'Well, then! And you've lived here your whole life.' I groaned. 'I don't know what it is, but this business with Imu Jonasson and Tom and Fatso, it's all connected, you can see that too.'

She tilted her head and put her hands on her sides. 'I can see that *too*?'

'Sorry, I didn't mean . . . I . . . sorry.' I threw my arms out. 'I'm just very, very stressed right now.'

Her eyes went back to being all Karen and mild again. 'I know, Richard. One more thing . . .' She stopped and touched her forefinger to her bottom lip thoughtfully.

'What?' I said impatiently.

'If what the sheriff says about town history is true, then we ought to be able to find out about Imu Jonasson in the local history almanacs.'

'Local history almanacs?'

'Yes. They come out every year. Family history, and random things that have happened in Ballantyne.'

'Where do we find them?'

'They're under B,' Mrs Zimmer said, pointing to the bookshelves at the back of the library. 'Forty-eight volumes. What are you looking for?'

'Anything about an Imu Jonasson,' Karen said, still out of breath after running all the way here from school.

Mrs Zimmer sneezed hard, twice. 'There's nothing about an Imu Jonasson there,' she said in a nasal voice, tearing a sheet from the roll of tissues in front of her on the counter.

'Oh?' Karen said. 'How do you know that?'

'Because I know Ballantyne,' Mrs Zimmer said. 'The way I know my library. I know, for instance, that you are Karen Taylor, daughter of Nils and Astrid.'

Karen nodded in confirmation, and Mrs Zimmer went on with her eyes fixed on me. 'And I know that we're missing one phone book.'

I felt myself blush. 'I . . . erm, I just borrowed it. I'll bring it back this afternoon.'

'I thought as much. How did you get it down from up there?'

'There was a tall ladder there, like a fire ladder.'

'Nonsense!'

'Nonsense?'

'Yes, we don't have any tall ladders here. And we don't loan out phone books. Or local history books. They're reference books that have to be read here. But, like I said, there's nothing about an Imu Jonasson.'

I turned to Karen, who was shaking her head sadly.

'Thanks anyway,' Karen sighed, and we started to walk back towards the door.

Mrs Zimmer cleared her throat behind us. 'There's nothing there because the publishers don't like publishing town gossip.'

We stopped and turned round.

'You know who Imu Jonasson is?' I asked.

'Of course.'

'Why of course?'

'Because he's the adopted son of Robert Willingstad who donated this library to Ballantyne in 1920. They lived in the Night House.'

'The Night House?' Karen asked.

'That's what people called it. The big mansion in Mirror Forest.'

'You say lived?' I said. 'So Imu doesn't live there any more?'

'As far as I know, Imu Jonasson hasn't lived in Ballantyne since he was committed to an institution. And that was decades ago.'

'Did he do something wrong?'

'Oh yes, but not before something wrong was done to him.'

'Like what?' Karen asked. She looked as tense as I felt.

'Oh, Imu was a bit different, and was tormented by the other children. Then, one Halloween, when everyone was out begging for sweets, they mobbed Imu, stripped him and tied him to the fence of the cow pen on the Geberhardt farm. Then one of them snuck into the barn and turned the electricity on. When they found Imu, he . . . he wasn't the same as he had been before, if I can put it like that.'

'And what was he like before?' Karen asked.

'He was a kind, thoughtful boy. A bit of a loner, he used to spend a lot of time here in the library. He said he was going to be a famous author.'

'And afterwards?'

'He got mean.'

'How?'

Mrs Zimmer gasped for breath three times in a row, but no sneeze appeared. 'He bullied the other children,' she said. 'To get revenge, I suppose, but he didn't just bully the ones who had tied him to the electrified fence. Once he stole a bicycle that one of the neighbours' children had been given as a birthday present, and threw it in the river. But most of all he liked scaring them. One time he dressed up as the dead father of one girl, and went and stood in the moonlight outside her bedroom window. When the sheriff caught him for stealing the bicycle and asked if he did it for revenge, Imu replied that he couldn't remember who had tied him to the fence, so he was taking his revenge on all of them.'

'He couldn't remember?' Karen asked.

Mrs Zimmer shrugged. 'They say that electric shocks can affect the memory. And I think it did other things to his brain as well.'

'Like what?' I asked.

'He became strange. Used to wear ragged clothes and kept to himself in Mirror Forest, where people used to say he hunted animals. One man claimed to have seen the boy squatting down as he ate a rat, a rat that was still moving, and when the boy looked up there was blood running from the corners of his mouth.'

'Oh, no,' Karen said, putting her hands over her ears, but not quite covering them.

'Oh, yes,' Mrs Zimmer said. 'Another man said he had seen the boy eating insects, that he was picking them up off the ground and chewing them like they were popcorn. And Imu developed strange interests. One day he came to see me, he was standing where you two are now, and asked if I had any books on black word magic.' She lowered her voice. 'His eyes were completely black and wild, his clothes were filthy, and he smelled terrible. Poor lad! It's hardly surprising that they had to send him to an institution.'

'So, have you?' I asked. 'Got any books on black word magic?'

Mrs Zimmer looked at me but didn't answer. We stood there in silence, and it might have been my imagination, but I thought I could hear something in the distance. Like wind blowing across a hollow trunk. Or the warning cry of an owl.

'Where?' Karen asked.

'Like I said,' Mrs Zimmer whispered, suddenly looking uneasy. 'We don't have a ladder that can reach that high.'

'But –' I began.

'And now you have to go.' She looked to where I thought I had heard the sound. 'We're closing.'

'Now?' Karen said. 'But it's only –'

'You should never rely on the clock, Karen Taylor. Now, quick, out with you!'

I saw the red car as soon as we emerged from the library. Because this time it wasn't parked in the distance, but right outside. It was obviously done with playing hide-and-seek.

'What is it?' Karen asked when she noticed I had stopped.

'A Pontiac LeMans,' I said. '1968 model.'

'I mean, what's wrong?'

'We're about to find out,' I said, because the door opened and a tall man got out, dressed in a black suit and a thin black tie, and with side-parted black hair that was so shiny and thick that it looked like it was made of porcelain, a bit like Superman's. I was in no doubt that this was the same man whose rear view I had seen in the meeting room at the police station.

'Richard Elauved,' he said, holding up a leather pouch with a metal star inside. 'I'm Agent Dale from the Federal Police.'

# 12

A MAN IN A WHITE doctor's coat was hovering around me as he attached wires to my bare torso. When Agent Dale and I arrived at the police station in the red car, he had led me into a small room in the basement. It looked like it had once been used as a recording studio, because it had padded walls and a single, large window in the wall between the rooms, with microphones on both sides. But obviously it could also have been used as a torture chamber.

'There's nothing to worry about, Richard,' Agent Dale said. He was leaning against the wall with his arms folded. He had explained that he was an investigator specialising in missing persons cases. That he and the man in the white coat had come to Ballantyne to find out what I knew about Tom and Jack.

White-coat had cold, clammy hands, and they clawed at my

chest, neck, back and wrists as he taped red, blue and orange wires to me, all of which led to a large, humming gadget on the table. They had told me that it was a lie detector, that they could tell if I was telling the truth or lying. And that it would best for me to tell the truth. If I didn't, there could be consequences. They didn't say what those consequences would be, but they let me understand that they weren't trivial.

'There,' white-coat said, sitting down on a chair on the other side of the table, adjusting his glasses and staring at a screen in front of him.

Agent Dale came and sat down. 'Any questions before we begin, Richard?'

'Yes,' I said. 'Did you and the sheriff agree to let me go free so you could spy on me and see if I gave anything away?'

Agent Dale looked at me for a long time before replying: 'Any other questions?'

'No.'

'Good,' he said, and put his hands on the tabletop between us. 'My first question is about Tom. We have a theory that he ended up in the river in Mirror Forest. The river has been searched, without result, so we believe he has been carried downstream, south towards Crow Lake. We've spoken to someone who was there back in the day when timber used to be floated down the river. They pointed out the place where the unfortunate rafters who got trapped beneath the logs and drowned used to get washed ashore. So we went there, and we didn't find Tom. But we did find this on the shore.'

Dale put something down hard on the table. It was Luke Skywalker. The plastic figure looked at me with its blue eyes.

'We've spoken to Tom's parents, and they say this isn't his toy.

But when we asked the owner of the local toyshop who sells these, he told us that his son recently had a figure like this stolen during a class party that Tom attended. So we believe that Tom had the figure on him when he ended up in the river. Do you know anything about that?'

'No,' I said.

The man in the white coat shook his head without speaking.

'The detector says you're lying, Richard.'

'OK,' I said, and swallowed. 'Then I'll say that Tom stole the figure and ended up in the river. What's the machine saying now?'

The man in the white coat shook his head again.

Dale frowned. 'Perhaps you should try saying something true instead, Richard? What's your name?'

'Richard Elauved.'

White-coat nodded.

'Anything else?'

'Tom was eaten by a telephone.'

The man in the white coat looked at the screen, then up at Dale. He nodded.

I saw Dale's jaw muscles tense, and he clenched one fist so hard that his knuckles turned white.

'What about Jack, what happened to him?'

'It got late, so he had to leave.'

'And you saw him leave?'

'Yes.'

'He was going home?'

'I assume he was going home, yes.'

The head above the white coat was nodding repeatedly.

'Any idea if he might have taken a detour?'

'I don't know about a detour. Fats . . . Jack was interested in insects, so he might have gone to the house in Mirror Forest. The magicicadas are swarming there at the moment, especially around the house.'

'Oh?'

'If I were you, I'd check out the guy who lives there, maybe he knows something.'

'And who's that?'

'I think his name is . . .' I swallowed. 'Imu Jonasson.'

White-coat shook his head.

'I *know* his name is Imu Jonasson,' I corrected, and white-coat nodded.

# 13

'SO THIS IS WHAT PEOPLE call the Night House?' Dale said, peering through the railings of the gate at the ramshackle house with the oak tree growing out of its roof.

'According to Mrs Zimmer in the library,' I said, and McClelland nodded in agreement.

'It looks pretty abandoned,' Dale said. 'But you're saying someone lives here?'

I shrugged and was about to shout out a warning when Sheriff McClelland grabbed hold of the handle. But nothing happened, he just pushed the gate open, and the three of us walked across the wet ground up towards the house. Now that it was bathed in moonlight and there was no fog, it looked a lot less creepy than last time, I had to admit. And there was no trace of the magicicadas now, either they must have partied till they dropped and crept back underground, or they had moved the party somewhere else. The pointed gables no longer looked like devil's horns, and the roots growing out of the big cracks in the foundations didn't remind me of boa constrictors. McClelland, being rather thick-set, felt the rotten wooden steps tentatively before going up to the door. He didn't bother knocking, just pulled the handle.

'Locked?' Dale asked.

'Swollen,' McClelland said, then grabbed hold of the handle with both hands, took the strain and pulled. The door let go of the frame with a deep, reluctant groan, and we stared into the darkness behind it. Inside the air was damp, and there were dripping sounds coming from several directions.

We stepped into what was an enormous hall.

All of a sudden it was back, the same eerie feeling I had felt last time when I was standing outside.

It looked like someone had run amok in there.

In the middle of the hall, on top of a heap of overturned furniture and a grand piano that had broken in two, lay a large painting. The gilded frame had snapped in several places, the canvas was wet and the picture covered with spiders' webs and dirt, so it was impossible to see what it was supposed to be. On the walls the patterned wallpaper had bubbled up or was hanging in strips, and there were several steps missing from the broad staircase that led up to the gallery that encircled the hall.

Dale went over to the grand piano while McClelland walked over to one of the doors, switched his torch on and peered inside.

'There's no way anyone is living here,' Dale said, pressing two of the yellowed keys. His voice, and the broken, jarringly off-tune notes of the piano echoed like we were in a cave.

'I don't know about that,' McClelland said in a low voice. 'This is actually the perfect home.'

Dale's eyes narrowed, he pushed his suit jacket aside and – like he was in a movie – drew a shiny pistol. With my heart pounding, I crept closer to him. Raising his arm, he took a couple of silent steps until he was standing right behind McClelland, looking over his shoulder. I crouched down so that I could see into the room as well. At first I could only see the remains of a bed that had been reduced to firewood, then I looked up to see what the sheriff was pointing his torch at. There, on a beam by the ceiling, were what looked like a row of black, slightly stretched underpants hung up to dry.

'The perfect home if you're a bat,' McClelland said.

At that moment one pair of underpants came loose. Dale let out a scream as it came towards us, then there was a noise like a pistol shot as the underpants flew over our heads. It took me a moment to realise that it *was* actually a pistol shot. We turned and watched the underpants as they flew a couple of jerky, inelegant circuits of the hall before disappearing into one of the rooms on the upper floor.

Dale cleared his throat. 'I didn't hear you say bat.'

'How do you know that's what I said, then?' McClelland asked.

'Deduction,' Dale said, tucking the pistol away beneath his jacket again.

We walked into the next room and stood there staring at the big, sturdy oak tree.

'Incredible,' Dale said. 'Growing straight up through the floor and right through the roof like that. There really is no stopping nature once it's made its mind up. How old is this house?'

'I only moved here ten years ago, so I don't know the full history of the area,' McClelland said. 'But none of the people I've spoken to know much more. This house is old though, there's no doubt about that.'

'There's no doubt about something else too – the fact that there's no Imu Jonasson here,' Dale said, turning towards me. 'Not here, and not in the phone book.'

I shrugged. 'I saw him. Here, and in the phone book.'

'The boy's lying!' McClelland snapped.

We had driven back to the police station, where they had put me in the padded room while they talked in the room on the other side of the window. Because the room was soundproofed, I couldn't hear anything at first, I just saw McClelland march up and down, talking with an angry expression on his face while Dale sat calmly on a chair. But then I tried pressing some of the buttons on a panel on the table, and the sound of their voices suddenly streamed out of the speakers in the walls.

'Everyone says he's a troublemaker,' McClelland went on, punching his palm with his fist. 'And now I've got four distraught parents and an entire town that's wondering why we aren't getting anywhere. All because this little hooligan won't tell us the truth. What am I supposed to do? He's too young for me to throw him in prison like I should, and torture is . . . well, we don't do that here.'

'The lie detector told us he's telling the truth about this Imu Jonasson,' Dale said. 'Or rather: he believes he's telling the truth. Unless . . .'

'Unless what?'

'Unless we're dealing with a full-blown psychopath in Richard Elauved.' The pair of them turned to look at me, and I had to really concentrate not to let on that I could hear everything they were saying. 'Psychopaths can fool even the most advanced lie detector,' Dale said.

McClelland nodded slowly. 'If you ask me, I think we're dealing with a hardened, unscrupulous young man of the very worst sort, Dale. The sort society needs protecting from.'

'Maybe,' Dale said, stroking his chin. 'Can you tell me about this Jonasson, please?'

'Imu Jonasson? I've only heard a few stories. I know his parents died in a fire, there was something bad there, and the boy brought it back here.'

'He didn't bring it here!' I shouted, but obviously they couldn't hear anything.

'He was sent to a correctional facility,' McClelland went on. 'As far as I know, no one here has seen or heard from him since then. Our problem isn't Imu Jonasson, it's this wretched Richard Elauved. Have you got any suggestions as to what we ought to do with him, Dale?'

'Send him somewhere where he'll have time to think and repent. A few weeks, months maybe, ought to do the trick.'

'And where might that be?'

'You just mentioned it yourself.'

'Did I?' McClelland frowned. Then his face lit up. 'Oh!'

I sat and listened as McClelland phoned Jenny and Frank and informed them of the 'emergency measure', as they called it, and asked them to bring in clothes, toiletries and anything else I might need for a short or longer stay in a correctional facility.

The landscape outside the car window consisted of flat marshland, bogs and trees. Mostly trees. Entire forests of them, in fact.

Frank was driving, and Jenny was sitting in the back seat. The reason why I had been promoted to the front seat went unspoken, but it wasn't hard to guess. When you drive your foster-son to an institution way out in the wilderness, you let him sit where he likes, a bit like letting a death-row prisoner choose his last meal. We had been driving for three hours, and had three more to go, according to Jenny.

Frank was humming along to the music from the cassette player.

*Take me home, country roads, to the place I belong.*

As if that was actually the case, that I belonged where we were going.

'It isn't a prison,' McClelland had assured Frank and Jenny.

'But it is a prison!' Karen had exclaimed when I told her where I was going.

'A year will soon pass,' Jenny had said to console me.

'That's a whole lifetime!' Karen had snapped angrily. 'And you haven't even done anything!'

She had promised to visit me, she even gave me a hug in the schoolyard when Oscar Jr and the others were watching. And even if I had come close to tears, I managed to hold them back, to deny them that satisfaction. No one in class, not even Miss Birdsong, had anything to say to me, which was probably just as well seeing as in all likelihood they wouldn't have had anything nice to say to me. They were relieved to get rid of me, that much was obvious from their gawping faces. Because they were properly scared of me now. That was something, at least.

'What does deduction mean?' I asked.

'Deduction,' Frank said, taking time to think. An entire verse of the song, in fact. Which was fine, we had plenty of time. Far too much time. 'Deduction is a form of logic. You find your way towards a solution by excluding everything that's impossible. Then what you're left with is what's possible. And if there's only one thing left, that's the answer. Do you see?'

'Yes,' I said, looking out of the window. I realised that meant removing the possibility that someone had been eaten by a telephone or transformed into an insect. After that, you're left with a liar who is probably responsible for the disappearances of two boys. That was logical. So logical that I would have thought it myself. If I hadn't seen with my own eyes that the impossible is actually possible.

Jenny had estimated our time of arrival down to the minute, possibly because the road – which mostly ran like a straight, monotonous line across the landscape – had very little traffic, hardly any junctions or deviations in the speed limit.

'Is this it?' I asked sceptically.

We had stopped in the middle of a field.

'Looks like it,' Frank said.

We got out of the car. The sky had clouded over, and a cold wind was blowing.

'Yes,' Jenny said, shivering as she stood there with her arms folded, looking at the white, fortress-like building behind the barbed-wire fence. We couldn't see or hear anyone else. There was just this barren landscape, this unwelcoming building, and the wind that made the sign above the gate creak as it swung back and forth on its chains. Some of the letters had faded or been worn away by wind and rain, but I knew what it said.

RORRIM'S CORRECTIONAL FACILITY FOR YOUNG PEOPLE.

# 14

MCCLELLAND HAD BEEN TELLING THE truth, Rorrim's correctional facility for young people wasn't a prison. Because here the people who made sure the doors were locked weren't guards, but 'safety officers', and those who supervised us were 'teachers', 'work supervisors', 'activity leaders' or 'principals'. It wasn't called serving time, but 'being caught by society's safety net', something we were told we should be seriously damn grateful for. If you broke one of the many internal rules you didn't get punished, you were 'corrected' or 'deprived of privileges', such as being allowed outside for a few hours, or *not* being locked up alone. As far as I know, no one was beaten or otherwise physically punished, but those who lost control – and with so many vulnerable youngsters gathered in the same place, that obviously happened all the time – were taken care of. The regulations didn't permit the use of handcuffs, but they could tie you to something, a chair or your bed, for your own safety, as they put it. When I went to bed at night I often lay awake, hearing the screams from the other rooms and wondering if I'd end up like that if I was there long enough.

Whenever parents and other relatives visited, they were often shown round by the Principal, to the classrooms, or the workshops for those who were better at practical things, and the gym where we let off steam and vented the worst of our aggression. There were no bars on the windows, guns or uniforms. And we – the 'residents', rather than inmates – were also allowed to wear our own clothes. Rorrim's buildings may have been as desolate as the surrounding landscape, but they were always clean and freshly painted white, seeing as cleaning and painting were among our main activities. Seen from the outside, Rorrim's must have looked like any other boarding school for young people, but those of us who lived there knew better.

Boys and girls were strictly segregated in different wards at night. With one exception, the twins Victor and Vanessa Blumenberg. No one ever told us why, but it was obvious enough. If you separated them for more than an hour, they both went berserk. No correction or loss of privileges stopped them, and the twins were big and strong, so that took its toll on both the fabric of the building and the staff. So much so that the Principal realised that the only solution was the path of least resistance – letting them share a room. Which was just as well, seeing as no one else wanted to, because of the rumour that little brother Blumenberg – who the twins thought was getting far too much attention – had been smothered in his sleep.

But there were so many rumours.

For instance, some said that Vanessa and Victor not only came from the same egg, but that they came from the same half an egg. That they had been born far too early, and that they had been joined at the hip, which was why they limped, one on the right leg, the other on the left. That they shared one brain, which was why they often just sat there in silence, dull-eyed and slack-jawed. They didn't talk much, not even to each other, but someone said they didn't need to, they could communicate telepathically.

But that was probably all rubbish.

At least I *hoped* it was rubbish.

Because I had been placed in the same room as the twins. Just me. The other rooms housed groups of four. With us, it was two against one. For the first few weeks they didn't speak or look at me, it was like I wasn't there. And that was fine with me. I was a light sleeper, and kept an eye on the pillows.

I was among the residents who received an education. We sat in a classroom where the teacher had given up in advance. It seemed that he was satisfied if he could just get through a school day without someone having a furious outburst, getting hurt or ending up even more stupid than when they had arrived. After that came lunch in the canteen, then some time in the fresh air. The weather always seemed to be the same, grey and oppressive, but no rain ever fell from those steel-grey skies. In the evening the others played table tennis or sat in the television room, but I kept to myself or went for a walk round the library. Karen had given me a taste for books, I had to give her the credit for that. The days were just as long and monotonous as the road from Ballantyne, so it was something of a change when I actually got the room to myself for a week. Victor had slashed the cook in the face with a meat cleaver when the cook accused him of stealing his wallet (which, naturally, he had done). While the cook was lying on the kitchen floor bleeding, Vanessa had kicked him, probably out of solidarity. Either way, the twins had each been locked up in their own little room (they weren't called cells), where they had to spend their days alone (it was called alone, rather than in isolation), and we could hear their screams all through the night. When they came back to the room they were different. They seemed broken, they stared down at the floor, I was no longer invisible, they actually moved out of the way when I wanted to get in or out of the room. One evening Vanessa asked what I was reading as I lay on my bed. I was so surprised at being spoken to that at first I thought I had misheard, but when I looked up from the book I saw her peering down from the top of our three-tiered bunk bed. I told her it was a book called *Papillon*, about a man who escaped from prison. From the bunk between us I heard Victor grunt:

'Escape.'

From that day on, we started to have simple conversations. Or rather, one conversation, because it was always about the same thing. Escaping. Victor and Vanessa wanted out. Had to get out, they said. They were going to die in there. When I asked what they were hoping to escape to, and if they were absolutely certain that there was something better out there, they just looked at me with glassy, uncomprehending eyes that I took to mean that they either thought it was a ridiculous question, or hadn't actually thought about that. In the end Vanessa replied:

'Out there at least they won't be able to keep us apart from each other.'

'You have to help us,' Victor said.

'Me?'

Vanessa nodded.

'What makes you think I can help?'

'You can read about how to escape,' Victor said.

'But you can do that too –'

'No,' Victor interrupted. 'We can't. Help us. Or else . . .' For the first time I saw something other than emptiness in his eyes. Something hard and cruel.

I gulped. 'Or else?'

'We'll kill you,' Vanessa said. 'We know how to do *that*.'

'Oh?' I said. 'The cook survived.'

'Because we let him,' Victor said in a low voice. 'You've got until Sunday.'

'Sunday? That's only four days away.'

Victor screwed his eyes up in concentration and I saw his lips move as he counted on his fingers.

'That's right,' he said.

It wasn't that it was impossible to escape from Rorrim's. Getting outside the fence wouldn't even be particularly difficult. It was getting any further than that. If you had someone you knew who could be waiting there with a getaway vehicle, then maybe. If you didn't, you had fifty kilometres of flat, open landscape to the nearest settlement, and no one picks up hitchhiking teenagers anywhere close to Rorrim's correctional facility for young people. They sound the alarm instead.

So I had to come up with a plan that solved both the how-to-get-out and how-to-get-away problems in one go.

The answer was the garbage truck.

It turned up every Friday morning, so, two days after the twins had given me their ultimatum, I just happened to be standing in the yard behind the kitchen when the garbage truck reversed in. I looked on as the two guys from the truck wheeled the nine green bins over to the truck and attached them, one at a time, to the hoist. One of the guys pressed a button on the side of the truck, and the other wore some sort of back brace as he watched the bins being lifted into the air, turned over and emptied into the back of the truck, to the sound of hydraulic groaning. The bins were one metre by one metre, and came up to chest height.

I went over to them and asked a few questions, sort of just out of curiosity, and they answered happily enough. That evening I outlined my plan to the twins as we lay in our bunks.

'We each hide in a bin bag in a bin,' Victor repeated.

'Yes,' I said. 'We push two of the bins into the kitchen and remove the rubbish to make room for you. You get into a bin bag, I tie the bags and push the bins back outside. I'll make some holes in the bags so you can breathe. And it's important that you don't make any noise when you land in the truck, because the guys stand and watch.'

I heard the bunk creak as they both nodded.

'The garbage truck drives to pick up more rubbish in Evans,' I said. 'Evans is thirty kilometres away, so there probably won't be anyone who'd suspect that you were from Rorrim's. So you'll be OK to hitchhike or take a bus from there.'

After a short pause I heard more creaking.

Then, after a longer pause, Victor's voice: 'That's seven days away.'

'That's right.'

'You had four.'

'To come up with a plan, not to actually escape.'

'Four. Seven days is a long time.'

'Well, if you kill me, there'll be no one to tie the bin bags.'

Another long pause. Then a strange sound that I hadn't heard before. It came from both of the bunks above me at the same time, a mixture of snorting, heavy breathing and what sounded like unoiled door hinges. I eventually realised that the twins were laughing.

That Sunday I had an unexpected visit. From Karen.

We were allowed to sit in the canteen, she had that same little notebook in front of her. As usual, she asked questions about me rather than telling me about herself. She asked how I was, and how I passed the time, about the people at Rorrim's, about the food, beds, the books I was reading. She made notes of my answers about what it was like being locked up, what I dreamed about at night, why I thought no one believed me. If I still remembered everything that had happened the same way – that Tom was eaten by a telephone and Fatso turned into an insect.

'Why are you writing everything down?' I asked.

Karen looked round as if someone might be eavesdropping in the empty canteen, then leaned forward and whispered: 'I want to try to solve the mystery of Imu Jonasson.'

'What for?'

She looked at me in surprise before replying.

'Because it would be good for you if we find him, Richard. And good for me. Good for all of us.'

'All?'

'Yes.'

'Why?'

'Because I think he could be dangerous if we don't do something.'

'What do you mean?'

Karen lowered her voice even more. 'There was something Mrs Zimmer didn't tell us about Imu Jonasson.'

'And what's that?'

'He wasn't sent to an institution because he drank rat's blood, smelled bad or stole a bicycle. He set fire to his parents' house.'

'What?'

'They both burned to death.'

'Is that true?'

Karen nodded, fixed her pink hair clip to the page of the notebook and closed it. 'I read it in the local history almanac. Not about Imu, exactly, but that there had been a fire where two people died. And now I think he's back in Ballantyne.'

'That's what I was saying!' I exclaimed, then calmed down when I saw that the 'activity leader' was watching us. 'I said I saw a man in that house in Mirror Forest.'

'You can't know if that was Imu Jonasson, Richard.'

'Yes, I . . .' I didn't know how to explain it to her, so I just said it. 'I recognised him.'

Karen looked at me, wide-eyed. 'How?'

'I don't know.' I put one hand on my forehead, it felt hot. 'I just knew I'd seen that face somewhere,' I whispered.

'Are you ill?' Karen was looking anxiously at me.

'No, there's just a lot going on at the moment.'

A car horn sounded outside.

'Same here,' Karen said. 'Sounds like someone's waiting for me.'

'What sort of someone?' I had been so surprised by the visit that I hadn't even thought about how she had got there.

'Oscar,' she said with a quick smile as she put her notebook in her bag.

'Oscar? He isn't sixteen, he can't drive.'

'This isn't the city, Richard, we aren't that fussy here. Oscar's over fifteen and has a provisional licence.'

'OK, then. So he can drive you to Hume, too?'

'Hume?'

'The cinema. To see one of those old films you like.' I could have bitten my tongue, but it was too late. I did at least feel a certain relief when she shook her head. I wondered how she had managed to persuade Oscar to help her visit me. I guess he thought that if she was going to do it anyway, it would be better if he was there to keep an eye on her. She stood up.

I went outside to the fence with Karen, where a 'safety officer' stared at us as he opened the gate. There was a Ford Granada parked outside. I took a step forward and saw Karen realise I was about to give her a hug. She pre-empted me and held her hand out instead.

'Look after yourself, Richard.'

I stood inside the fence and watched as a cloud of dust flew up behind the car when it drove off. It was summer, the wind was blowing, and the same grey clouds covered the monotonous, colourless landscape, making it neither hot nor cold, neither dark nor light.

# 15

THE DAYS FOLLOWING KAREN'S VISIT crawled by. My mood was even gloomier than usual, and the twins' impending escape filled me with neither joy nor excitement.

One night I dreamed I was standing at the top of the tower at the fire station. It was dark, and all I could see in the car park below me was the rotating blue light on top of the fire truck. I could only just make out the people down below, but I could hear them perfectly well. There were a lot of them, and they were chanting:

'Jump, jump, jump!'

I wanted to do as they said, but how could I be sure that those voices wished me well?

'Jump, jump, jump!'

Maybe they just wanted the excitement of seeing someone fall so far. Maybe they were starving and wanted to eat me. Or were they right? Did I have to jump to save myself? Maybe I didn't have a choice. But it's hard to jump, it's hard to trust anyone. Just as I made a decision, I woke up. During the day I didn't think much about the dream, but when I went to bed again I could still hear the voices, it was like a chorus, and I hummed along: 'Jump, jump, jump!', until I realised it was a sad tune and stopped.

Then, on Wednesday, two days before the escape attempt, I received a letter that turned my mood upside down.

Lucas was the only person at Rorrim's that I spoke to more than was absolutely necessary. He had worked there for forty years, as a combination of caretaker and librarian. What we talked about most was books. He tossed the letter on the table in front of me in the reading room.

'Girl's handwriting,' he said simply, then walked off.

It was from Karen.

*Dear Richard,*

*I'm on the trail of Imu Jonasson! I think I know where he's hiding, but I need your help, you're the only person who knows what he looks like now. Is there any way you could get a leave of absence for a couple of days and come back here, do your thing?*

*Yours, Karen*

*PS I know it seemed a bit cold when we said goodbye, but I know Oscar was watching. He's got it into his head that he and I are going to be together, and I couldn't bear the thought of an awful atmosphere the whole way home. Not that a hug would have meant that you and I were together, but you know what jealous alpha-male types like Oscar are like.*

I read the letter a couple more times. Twelve, to be precise. And I came up with the following preliminary analysis:

– Karen chose to open the letter with 'Dear Richard' instead of 'Hi Richard', which is probably what I would have used if I'd been writing to her. 'Hi Karen', I mean.

– Karen had actually wanted to give me a hug.

– Karen *doesn't* think I'm an alpha male.

– Karen takes care to emphasise that any hug would have been friendly, just as I would have done. But in my case it would have been because I was terrified not of her misunderstanding, but of her actually understanding.

– Karen emphasises that she doesn't want to be Oscar's girlfriend. Does she do this because she thinks I'm jealous of them driving here together? Why does she take my feelings into account?

– Karen doesn't want Oscar to be jealous. Why does she take his feelings into account?

I put my head in my hands. Damn, it was messy in there.

Then I read the letter again. And decided that the most important thing was that Karen wanted me to get to Ballantyne.

'Good news?' Lucas asked with a sly smile as he handed me the broom, which meant I had to sweep the floor of the little library before it shut for the night.

'A friend of mine in Ballantyne,' I said. 'She wants me to go and visit her.'

'Do you want to visit her?'

'Very much.'

'Well, then,' Lucas said, taking the broom back off me. 'Then you're going to need a leave of absence.'

'Is that possible?'

'If you write for permission to visit family. If you've behaved reasonably well here, permission is usually granted. Sit down, I'll get a pen and paper.'

No sooner said than done.

While Lucas swept the floor, I wrote a concise request.

*Dear Principal,*

*I would hereby like to apply for permission to go to Ballantyne next weekend to visit my foster-parents. I would like to point out that I have no demerits for bad behaviour.*

*Regards, Richard Elauved*

'Fine,' Lucas said, leaning on the broom. 'Just hand that in to the admin office and I'll make sure it gets a recommendation, if that's actually required for any reason.'

I ran out on light feet and crossed the yard to the administration block. I saw the safety officer at the gate watching me, and the safety officer in the clock tower following me with binoculars, they weren't used to anyone running here. I rang the doorbell of the oblong, two-storey office building, and Mrs Monroe's metallic voice answered. I explained why I was there, and she appeared a few moments later to open the door. Mrs Monroe was a grumpy, comical, overweight woman who had a violent temper and was addicted to chewing gum. She claimed that the only privilege women had in a male-dominated world was being allowed to cuff the ears of cheeky young boys. I handed her the sheet of paper, she glanced at it, then pointed to the stairs. I looked at her questioningly.

'Quick, quick, I run around enough as it is,' she snapped. 'The Principal's office is the one with the red door. No nonsense. I'm giving you twenty seconds.'

I ran up and knocked on the door. Inside I heard the Principal's voice, it sounded like he was talking on the phone. His voice was soft, like it always was, especially when he was angry. I knocked again. As I waited I looked at the nearest of the framed photographs that hung in a row along the wall of the corridor. They were marked with different years, but were confusingly similar to each other: forty or fifty people lined up on the steps in front of the main building, evidently the residents and staff who had been at Rorrim's that year. I heard the Principal say 'yes' and 'oh dear' on the phone as footsteps approached the door. At that moment my eyes were caught by one of the faces in the photograph nearest the door. Or rather, if it hadn't been a photograph, I would have said that it was the face that actually caught sight of me.

I knew the moment I saw it that I shouldn't have been surprised, but even so, it felt like someone had stabbed an icicle into my guts.

The pale face was staring straight at the lens, at me. The way it had stared at me, framed by a window in Mirror Forest. The blood-red door in front of me swung open, and there stood the Principal.

He was tall and thin and had this gentle look that fooled everyone at first.

'I understand your concern, Mrs Larsson,' the Principal said. I saw the spiral telephone cord stretched tight and quivering from the desk in the surprisingly small office, I had never seen inside before. The Principal glanced at the sheet I was holding out to him, looked briefly at me, then nodded without taking the phone from his ear, and closed the door again. I took another look at the photograph on the wall. It was him. Then I ran back down the stairs.

'Twenty-five seconds,' Mrs Monroe said sullenly, blocking the doorway with her immense bulk. 'Did you steal or wreck anything?'

'Not today,' I said.

Mrs Monroe raised an eyebrow, and I saw her getting her right palm ready as her red upper lip curled back in a leer. But then the flesh on her body began to tremble and her lips suddenly formed a grin. She stepped aside.

Lucas was still sweeping the floor when I came running back into the library.

'Was there ever a boy here at Rorrim's called Imu Jonasson?' I asked, out of breath.

Lucas looked up. 'Why do you ask?'

'I just saw him on a photograph in the admin block.'

'Then you already know, so why are you asking?'

'Because I've only seen him as an adult. And people do change, after all.'

'Are you sure about that?'

'Aren't you?'

Lucas let out a deep sigh. 'Well, I work here because I hope it's true, that young people at least can change. But obviously you can't help having your doubts on bad days.'

'Do you remember Imu Jonasson?'

'Oh yes.'

'What happened to him?'

'You tell me. I don't think anyone here knows.'

'What do you mean?'

Lucas let out an even deeper sigh which made me think of the dripping sounds inside the house in Mirror Forest. He put the broom down against the wall.

'Cup of tea?'

# 16

'A LOT OF YOUNG PEOPLE have come and gone from here over the course of my forty years,' Lucas said. He still hadn't touched his cup of tea. 'An oldie like me can't remember them all, but a lad like Imu Jonasson isn't easy to forget. The first time I saw him was when he came here to ask for a book about magic.'

'Black word magic?'

Lucas looked up at me. 'Yes, actually. But we don't have books like that here.'

'Books like what?'

'Books that can give young people . . . ideas. What I didn't know was that the boy already had ideas I couldn't even begin to imagine.'

'What do you mean?'

'Imu Jonasson wasn't just a broken boy, Richard. He was evil.

Do you understand? Evil.' Lucas looked at me as if to assure himself that I had understood the full weight of the word. 'His evil is still ingrained in the walls here. When he escaped, everyone here breathed a sigh of relief. No one said anything, but everyone knows that the Principal at the time waited two days before sounding the alarm, to give the boy a chance to get away, so he wouldn't be sent back here.'

'And he did get away?'

'He did.'

I sipped my tea. 'What did he do that was so bad?'

Lucas folded his arms and measured me with his gaze, as if contemplating something.

Lucas turned the key in the rusty lock and shoved the door open. The basement air was cold and raw around us. A spider's web stuck to my face as we stepped into a tiny broom cupboard of a room, just two metres square. A narrow bed was the only furniture.

'We used to keep Imu Jonasson down here, it was a sort of . . .' Lucas tried to find a different word, but gave up. 'Isolation. For those who got violent. But after he escaped, this room was only used three times before management decided to stop using it altogether.'

'Why?'

'Because the three people who were put in isolation in this room after Imu Jonasson all tried to kill themselves after spending just one day here. The first two were observed at breakfast, sitting there repeating simple words and phrases, then later the same day one of them tried to hang himself in his room, and the other jumped off the roof but survived.'

I shuddered. Kill themselves? The room was extremely dark,

there was no window, the paint was peeling, and the scratches on the walls indicated that someone had tried to cut into them with a knife. All the same, a bit of vandalism and graffiti was hardly unusual for Rorrim's.

'We believe that the words they were repeating were taken from what you can see Imu Jonasson carved into the walls in here,' Lucas said. 'Best not to look at them too long or too closely . . .'

Only once my eyes had got used to the gloom did I see that the scratches were words and numbers. They were closely written, covering the floor and ceiling. Yes, there was even writing on the ceiling. I pointed upwards questioningly.

'We have no idea,' Lucas said. 'There was nothing he could stand on in here to help him reach. He didn't have anything sharp either. The only possibility is that he used his fingernails.'

'His nails?' I said in disbelief.

'Don't ask me,' Lucas said.

I had automatically begun to read, there was one word that began P-A-K-S, but I quickly made myself look away.

'What happened to the third person who was put in here?'

'We painted the walls so the words couldn't be seen. But when we came back the next day, he had scraped the paint off with his teeth and fingernails, and had tried to smash his head against the wall. Like he couldn't bear what was inside it. The blood . . . Poor lad. If these walls had been made of brick . . .' Lucas shook his head.

'But now you've painted the walls again?'

'Just one coat, as you can see. We used professional decorators, but after that first coat they left and refused to come back. So we keep it locked, and . . .' Lucas trailed off, as if he had heard something I hadn't noticed.

'You haven't told me how he escaped.'

'Because we have no idea,' Lucas said, looking down the basement corridor, into the darkness where the light from the bare bulb above us couldn't reach. 'When we got here that morning the door was locked, but Imu Jonasson was gone. No one confessed to having let him out. The safety officers that night swore they had stayed awake, and hadn't seen or heard a living soul leave. Apart from a magpie they saw flying in the moonlight, from the main building and over the fence. Not that magpies have souls, but they probably only mentioned it because we don't get magpies out here.'

'Maybe the Principal let him out to get rid of him?'

'Maybe.' Lucas looked like he was straining his eyes, as if he thought he'd seen something in the darkness at the end of the corridor. 'OK, Richard, let's go back up.'

As he locked the door to the basement stairs, he said: 'It would be good if you didn't tell anyone I showed you the room. It isn't that I'm not allowed, but I don't want to spread fear among so many impressionable souls.'

'Of course,' I said, managing to stop myself from asking the obvious question. If he didn't want to scare people like me, why had he shown me the room?

That night I lay awake thinking about Karen. And what she might be on the trail of. And the photograph with the face that seemed to be looking at me. And, in the end, just before I drifted off to sleep, about a magpie shrieking in a forest. I woke up again, or at least I thought I was awake, because the phone in the corridor was ringing. I lay there listening to the sound, and Victor and Vanessa's undisturbed breathing. Should I wake one of them?

No, they had gone to bed early to make sure they were ready for their escape after lunch the next day, something I had almost forgotten after everything that had happened earlier. I waited for the ringing to stop, but it didn't. After what happened to Tom I had kept well away from telephones, but the ringing was so intrusive and insistent that I thought I was going to snap if it didn't stop soon or no one answered it. In the end I swung my legs out of bed, put my feet on the cold floor and crept out into the corridor.

The telephone was attached to the wall between the toilet and the emergency exit. It could only be used for incoming calls that had been transferred from the admin block. Those calling were usually the parents, friends or partners of residents who had any of those. Frank and Jenny had called a few times, but I had always found an excuse not to go to the phone and said that we could speak next time they visited me, which they did once a month. I didn't think how strange it was that it was ringing in the middle of the night when there was no one in the office, just like you never think about being able to fly or that the sky is green when you're dreaming. All the same, I felt my hair stand on end and my body resist the closer I got to the black, frantically ringing object.

I stopped in front of the phone, undecided.

My hand refused to lift up, and my feet wouldn't go back to the room and my warm bed.

The ringing sound got louder and louder with each ring. How come none of the others had come out into the corridor? I stared at the hard, vibrating plastic.

Then I answered it. I held my breath as I cautiously raised the receiver towards my temple, not quite close enough for it to touch my ear.

‘Hello?’ I said, and could hear the tremble in my own voice.

I heard someone take a breath. It was a light, soft voice, and at first it was hard to tell if it belonged to a man or a woman.

‘I’m just telling the truth.’

‘Hello?’ I repeated.

‘I want in.’ It was a man. ‘And you want to let me in. Because you’re mine. I’m just telling you the truth.’

‘I . . .’

‘That’s what they can’t stand. The truth. Letting it in.’

‘I have to go,’ I said, and was about to hang up when I heard the voice say her name.

‘What?’ I said, even if it had been clear enough.

‘Karen,’ the voice repeated.

‘What about Karen?’

‘She thinks she’s going to find me. But I’m the one who’s going to find her.’

‘What do you mean? Who are you?’

‘You know. She’s going to burn. The girl you love is going to burn. There’s nothing you can do about it. Because you’re small and weak and a coward. You’re garbage. Do you hear? You’re garbage. And you’re going to let me in.’

I quickly hung up. My whole body was shaking, as if I were ill or running a fever. There was a word carved into the wall above the phone; I recognised the writing and closed my eyes before I had time to read anything. I had to get back to the room. Keeping my eyes closed and with my fingertips running along the walls, I made my way along the corridor with my heart pounding in my chest and those words ringing in my ears. Garbage. Burn. Garbage. Burn. Don’t look, don’t read. It had got cold, and the air felt clammy and damp when my fingers finally slid over a gap, over something they recognised as a door, then found the door handle. I pushed it down and pulled the door towards me.

The door was locked.

I opened my eyes. It wasn't the door to the bedroom. I looked round. I had ended up back in the basement, and this was the door to the room where Imu had been kept. There was a key in the lock. Garbage. Burn. Garbage. I gripped the key between my thumb and forefinger, turned it and opened the door. I stared into the darkness. I couldn't see anything, but I could sense something breathing in there. Then I let go of the door and ran. And ran. But my legs felt like they were stuck in something. In garbage. I sank into the garbage.

I woke up with a start. Something about the room was different. The light. The light from the window. I sat up on my bunk, looked around and realised that, for the first time since I had arrived at Rorrim's, the sun was shining. Victor and Vanessa were sitting swinging their legs above me.

'Did you hear the phone ringing during the night?' I asked as I rubbed the sleep from my eyes.

They looked at me and shook their heads.

'Good, I just wanted to make sure it was a dream,' I said as I stood up and began to get dressed.

'Remember to wait until twenty minutes after the end of lunch before you come to the kitchen,' Vanessa said. 'The cook will be having his nap by then.'

I nodded. I had been through the relatively simple plan with the twins at least twenty times, and now they had begun repeating the details and telling me what to do as if they were the ones who had come up with it.

During breakfast I asked some of the others who lived on our corridor if they had heard a phone ringing last night, and when they all said they hadn't, I dismissed the whole thing.

During the lessons before lunch I was only half listening as I went through Karen's letter in my mind again, word for word. I was thinking about how I was going to get to Ballantyne once my leave of absence was granted. I had never seen any buses here, but surely there had to be some on the main road? Maybe I could get Lucas to drive me there. A thought suddenly struck me: if my involvement in the twins' escape was discovered, I definitely wouldn't be granted leave of absence. I looked at the time, still an hour to go before lunch. Briefly I considered telling the Principal about the escape plan, saying I had never intended to help them, just pretended to for my own safety. But I quickly dismissed that idea. I may have been many things, but I wasn't a sneak. OK, maybe it was more that I had seen what happened to sneaks. I would just have to hope that everything went according to plan.

# 17

AT LUNCH I EXCHANGED GLANCES with Victor and Vanessa every time they came limping in through the swing door from the kitchen. Instead of aprons, the kitchen staff at Rorrim's wore long, white coats and tall, pointed chef's hats that made me think of the Ku Klux Klan. There were two cooks working, plus the twins who carried in metal trays of fish, potatoes and boiled vegetables to the counter, and removed the trays of washing-up as it mounted up. Every time our eyes met, they nodded, everything was under control. I looked at the clock above the swing door; the garbage truck was due an hour from now.

When I had finished eating and was putting my plate and cutlery in the rack on the counter, Lucas came up to me.

'The Principal wants to talk to you.'

My heart leapt in my chest: my application for leave.

I looked at the time again. Still three-quarters of an hour before the truck arrived, no need to stress. I crossed the open space to the admin block even faster than last time. The safety officers at the gate and in the clock tower saw me, but seemed less interested than last time. A green car of a type I had seen before was parked outside the barbed-wire fence.

This time it wasn't Mrs Monroe who opened the door but the Principal himself.

'Follow me,' he said in that disturbingly soft voice.

We went upstairs in silence. It struck me that this could hardly be standard procedure for granting a short leave of absence. Was something wrong? Had he called Frank and Jenny, who didn't know anything about my application? Or – even worse – had the twins told someone about the escape plan, someone who had talked?

The Principal held the red door open for me, and I stepped inside. And stopped dead when I saw the face of the man behind the Principal's desk. He was sitting with his hands clasped behind his head, and gave the Principal a silent nod. The door closed behind me and I realised that I was alone with the man behind the desk.

The car outside the fence. The same model, different colour.

It was Agent Dale.

'I hear you've applied for a leave of absence,' he said. 'Had enough of Rorrim's for a while?'

I didn't answer.

'I also hear that you've been exhibiting exemplary behaviour. Seeing as most people here have their applications granted despite demonstrating far worse behaviour than yours, that shouldn't be more than reasonable. In fact, we're willing to agree to a longer leave of absence. What do you say to that?'

I said nothing to that, I just swallowed.

'Possibly even get out of here for good. Doesn't that sound tempting, Richard?'

'Yes,' I managed to say.

'Great!' He removed his hands from behind his head and clapped them together. 'Let's get that organised, then. There's just one condition.'

I waited.

'That you tell us what *really* happened to Tom and Jack.'

I lowered my head and looked down at my trainers. I swallowed again.

'I did . . .' I said quietly.

Dale brightened up and pulled something out from beneath his jacket. Not a pistol this time, but a small black tape recorder covered in perforated leather. He put it on the desk between us. 'You did what? Pushed them in the river?'

'No.' I raised my head and looked at Dale. 'I *did*. As in, I already told you what happened. *Really*. You know . . . the telephone and all that.'

Dale looked at me for a long time. Then he let out a deep sigh, touched his fingers together and shook his head slowly.

'Richard, Richard, please don't tell me I've driven all this way for nothing.'

I wasn't going to get my leave of absence. I felt my throat tighten.

'You have to let me go to Ballantyne, Agent Dale. Just for two days. Give me two days to find out what happened to Tom and Jack, please.'

Dale looked at me intently.

'You know, I think you're even more hardened now that when

I first met you, Richard. Now you've learned to lie so that even a federal police officer almost believes you. Is that the sort of thing you learn here at Rorrim's?'

For a moment I felt tempted to give him what he wanted, and say that sure, I killed Tom and Jack. But I didn't think that would make him grant my leave of absence.

'Please . . .' I whispered, feeling that I was close to tears.

I saw Dale hesitate.

'How are things going here?' I hadn't heard the Principal come in, but now he was standing in the open doorway behind me.

Dale stood up so abruptly that the springs in the Principal's desk chair creaked. He looked annoyed and desperate. 'He's all yours, Principal. He'll give up eventually.'

I made the decision as I was walking back to the main building. It wasn't hard.

I went into my room and put my hand behind my cupboard where I had hidden what little money the twins hadn't yet found.

Then I left the room for what I hoped was the last time.

That was when – on the way out – I noticed that the telephone receiver wasn't sitting on top of the phone, but hanging from its cord towards the floor. It was making a sound, wasn't it?

I walked closer, then stopped abruptly. I felt every hair on my body stand on end.

The sound. Slurping. The same sound as when Tom had been eaten.

Then the slurping stopped, as if the voice had heard me coming. It began to talk instead.

'You're garbage. She's going to burn. You're garbage –'

I turned and walked quickly towards the exit. The voice behind me started shouting, and the sound got distorted.

'She's going to burn. You're –'

I put my hands over my ears and ran out into the sunshine.

'I'm coming too,' I said once Victor, Vanessa and I had wheeled not two, but three dustbins into the kitchen from the yard.

They looked at me, then at each other, and then they just nodded. OK, pretty much.

The two cooks had gone for a nap as usual after lunch, leaving the twins to do the washing-up. They wouldn't be back until it was almost time for dinner, and there was still time before the garbage truck arrived.

We removed some of the rubbish so there was enough room in the bins. Victor and Vanessa kept their klan costumes on to save the clothes underneath getting messed up, then they each climbed into one of the bins and pulled a bin bag over their head. I made a dozen holes in the black plastic before they crouched down and I tied the bags.

I pushed the three bins back outside to their position in the yard. I knew we couldn't be seen from the gate or the clock tower, but I still looked round to make sure no one was looking. Then I climbed into the third bin, closed the lid over my head and crawled into the bin bag I had left open inside. It was harder to tie my own bag, but somehow I managed it. Then it was just a matter of waiting.

It was quiet. So quiet that I couldn't block out the words from the telephone receiver.

Finally I heard the garbage truck. Then footsteps. I lost my balance as the bin began to move, and heard the sound of wheels on tarmac. The sound of hydraulics. I knew I was being lifted into the air and felt my stomach tremble. Soon I would be tipped out. When it came, it happened so fast that I didn't have time to think, I just registered that I had landed on something surprisingly soft. But at least the voice in my head had fallen silent.

But once the garbage truck had started to move and I was getting drowsy after ten, fifteen minutes of being rocked back and forth, the voice started up again. To shut it out, I started to sing quietly.

'*It's a long way to Tipperary. It's a long way to go. It's a long way to Tipperary. But my heart's right there.*'

I kept repeating the words, over and over, trying to think about anything else. About Karen and me lying on the school roof looking up at the clouds in the sky. About floating down a river on your back. About swimming ashore on a South Sea island where there are other youngsters who will become your friends.

The sun had come out, the temperature was rising, and the inside of the bin bag was beginning to feel damp. And with the heat came a rising stench of shit. Of nappies. I assumed I was lying a little way from them, seeing as the stench came and went, but someone – probably Victor – was clearly lying closer, because I soon heard the unmistakable sound of someone throwing up. The thought of him being sick inside his own bin bag was almost enough to make me throw up too. Because our agreement had been clear, no one was to get out of their bin bag until we were emptied out at the tip, and even then we had to count to one hundred before we tore the bags open. If one of us got caught, we would all be done for.

After a while Victor started shouting something, and I was worried the men in the cab would hear us. But then I heard

Vanessa's voice, saying something quietly that I didn't understand, and then he calmed down.

I couldn't see the hands on my watch, but I think something like an hour had passed when the garbage truck slowed down and turned sharply left, then changed gear. At the same time I detected a new smell. I stiffened.

Smoke.

I hadn't asked because the thought hadn't even occurred to me. That the landfill could actually be an incinerator. That the contents of the truck would be tipped into a furnace at the end of the route, where everything would be burned up. And yet it was as if I had got the answer to a question I hadn't asked, as if a prophecy I had forgotten about was about to be fulfilled.

It wasn't Karen who was going to burn – it was me.

My heart was beating faster and faster, but I didn't move. I don't know if it was apathy, that I just couldn't take any more, or if some part of me accepted that this was going to be my fate. The garbage truck braked and came to a stop, the gearbox screeched, we reversed, and the next moment I was moving, sliding slowly, then faster. And then I was in free fall again.

And, once again, I landed on something soft.

The smell of smoke was more intense, but I couldn't hear the crackle of flames. Instead I heard the garbage truck start moving again, I heard the tyres crunch on gravel as it slowly drove away. When everything was still, I heard low muttering off to one side of me.

'Twenty-two, twenty-three, twenty-four . . .'

I lay there listening out for other sounds that could tell me anything about the situation.

Nothing.

I stuck one finger through one of the air holes in the bin bag and put my eye to it. All I could see was a rolling, colourful sea of garbage and a thin plume of smoke rising from behind one wave of rubbish.

'Thirty-six, thirty-seven . . .'

The next moment something landed on my bin bag, and something sharp, like a claw, cut through the plastic and grabbed me by the shoulder. I couldn't help crying out and pulled myself free. My scream was answered by a cold shriek, and a moment later the attacker was gone.

I peered out of the hole it had made and saw a big, fat seagull flapping away. Seeing as I was already exposed, I got up on my knees and looked around at the unending horizon of rubbish, only interrupted by the ramp the truck had dumped its load from. It wasn't until I stood up that I could see the gravel road winding through the treeless moorland towards the main road, where a lumber truck was silently passing by. At the other end of the dump, a little more than a hundred metres away from us, I could see a wrecked car. And a wooden shed with a thin, rusty pipe sticking out of it. A column of white smoke rose into the sky. And there was a man.

I ducked down, but I knew it was too late. The man, who was sitting on a camping chair in front of the shed, must have seen me. I crawled over to the bin bag that had now counted to forty-five, and tore it open. Vanessa stopped counting and looked up at me.

'We've been spotted, we have to run,' I whispered. 'Where's Victor?'

Vanessa pointed firmly towards a bin bag that lay a short distance to our right. Seeing as all the bags looked the same, I had no idea how she could know he was in that one, but I wasn't about to ask.

When all three of us were out and I still hadn't heard anything from the wooden shed, I quickly stood up before ducking back down again. The man had something on his head, it looked like a felt hat.

'He's still sitting there,' I whispered. 'Maybe he hasn't seen us after all. Maybe we can crawl out towards the main road without him seeing us.'

Vanessa wrinkled her nose. 'You mean we have to crawl through the rubbish?'

I don't know when Vanessa had become too good for that, but maybe it was just the thought of more nappies.

'Rats,' she said, as if in answer to my thoughts.

'How do you know –' I began.

'All rubbish dumps have rats,' she said simply. 'They're big, and they bite.'

Something told me she was speaking from experience, so I kept quiet while I tried to think of another way of getting out.

Behind us I heard Victor say something, and he wasn't whispering. I turned and saw to my horror that he was standing up, fully visible.

'Down!' I hissed.

But Victor remained standing. And as if that wasn't enough, he started waving his hands above his head.

I grabbed hold of Victor's cook's tunic and tried to pull him down. 'What are you doing?' I hissed.

'He's blind,' Victor said.

'He's what?'

'Blind. He can't see.'

'I know what . . .' I stood up and looked over at the man. He was sitting there motionless. But how could Victor know he was blind?

'He's right!' The call came from the man in the camping chair, and it echoed across the dump. 'Blind as a bat!'

# 18

'ONE BLIND, TWO LAME AND one scared,' the man in the camping chair said with a smile.

Vanessa, Victor and I were lined up in front of him. None of us had yet said a word, we were just looking at him. He was wearing a suit that was slightly too big for him, with a white shirt, a felt hat and a pair of white gloves. The face beneath the felt hat was black, but the beard and smile were white. His eyes had a film that reminded me of the lake in Mirror Forest, where the surface was covered with frogspawn that I had thrown stones at to see if I felt guilty about it. I did. Before throwing another stone.

Vanessa, Victor and I looked questioningly at each other.

'These,' the man said, pointing at the biggest pair of ears I had ever seen; they looked like saucers. 'You two shuffle when you walk, and you . . .' he said, pointing at me with a black walking stick topped with a shiny brass ball, 'are taking quick, shallow breaths. Relax. There's nothing to be frightened of here. You came with the garbage?'

'No,' Vanessa said quickly.

'It was a rhetorical question, my girl. That means I *know* you arrived with the garbage. No one opened any doors on the rubbish truck, and you walked over here through the landfill, not along the road.' He pointed at his huge ears again. 'No one sneaks up on old Feihta. So, what are your plans?'

'We're heading south,' I said. 'Or north. It depends. How can we get away from here?'

'Seeing as you haven't got a car, it'll have to be the bus.'

'Which leaves when?'

'Once a day. I'm afraid it left two hours ago.'

The three of us who could see exchanged a glance.

'We could hitchhike?'

The black man in the camping chair let out a hearty laugh.

'What's so funny?' I asked.

'Well, no one round here has hitchhiked or picked up a hitchhiker for the past thirty years, not since the Hardy shootings. Believe me, you're not going to get a lift.'

'Because a hitchhiker shot a driver called . . . what, Hardy, thirty years ago?'

'Yes, but it was worse than that.' The blind man sighed. 'Hardy shot the hitchhiker too. That's why no one hitchhikes *or* picks up hitchhikers here.'

'Damn.'

'Damn is the word. Do you want to hear the rest of the story?'

'No thanks,' I said. 'We need to get going.'

'The bus doesn't leave for another twenty-two hours,' the man said dismissively. 'So, the police said that Hardy – who had served time for robbery – was looking for a victim. And the young hitch-hiker was doing the same.'

I looked at Victor and Vanessa, who just shrugged their shoulders.

'They both had guns,' the man went on. 'So they shot each other while the car was still moving. The car just kept rolling until it hit the Winterbottom village sign, where the skulls of the two dead bodies were smashed against the windscreen, forming two identical blood-red, rose-shaped shatter-patterns on the glass.'

'Pah!' Victor snorted.

'That, my lame friend, is as true as my name is Feihta Rice.' The blind man turned and pointed his stick towards the car wreck I had noticed, a white Toyota. 'Afterwards they dumped the car here. Because no one wanted a car people had been murdered in, even if it was in decent condition. Come and see, those red roses are still there. Help me up, darling.'

Feihta Rice held out one gloved hand, and Vanessa found herself, rather bewildered, helping him up from the camping chair. He staggered towards the car on long, thin legs, and after exchanging another glance and shrugging our shoulders, we followed. Sure enough, the front windscreen of the Toyota had two rose-shaped shatter-patterns, there was a large dent in the bumper and grille, and there were streaks on the paintwork. But apart from that the car looked OK. I also noticed that the keys were in the ignition. 'And it still works, you say?'

'Like a Swiss watch.'

I looked at the twins. 'Can either of you –'

'I can!' Vanessa said.

Victor nodded in confirmation.

I felt the money in my pocket. 'How much do you want for the car, Mr Rice?'

'The car?' He raised his grey-white eyes towards the sun up in the sky for a moment. 'A thousand dollars.'

'Pah!' Victor grunted.

'Mr Rice,' I said, 'you can't even drive the car.'

'The price, my frightened friend, isn't determined by how much the car is worth to me. It's how much it's worth to you. And that's probably quite a lot, because you're fugitives with the police hot on your heels.'

I saw Victor's eyes open wide as they stared at me.

I cleared my throat. 'What on earth makes you think that, Mr Rice?'

'Because you smell of garbage, because you don't know where you are, and because of the sound of police sirens rapidly coming closer.'

'Police sirens?'

He pointed to his ears. 'I'm guessing they'll be here in three minutes.'

I swallowed. Closed my eyes. Tried to think. So, what had happened after I left the Principal's office? Obviously Agent Dale wasn't going to drive all the way home again without making one more attempt to persuade me to confess. But when no one could find me, the alarm would have been sounded. And then, when they realised that the twins were also missing, Agent Dale would have used . . . what was it called again? Deduction! He would have ruled out the impossible until he was left with the possible, and that way he would have figured out how we had escaped. And the police car, which I still couldn't hear, could obviously drive much faster than the garbage truck.

I cleared my throat again. 'Mr Rice, would you consider lending us the car and not saying anything to the police about us being here?'

'I don't think so, no,' Rice said.

I looked at Victor and Vanessa. Victor nodded slowly, as if he was trying to tell me something, then put his hand inside his cook's coat and pulled out what I saw to my horror was a large kitchen knife. I shook my head wildly, but Victor just shook his head slowly back, as if to tell me that the decision had already been taken. He took a step closer to Feihta and raised the knife to attack.

'Here's the money for the car!' I blurted, sticking the seven notes I had in Feihta's hand.

Victor froze for a moment, standing there dressed in white with the knife pointing towards the man in the felt hat. The sun glinted brightly off the blade.

Feihta leaned the walking stick against the car and ran his fingertips over the money.

'This is only seven hundred,' he said.

'It's called haggling,' I said.

'It's called trying to trick a blind man,' he said. 'You're going to have to come up with something better than that, lad. And don't try telling me this is all you've got. The police will be here in two minutes, so get a move on.'

'OK,' I said, and tried to moisten my mouth with my tongue. 'I need to get home to my girlfriend so I can help her.'

'Better than that!' Rice declared.

'I need the rest of the money to buy her something nice!' I blurted back.

'Not good enough!'

I took a deep breath and shouted as loudly as I could: 'Give us the car or one of us will stab you with a knife!'

'There you are!' Rice said. 'The car's yours!'

He picked up his stick and walked away from the car as Victor, Vanessa and I hurried to get into it.

Vanessa turned the key in the ignition.

Nothing happened.

She tried again. Still nothing.

Rice tapped his stick against the side window and I wound it down. 'The battery's dead, lad.'

'You didn't mention that!'

'The car was sold as seen. But I've got jump leads and can let you have a charge from my battery. Five dollars. Interested?'

'I haven't got –' I began.

'Here,' Victor said from the back seat, holding a hand containing a crumpled five-dollar bill out through the window.

'See?' Feihta Rice said, straightening out the note. 'But it might take a while, and that's something I don't think you've got. So I suggest that you lie down in the back seat until my next visit is over.'

Up above us the cold cry of a seagull cut through the air, and now I could hear it as well, the low note carried on the wind. The police siren.

Vanessa and I crawled over the seat and lay on top of Victor, who was already lying on the floor. I heard the door open and something was laid on top of us, a blanket that smelled faintly of garbage.

The police siren grew louder. Then it was switched off, presumably when the car turned off the main road. In the silence that followed I could hear the others breathing. I could feel their chests rise and fall. The gravel crunched. Then the growl of what sounded like a butch, eight-cylinder car, followed by doors opening and closing. Voices.

'We can't trust him,' Vanessa whispered.

'We should have killed him,' Victor whispered.

'Shhh!' I said. 'They're coming this way.'

The footsteps of three, maybe four people.

'That's all very interesting, Mr Rice.' It was Agent Dale's voice. 'But I wasn't working back then, if these Hardy murders happened thirty years ago, and I'm not here to listen to stories but to find three escaped youngsters. So let me ask you again, have you seen these escapees or not?'

I held my breath, and felt the twins doing the same.

Feihta Rice's voice sounded as solemn as a priest's as he replied: 'I swear on my mother's grave and the Holy Virgin Mary, Agent Dale. I haven't set eyes on the three escapees you're talking about. And you can put me in prison if I'm lying. But . . .'

'But?' Agent Dale sounded hopeful.

'But take a look at these two roses. Completely identical! Isn't that unbelievable?'

Agent Dale let out a low groan. 'Unbelievable is the word,' he said.

I heard footsteps moving away, and began to breathe again. The car doors opened and closed again. The engine started up, followed by the sound of a green Pontiac LeMans driving away.

'Thanks,' I said as I drank the lemonade from the glass Mr Rice had put down on the table in front of me. A fly buzzed and landed on the windowsill. I opened the window to let it out.

'Why didn't the others want any?' Mr Rice asked. He was

sitting on a sofa bed beneath some bookshelves. His shack consisted of one room that was a combination of living room, kitchen and bedroom, but it was cosy, clean and furnished with all manner of ingenious, home-made solutions, such as the large magnet that had various tools, keys, cutlery, coins, a tin-opener and other things you might need in a hurry attached to it.

'They don't like being inside,' I said, looking out at the two twins. They had taken off their cooks' tunics, and were now each sitting on a oil drum in front of the open hood of the car, staring at it as if they could *see* the electricity passing through the charging leads to the battery.

'Thank you, by the way,' Rice said.

'What for?'

'For stopping the lame lad from sticking that knife into me.'

I stared at him in astonishment. 'How do you know . . . ?'

'Oh,' he said, tilting his head. 'Steel has a song of its own. And fear has its own smell. I don't need to see to know. All sorts of things are going on around us the whole time that our senses don't pick up on. I know that, because I'm missing one sense that other people tell me exists, even though I don't know what it means to see things. But you don't have anyone to tell you what you lack in terms of senses.'

'So you think things happen that we can't notice or understand?'

'I *know* it, lad. Just take the Hardy shootings. Who can explain how that boy just disappeared?'

'Disappeared? I thought you said he died?'

'Oh, I don't know about that. From what we can tell with our senses, I dare say he was dead, but people like him don't die from a pistol shot. When the medical officer arrived at the mortuary the morning after the shooting, the bird had flown. And I mean that literally. Flown like a bird.'

Like a bird. Thirty years ago. I saw the hairs on my arms stand up. 'What was his name?'

Mr Rice shook his head. 'They never found out. But he wasn't from round here, because no one in or around Evans was reported missing.'

'But you have an idea of who he was, don't you?'

He shrugged. 'A few days later we heard that a boy had escaped from Rorrim's. And sure, it sounded like he was one of them.'

'*Them?*'

'People who can change into flying creatures. People who can only be killed one way.'

'How?'

'With fire. They have to be burned.'

I looked at Rice, sitting on the sofa bed with his felt hat next to him. The strip of sunlight from the window made his shiny, sweaty scalp glint as he stared out into the air in front of him. It dawned on me that there were all sorts of things I couldn't see. Possibly didn't want to see either.

'That money I gave you, those were only ten-dollar bills,' I said.

'Yes, I know the difference between a ten-dollar bill and a hundred-dollar. The battery should soon have finished charging.'

'Why are you doing this, Mr Rice? Helping us?'

'Oh, I don't know if I'd have helped the other two, I think they're lost causes, poor things. But there's hope for you.'

'Hope for what, though?'

'That you'll find yourself. Your real self. The nice, kind boy you're trying to hide.'

'Me, kind?' I laughed out loud. 'You don't know what I've done,

Mr Rice. You know, I made someone who wanted to be my friend turn into an insect? And after that, I tried to stand on him, to crush him on the floor just because . . . well, I don't even know why.' My voice had developed a strange little tremble.

'We do a lot of stupid things when we're scared,' Rice said. 'But now that you're feeling safe, you just let a fly out of the window. Which one do you think is the real you? If you could just manage to get rid of what you're afraid of, I think you'd discover a different person, one you like, the person you were before. And then you wouldn't have to be the person you hate so much that you have to be unkind.'

Something was stinging my eyes. 'He said . . .'

'Yes?'

I had to swallow several times before I could get the words out. 'He said I was garbage.'

'Hmm,' Rice said. 'Is that what he said? Well, I know a thing or two about garbage, and you know what, Richard?' He leaned forward and put one hand on my shoulder. 'You're not garbage.'

I closed my eyes. His hand was big and warm and his voice was right beside me as he repeated:

'You're not garbage. You're-not-garbage. OK?'

I nodded. 'OK,' I said in a thick voice.

'Let me hear you say it.'

'I'm not garbage.'

'Good. Say it one more time. Slowly. And really feel it.'

'I. Am. Not. Garbage.' I felt it.

That was that.

Or rather, that wasn't that, because something was missing. I suddenly felt as light as a feather.

'Better?'

'Yes.' I opened my eyes again. 'What did you do?'

Rice was smiling broadly. 'It was you who did it, Richard. Let's just call it white word magic, the sort that works against the black.' He pulled his gloves on again, picked up his walking stick and tapped it on the floor twice. 'Shall we go out and get you on your way?'

I stood up, but stopped just as I was about to duck to get out through the low doorway. 'There's one more thing I can't help wondering about. The voice said he was going to burn her.'

'What voice?'

'Imu Jonasson's.'

The light from the window disappeared, a cloud must have drifted in front of the sun, and I saw Feihta Rice's face change as if he were suddenly in pain.

'Imu,' he repeated, closing his eyes. The skin of his eyelids was thin, almost transparent, and reminded me of a pair of bat's wings. They began to twitch and tremble.

Outside came the sound of a seagull's cold cry.

# 19

'FASTER!' I YELLED.

'This is as fast as it can go,' Vanessa yelled back as she hunched over to see through the two rose-shaped shatter-patterns in the windscreen.

Sitting in the back seat and leaning forward between me and Vanessa, Victor was looking on, silent and even paler than usual. Heavy clouds had filled the sky ever since we left the dump, promising rain. A lot of rain. And it would soon be getting dark as well.

I looked at the time.

Feihta Rice had said that he – Imu – had taken her. I don't know what he saw on the inside of those trembling eyelids of his, but he had said that Karen was in danger, that she had been captured by one of the evil words, that he didn't know which word, but that I needed to find the word that could set her free. That I needed to drive Imu out of her. And that it was urgent, that a storm was coming, and that darkness – this stuff the sighted were always talking about – would soon be upon us all, and then it would be too late.

We passed a sign saying we were still eight miles from Ballantyne, then the headlights caught something shiny and metallic on one of the telegraph poles.

'Stop!'

Vanessa glanced at me, then put her foot on the brake.

'What is it?' Victor grunted.

'It's almost dark,' I said. 'We're not going to make it. I need to . . .'

I jumped out of the car and ran over to the pole. Obviously it struck me as odd that in the middle of nowhere, far from the nearest house, there was a phone attached to a telegraph pole. But presumably it was meant for people whose cars broke down or had suffered some other emergency.

I searched my pockets in vain for coins. I knew the twins were broke. Victor had got thirsty and ordered Vanessa to stop at a filling station, then made me empty my trouser pockets. Only when it was obvious that none of us had any money at all did he let Vanessa drive on.

I kicked the post angrily and looked up at the wires that ran south towards Ballantyne. Towards Karen. Towards Mirror Forest. I picked up the receiver and yelled into it:

'Come and get me, then! Come on, you horrible troll, take me, not her!'

But all I got in response was the long-drawn-out dialling tone. The dialling tone. I stared down at the emergency numbers printed on a sign on the device. RESCUE CAR was one of them. I dialled the number. It rang. It actually rang! The third ring was interrupted by a voice:

'Karlsen's tow trucks.'

'My name is Richard Elauved,' I said, and realised I was going to have to make a real effort not to talk too fast. 'I know this isn't your problem, but I've just left my house in Ballantyne and I forgot to turn the oven off, it's full of food. It's going to catch fire, if it hasn't already.'

'How old are you, Richard, and where are your parents?'

'Seventeen,' I lied. 'My parents are at our cabin, that's where I'm going.'

'OK, we can drive there, or call the police and –'

'No, there's no time, it's roast pork, the fat might already have caught light, and you, I and police are all too far away. I need to call the neighbour and get them to go in, but I haven't got any loose change. Can you transfer me to their number? I've got it here.'

'Give me the number, I'll call them and give them the message.'

'That won't work, they only speak Swedish.'

'Swedish?'

'They're very old.' I blurted out the few random Swedish phrases my dad had taught me, something about meatballs and smorgasbords. And trousers.

'*Put your trousers on!*' I said in Swedish.

'Sorry, young man,' the woman said, I could tell she was starting to find my story a bit complicated, 'but this isn't a telephone exchange. I'm hanging up now, and you can call the police instead, you can do that without having to pay.'

'Hang on!'

'What?'

I took a couple of deep breaths. I had to get oxygen to my brain, I had to think. But every time she said the word police, I saw the faces of McClelland and Agent Dale, and I started to panic and my mind went blank. I took a really deep breath and tried to think about Karen instead.

'You have another phone in the office, don't you?' I said.

'Er, yes.'

'Can you call my neighbour, then put the receivers next to each other?'

I heard the woman at the other end hesitate.

'It's my mum's roast pork,' I said with a tremble in my voice that was almost entirely natural. 'I was only supposed to be heating it up again. It's the best roast pork in the world, she only cooked it yesterday before she and Dad left. Then, with all the packing and everything, I completely forgot about it. The best mum in the world too.' I sniffed and wondered if I was overdoing it. 'And now her house is going to –'

'Give me the number, Richard.'

I listened while the woman made the call. I heard her say: 'Mrs Taylor, I have Richard here,' and then to me: 'Here she is.'

'Karen?' I said.

'Karen is in her room,' the voice said. 'Is this Richard from school?'

'I need to talk to her, Mrs Taylor.'

'I'm afraid she's not well and can't be disturbed. Is that Richard Elauved? The one who –'

'Not well?' I interrupted, hoping that I had also interrupted her train of thought for a few seconds. 'What sort of not well?'

'It's . . . we're taking care of it. Was there anything else, Richard?'

'Is she behaving strangely?'

'I need to hang up, Richard.'

'Hold on! Is she repeating the same word over and over again?'

There was silence on the other end of the line.

'What word is it?' I asked.

No answer.

'Mrs Taylor, this is important. I don't know if I can help, but I know I can't help if I don't know the word.'

I heard Karen's mother breathe shakily into the receiver, then she started to cry.

'It isn't a word,' she hiccuped. 'It's just . . . it sounds like she's saying "imu". She just sits there staring at the wall, saying it over and over again. The doctor's prescribed tranquillisers, but she won't take them. She –'

'Mrs Taylor, listen to me. You need to stay with her. She might try to harm herself.'

'What is this?' Mrs Taylor sounded suddenly furious. 'What's this got to do with you, Richard Elauved? Have you given her something? Is it drugs? LSD?'

'Don't let her out of your sight, Mrs Taylor. I'm hanging up now.'

I heard rumbling from the cloud above me, and felt the first raindrops.

'Put your foot down,' I said as I got back in the car.

The rain was pouring down, and the Toyota's windscreen wipers were whipping back and forth. Through the film of water the road seemed to be swimming and bending in front of us, and I was just able to make out the sign saying that we were driving into Ballantyne. It was pitch-black, and the rain was hammering on the roof so hard that I had to shout out the directions. The fuel light had started flashing red. We had made it, but I hoped there was enough petrol left for what else I had in mind. Beyond the library the main street was empty of people and flooded with rainwater.

'Here,' I said when we had just passed the little centre, where the street lights stopped. We parked and got out of the car. The rain was easing up; perhaps the sky was finally starting to run out of water. The trees stood like a dark, silent wall in front of us. Mirror Forest.

'What if it doesn't burn?' Vanessa said. 'Everything's completely soaked.'

'It *will* burn,' I said. Maybe there was something about the way I said it, but Vanessa and Victor stepped away from me.

I opened the boot, took out the jerrycan and the hose, stuck it into the petrol tank and started to suck. When the salty taste of petrol reached my mouth, I spat it out and put the end of the hose in the can. It spluttered and trickled for a while, then stopped. I shook the can. Not much, one litre maximum, but maybe that would be enough. I took out the box of matches Mr Rice had given me and wrapped it in a plastic bag, then tucked it away in my trouser pocket. Then we started to walk.

It had stopped raining altogether now, but it was so dark that I couldn't see much. Luckily the gravel on the path was pale in colour so we had something to aim at.

Everything was so different here now. Like in a cinema just before the film is about to start: pitch-black, with the dripping from the trees sounding like expectant whispering, the rustling of sweet wrappers, the sound of chewing, kissing, suppressed squeals.

That was when the thought occurred to me. That I was going to ask her to the cinema. That was what I was going to do. If this turned out OK. I swung the petrol can in time with my steps and tried to hold on to that thought. She would say no, obviously, but I didn't need to think about that right now. Because this wasn't going to turn out OK. There was no way it was going to turn out OK. I almost had to laugh. Because no matter how hopeless it seemed, I still had to try. I mean, what else can you do?

And then – just like when the show begins in a cinema – the curtain of cloud was pulled aside and there was light.

'Wow,' Vanessa said.

Victor said nothing, but his mouth was hanging open more than normal.

Because there, bathed in moonlight, lay the house.

The devil's horns on the ridge, the oak tree through the roof, the black, blind windows reflecting the moonlight.

The Night House.

I walked up to the gate with the initials B.A. and kicked it with the sole of my trainer, and eventually it gave way with a shriek.

'Come on,' I said.

# 20

VANESSA, VICTOR AND I WALKED up to the house in single file while I kept a wary eye on the big window below the devil's horns. It was dark, and there was no face in sight.

When we reached the front door I heard Vanessa and Victor stop behind me. I turned round.

'We're not coming in with you,' Vanessa whispered.

'What? You said you wanted to come in to see if there was anything worth stealing.'

'We've changed our minds,' she said.

There was no time to discuss it, and I could see from the determined looks on their faces that there was no point trying. So I took hold of the door handle and pulled it as hard as I could. The door opened with a jerk, and an indeterminate damp stench of decay and death hit me.

'Wait,' Vanessa whispered. 'Car keys.'

I turned towards them again. Victor had drawn his knife.

'Now,' he said.

'In case you don't come out again,' Vanessa said with something resembling an apologetic smile.

I felt in my pocket and gave her the keys. They were hardly going to get far in a car without any petrol, anyway.

So I stepped into the house alone.

The moon was shining in through the big window, bathing the hall in a magical, almost unreal light. Opening the door must have caused a draught, because dry leaves began to scrape across the floor, and suddenly I heard a loud bang behind me. The door had slammed shut.

I held my breath and listened. Had the bang woken anyone? All I could hear was the same dripping sound as before. And a creaking, as if someone were moving over floorboards, only this noise came from beneath the floor. I looked down. It was probably just my imagination, but in places it looked as if the floorboards were moving. I raised my head and looked around. Nothing seemed to have changed since last time. Apart from the door to the room where the bats had been sleeping. I couldn't remember us closing it before we left, but now it was definitely closed.

I walked over to the wrecked grand piano and the pile of furniture, unscrewed the lid of the jerrycan and poured half the contents over the heap. I emptied the rest on the floor. Then I got the matches out. As I was lighting one of the matches I heard a deep sigh, like when you pull your foot out of a bog. I quickly looked around. Then I tossed the match, and a moment later the flames flared up. I stared in fascination as the fire spread across the floor and licked its way up the wallpaper.

A sound like a pistol shot came from the piano, followed by a high note. Then another shot and a slightly lower note, and I realised it was the strings of the piano snapping. A tall flame leapt up when the fire reached the canvas of the ruined painting. At first the heat made it curl up, then straighten out. As if the fire had burned away the layers of dirt, damp and spiders' webs, time and neglect, until a portrait emerged. A man dressed in the sort of clothes I had seen in a book at the library, the one about Hamlet. So maybe the painting was hundreds of years old. But what didn't make sense was the fact that I had seen the face on it twice before. Once in the window of this house, and once in a photograph at Rorrim's correctional facility. But on the other hand, that obviously matched what Feihta Rice had said about an eternal being that could only be destroyed by fire. I shuddered as the face in front of me came to life and grimaced in rage as the paint melted and began to run. Then the man was consumed by the flames.

There was a small bang. Not from the grand piano this time, but from over by the stairs. I saw something like a snake pushing up between two floorboards. There was another bang, closer to me, and another stem curled up through the floor into the moonlight, twisting and turning, as if it was blindly searching for something. I didn't need to go any closer to see what it was. I didn't want to go closer. It was the roots of the tree.

At that moment I heard a scream from behind one of the doors on the gallery. It could have been an animal, it could have been a person. Either way, it was the sort of scream that not only cut through your marrow and bone, but through your heart and soul as well. The sort of scream that contains everything. Despair. Fear. Rage. Loneliness. It hung in the air long after it had stopped.

A door slid open. And I heard another sound. A low crackle, like when someone takes off a stiff coat. A very big coat. In the light of the flames that had climbed the wallpaper up to the ceiling, I saw something big moving in the doorway. A big, thin, leathery wing.

In short: it was high time to get out of there.

'Come on!' I ran down the steps in front of the house.

Victor and Vanessa were standing there as if frozen to the spot, staring at something behind me.

'Come on!' I repeated, turning round to see what they were staring at.

The roots. They were coming out of the ground along the whole facade of the house, creeping over the ground towards the twins' feet, thin and wavering, like snails' antennae. But further back the roots were as thick as anacondas.

'They're out to get you!' I roared. 'They want to eat you for dinner!'

At last they seemed to realise, and they turned and began to run after me. I could already hear the crackling of fire from the house but didn't look back, I just ran as fast as I could. As I approached the gate I saw that it was moving. It had to be the wind. I couldn't feel any wind, but it had to be the wind! With a low wail, the wrought-iron gate slowly swung closed, and clicked shut just as I reached it. I kicked at the struts, but this time the gate didn't open. I turned and saw the twins running towards me. If the situation had been different, I would have thought the sight of their limping, lurching attempt at running was funny, they were only just managing to stay out of reach of the roots that were crawling after them. I grabbed the handle of the gate to push it down, then seized one of the railings with the other hand to give it a shove.

It was like being hit between the shoulder blades with a sledgehammer.

It was a pain unlike any I had felt before, it ran from the top of my head all the way down to my toes, it was inside me, enveloping me, it was everywhere all at the same time. An electric shock. Volts, watts, amps, whatever they were, pulsing through my body, but I couldn't even scream, because my jaw was locked tightly shut. The muscles in my body were all tensed and I couldn't let go of the handle of the gate. Quite the contrary, it felt like my grip was only getting tighter, as if I were trying to squeeze juice out of black wrought iron.

'Open it!' Victor cried behind me.

'Hurry up, it's coming!' Vanessa wailed.

'The idiot isn't moving, he's just standing there shaking,' Victor said.

'So get him out of the way!'

In spite of the intense pain, I could both hear and think, but I couldn't open my mouth to warn them. I felt Victor's hands grab me by the shoulders, I heard a groan, and then Vanessa's scream. I managed to turn my head just enough to see them. Like I said, in different circumstances, I'm sure I would have laughed. The three of us were all part of the same electrical circuit, a shaking, dancing chain of three silent rag dolls. We were the cinema show now, lit up by the moon and the flames that had burst through the roof of the house to colour the underside of the loose clouds yellow. A horror film with roots that were creeping closer and closer, with a howling sound rising and falling inside Mirror Forest, like some moonstruck werewolf.

I felt Victor tugging at my shoulder, as if he was trying to pull himself free. But then I realised that someone was pulling at him. The grip on my shoulders loosened, but kept hold of my shirt. I felt it tear as it was pulled off me, and heard their screams. The fact that they could scream must mean that they were free from the electrical circuit. I turned my head again and saw the twins being dragged back across the ground towards the burning house. Thin roots were wound round their legs, and they were kicking and trying to grab hold of the gravel, like desperate cattle caught in lassoes. What fate awaited them? Were they going to be eaten like Tom or disappear like Fatso and his magicicadas? Or were they going to be consumed by the flames? I didn't know if that was better or worse than my fate, being fried here until my brain and my heart exploded, because I could feel that that's what was starting to happen. But I could also feel something else. I looked down. One of the pale, naked roots had twined round one of my legs. And then came another one, coiling up past my ankle, once, twice, three times, before it tightened and began to pull. At first gently, then harder. Then very hard. My shoes slid backwards on the gravel, and my body and head fell forward. My arms were stretched out, and the hand that was holding the rail slid down until it was stopped by the initials B.A. But both my hands were held tight, without me being able to do anything about it.

The roots were stretching me out as if I were made of rubber, my back was screaming, my head aching, my shoulders felt like they were about to pop out of their sockets. And in addition to all that, it sounded like the werewolf was coming closer and closer.

My feet left the ground, and at that moment it was as if someone flicked a switch in my body. A fuse box. I was no longer earthed. Without contact with the ground, the electricity was no longer running through my body.

For a brief moment I felt immense relief.

Until I realised that this meant my muscles were no longer locked.

A moment later my solid grasp of the gate gave way. My face hit the ground and I was dragged backwards.

My mouth filled with soil and grit. I was rolled over onto my back, and I reached forward to try to pull the root off one of my legs. It was hopeless, the root was clinging on to me like a vice.

Something was glinting on the ground ahead of me, and as I was dragged past it, I saw that it was Victor's knife. I reached out for it but it was too late, I only managed to touch the bloody blade with one of my fingers. The blade hadn't been bloody before, and I realised that he must have cut himself trying to slash at the roots.

I could no longer hear Victor or Vanessa screaming, and the howling from the werewolves that were on their way had also stopped.

But I could hear the flames. The crackling had risen to a roar that was getting steadily closer. I closed my eyes, I could already feel the heat from the inferno I was heading towards. And I realised that what they said was true, your whole life really does pass before your eyes when you know you're about to die. Obviously it was a disappointingly brief performance, and I wasn't even the hero. In fact, second only to Imu Jonasson, I was actually the biggest villain, and one that no one was really going to miss, not really. No one would ever know that Richard Elauved in the end, in spite of everything, had actually tried to save someone, had actually risked his life for Karen Taylor. But even if I was the only person who knew it, there was a strange sort of comfort in knowing that I'd tried my best. A comfort in repeating the words as I was dragged towards my doom: 'I. Am. Not. Garbage. I. Am. Not . . .'

Something flew through the air, and I heard a deep thud.

'The other foot too!' a familiar voice said. 'Quick, they're coming back, they're everywhere!'

'I know!' another, even more familiar voice said.

I opened my eyes. In the yellow light of the moon and the fire I saw the large blade of an axe being raised above me, then saw a figure dressed from top to toe in bright red swinging it down towards me. Another swing, another thud. The ground beneath me was still. Or rather, obviously, I was lying still. The red-clad figure tossed the axe aside and bent down over me. I looked up at his face beneath his red fireman's helmet.

'Hi, Dad,' I said.

Frank looked at me in surprise.

'Can you stand?'

I tried. I shook my head.

'We need to get away from here!' the voice behind us called.

'Ready for a fireman's lift?' Frank asked, grabbing hold of me.

'Ready,' I said.

Frank lifted me off the ground and heaved me over his shoulder, then began to run back towards the gate. I raised my head and saw Agent Dale running right behind us. And behind him I saw something fill the large window of the house. It was big, black and had wings the size of sails. And in the middle of all that black, a glint of white piranha teeth. Then there was a damp thump, and suddenly the whole creature was on fire. And it screamed. One last scream, a scream that was not of this world.

I saw Agent Dale spin round without stopping, and when he turned again his face was as white as a sheet.

When we reached the railings I saw the fire truck outside. It still had its blue lights on, and I could see where the werewolf's howling had come from. Frank sat me down on the fireman's ladder that had been set up over the fence, and I was met by more firemen when I scrambled over to the other side. They patted me on the shoulder as if I had rescued someone, gave me a blanket and helped me into the back seat of the fire truck. Soon after, Frank and Agent Dale got in as well.

'Aren't you going to put the fire out?' I asked.

'It's probably too late for that,' Frank said. 'Fortunately the surrounding forest is so wet that we aren't going to have to deal with a forest fire as well.'

I looked towards the Night House. It was burning all over now, even the oak tree was in flames.

'But the twins,' I said. 'They were dragged in there . . .'

'It's probably too late for them too,' Agent Dale said, running one hand over his hair and shaking his head.

Something about the way he did that made me think that he believed me now. Not just about what had happened to the twins, but about Tom and Jack too.

'I think Imu Jonasson is finished,' I said.

Agent Dale nodded slowly. 'I think so too, Richard.'

There was a rumble above us and the moon disappeared as the clouds swept in front of it. The performance was over. And soon the rain was pouring down again.

# 21

IT WAS STILL RAINING WHEN Agent Dale and I got in his green Pontiac and drove from Mirror Forest towards the Taylors' house. Agent Dale told me about the pursuit, and how he had carried on alone from the dump with blue lights and blaring sirens all the way to Ballantyne, which he had assumed was my final destination. There he sat and waited in the police station until he heard the man in the fire tower shout down that he could see there was a fire in Mirror Forest. When Agent Dale heard it was the old house burning, he jumped in his car and followed the fire truck.

After that it was my turn to tell my story.

And this time I told him absolutely everything.

From when Tom and I walked into the forest, and I persuaded him to make a prank call. How Jack was transformed into an insect when I was teasing him, and how I got scared and tried to squash him. About the words Imu had carved into the wall at Rorrim's, and how they had made the people who read them try to kill themselves. About the voice on the phone, and our escape, and what I had seen in the house when it started to burn.

Agent Dale listened without interruption, only asking brief questions when there was something he wasn't sure he had understood correctly.

'That's quite a story,' he said when I had finished.

'I know. Too unbelievable to be true, right?'

'Yes,' Dale said seriously. 'If I hadn't seen what I've seen this evening, I wouldn't have believed you. My problem now is that no one at headquarters is going to believe *me*.'

We pulled up in front of the Taylors' house. I saw there was a light on in the window of Karen's room on the top floor.

'Looks like the sheriff is here,' Agent Dale said, nodding towards a car parked in front of the barn.

At that moment McClelland came rushing out of the door of the farmhouse, closely followed by Karen's father.

Agent Dale opened the car door and started to get out.

'Hi, Conan, what's going on?'

'It's the daughter,' McClelland said. 'She's run away.'

'Run away?'

'We'd locked her in,' her father said, pointing up at her window. 'She must have jumped out.'

'From there?' Agent Dale said. 'That's . . . very high.'

'The ground is wet from all the rain, so she evidently didn't hurt herself badly,' McClelland said. 'She managed to get away from here, anyway, her parents say they've looked everywhere. We've called out a search party, they're gathering at the police station now.'

'Richard and I will join you,' Agent Dale said.

'No!' The shuddering, tear-choked cry came from the front door. It was Mrs Taylor. 'Richard Elauved isn't going *anywhere* near our Karen. Nothing bad ever happened in Ballantyne before he came, or after he left. Keep him away! He's . . . he's . . .'

I didn't actually hear what she called me, because I turned to Agent Dale and said we should drive to the library. I said we needed help from the fire truck, and Agent Dale used the police radio to contact them. They replied that the rain had extinguished the fire in what was left of the house, so they could set off at once.

'Why here?' Agent Dale said as we stopped outside the dark library.

'Because just finding Karen isn't going to be enough,' I said. 'We're going to have to deprogramme her too, or she's going to keep trying to find ways to harm herself.'

'You're saying she's been programmed like the youngsters who were locked in the room where Imu wrote on the walls?'

'It's called black word magic. And there are books in here. But if we're lucky, they won't just be about the poison in black word magic, but the antidote as well.'

'Which is?'

'White word magic.'

At that moment the fire truck pulled up next to us. Frank jumped out brandishing his fireman's axe, and ran up to the main door with me and Agent Dale while two of the other firemen got the ladder from the back of the truck. Frank raised his axe, then lowered it again.

'It's a nice door,' he said. 'Do you really think it's so urgent that we can't just get Mrs Zimmer to open up for us?'

'Yes!' I cried.

Frank sighed, raised the axe and was about to swing it when the door opened.

'No!' Mrs Zimmer cried, and sneezed loudly.

I froze and let out a yell, as if I were the one about to be cut in two.

'Frank Elauved,' Mrs Zimmer said, staring at the axe blade that had stopped a few centimetres from her small, white-haired head. 'What's all this?'

'This,' Frank said, clutching the axe tightly, 'is a Pulaski, the finest fireman's axe there is. But why aren't you at home in bed, Mrs Zimmer?'

'The sirens,' she said. 'In weather like this, it isn't the forest but buildings that are burning. And nothing burns better than books. So I was worried there might be a fire here.'

'The fire's been put out,' Frank said. 'Perhaps you could let us in?'

'I'm not so sure about that,' she said, looking at the two firemen who had just appeared, carrying a long ladder. 'What do you want?'

'To borrow some books,' Agent Dale said, reaching inside his jacket and pulling out the leather folder containing his metal star. 'In the name of the law.'

Mrs Zimmer reluctantly opened the door.

'Here,' I said once we were inside, pointing up at the wall where the bookshelves disappeared into the darkness above the lights that Mrs Zimmer had turned on.

'Are you really going up there?' Mrs Zimmer asked, standing there with her arms folded over her dirty-green frock coat.

'Why not?' Agent Dale asked.

'Because . . .' Her mouth contorted in a grimace. 'Because it isn't safe these days.'

'What do you mean?'

'The Taylor girl was here a few days ago with her fishing rod, asking about books on trout fishing. I have a feeling she knew I was going to have to look in the other end of the library, because when I got back, she and one of my books were missing.'

'Which book?' I asked. And answered my own question when Mrs Zimmer pursed her thin lips tightly shut. 'The book on black word magic.'

'Since then things have been . . . unsettling here,' Mrs Zimmer said with a shudder. 'Lots of rustling and noises, books moving about and falling to the floor on their own even though there isn't a living soul in here. It's as if someone is looking for something that's gone missing.'

'That's why you're here,' Agent Dale said. 'Not because of the sirens. You're here day and night. You're sleeping here.'

Mrs Zimmer groaned. 'I have a sofa in the office. I lied because I didn't want you to think I'd gone mad. But this is my library, I've worked here my whole life and I've never lost a book or had one left in the wrong place.'

'Like a book about black word magic,' I said.

'It used to be there,' Mrs Zimmer said.

Frank switched a torch on and aimed it at where she was pointing. Sure enough, there was a gap in the row of books. My heart sank.

'Gone,' Agent Dale sighed.

'Stolen,' Mrs Zimmer corrected.

'Then we don't need the ladder,' Frank said to his men, who turned on their heel and began to walk out again.

'Hold on a moment,' I said. 'What's that white book, just to the right of the gap?'

'Surely that's obvious?' Mrs Zimmer said. 'That's the second volume on word magic. The one about white word magic.'

I looked at Frank and nodded.

'Guys!' he cried. 'We're going to need the ladder after all.'

Agent Dale and I were sitting in the reading room leafing through *A Compendium of Word Magic, Volume II: White Word Magic* beneath the light of an arched reading lamp.

Frank and the other firemen had left to take part in the search for Karen, and Mrs Zimmer had gone off to her office to make tea for us.

The pages were thin and the print so small that it strained our eyes.

It explained how to lift local and international curses, and provided general and specific incantations, formulas for reversing curses, to change people who had been turned into frogs back into people again. There were recipes for how to make storms disappear, how to get rid of scabies, how to clear traffic jams. But nothing about what I was looking for.

My head was starting to ache and I rubbed my temples as my eyes scanned down the page looking for the three letters I-M-U. I turned the page and looked at the page number: 12. Twelve pages, and those had taken us twenty minutes. There were 811 more pages. I groaned and pushed the book away.

'You can't see anything?' Agent Dale asked.

'We'll be here until dawn if we have to go through the whole thing,' I said. 'And we don't have that much time. For all I know . . .' I swallowed. I left the sentence unfinished, but I could see that Agent Dale understood: . . . *it's already too late.*

I groaned and banged my head on the open book.

He patted me on the back. 'Come on, Richard, let's give it a try anyway. After all . . .' He left the sentence unfinished, but I understood: . . . *it's the only thing we can do.*

He was right, I just felt very, very tired.

'The index.'

I smelled tea and looked up, to see that Mrs Zimmer had placed a steaming cup on the table next to my head.

'What?' I said.

'The index,' she repeated. 'If you're looking for something, look in the index. It should all be there, in alphabetical order.' She turned towards Agent Dale. 'I love it when things are in alphabetical order.'

I sat up and turned to the back of the book. And sure enough, there was an index. I leafed through until I found the entries for the letter *I*, then ran my finger down the page.

*I*carus, wings of; *i*maginary experiences, *i*mmaterial worlds, *i*mported word magic and . . . *I*mu. Or, to be more precise:

*Imu . . . p.214, p.510.*

I looked up page 214, and searched till I found the word.

*IMU is an incantation in black word magic that makes the person under the spell believe that he or she is identical with the spell-caster. As in I AM YOU. A person cursed with IMU will, like a mindless robot, seek to hide in a place that only he or she knows, and there seek confirmation that I AM YOU by performing something that makes him or her resemble the spell-caster. This latter is often pre-programmed by the spell-caster.*

That was all. I looked up page 510, and searched the page. There!

*IME is the counter-incantation to IMU, see: reversing incantations. The counter-incantation can only be used once the spell-caster and the recipient are one and the same person. One must get the recipient to say the words IME, as in I AM ME, for the I AM YOU incantation to be lifted.*

I noticed Agent Dale reading over my shoulder.

'Thanks for the tea, Mrs Zimmer,' I said, standing up.

We got in the car and Agent Dale grabbed the microphone of the police radio that was fixed to the dashboard.

'This is Agent Dale. Any news about Karen Taylor? Over.'

The radio crackled for a few moments, then McClelland's voice appeared. 'Nothing at the moment. Someone thought they saw her running towards the school, but it's locked up and we didn't find anything. We're going house to house now.'

'Have you tried Oscar Jr?' I asked.

'We've just been there,' McClelland said. 'He hasn't seen her, and has no idea where she might be.'

'Let us know as soon as you hear anything,' Agent Dale said.

'Will do.'

'Thanks. Over and out.'

Agent Dale hung the microphone back in place. I stared blankly out of the window. It had stopped raining again, it was like someone was having fun turning the tap off and on again up there.

'Maybe she's hiding out in a basement somewhere,' Dale said. 'Somewhere only she knows about.'

I tried to think of where that might be. A very dark basement. Or . . .

The moon suddenly decided to shine down on us again while I stared at the silent radio. Maybe it was like standing over a saucepan when you're starving and impatient, it never boils when you look at it. So I looked up at the sky above us instead. The clouds had broken up, and stars were peering out between the tattered remnants.

Basement. Living room. Or loft. Or . . .

One of the clouds looked like Chewbacca, the guy with fur in . . . no, not a guy, a Wookiee.

'I know!' I yelled.

Agent Dale jumped.

'What do you know?'

'I know where she is! Get going, straight ahead!' I grabbed the blue light from the compartment in the door, leaned out of the window and clamped it on the roof.

# 22

I TUGGED AT THE MAIN door of the school.

'Locked,' I said, putting my face to the frosted glass next to the door. There was no movement in the darkness within.

'Out of the way, I'll deal with that,' Agent Dale said.

He pushed his jacket back and drew his pistol. I put my hands over my ears. He turned the pistol round, holding it by the barrel, and broke the glass with the butt. Then he reached in and unlocked the door.

'I thought you were going to . . .' I began.

'I know what you thought,' he said. 'That only works in films.'

We ran along the corridor and up the stairs.

I was gasping for breath when we reached the door to the roof. I carefully took hold of the handle and pushed it down. There was no glass we could break here.

'A *bit* of shooting, maybe?'

Dale sighed and pushed his jacket back again, but what he pulled out was much smaller than a pistol, more the size of a paper clip.

'Out of the way.'

He pushed the end of the paper-clip thing into the lock and began to twist it. He was concentrating hard, with the tip of his tongue sticking out of the corner of his mouth.

'Only in films, right?' I whispered.

'Only in films.'

There was a quiet click from the lock and he carefully pushed the door open. We held our breath. The only sound we could hear was the low muttering of a girl's voice.

'Wait here,' I whispered.

I pushed the door fully open and stepped over the high sill and out onto the flat roof. The last of the clouds were scudding across the sky, and above us the stars sparkled like jewels on black felt. It was a beautiful night. Karen was beautiful too, even the wet hair sticking to her head and the nightdress streaked with mud. She was standing on the raised, tin-lined edge of the roof, facing me, with her back to the schoolyard below. She didn't seem aware of me, her eyes were closed and her face turned to the sky as if she was sunbathing, but her lips were moving. I walked slowly towards her, and as I got closer I could hear the words she was repeating:

'I AM YOU, I AM YOU, I AM . . .'

I moistened my lips and began to whisper quietly:

'I AM ME, I AM ME, I AM ME . . .'

When I was three metres away from her, Karen suddenly opened her eyes like a robot that had just been switched on. I stopped so as not to startle her, in case she stepped back and fell. She looked right at me. I could see that it was Karen, but the girl I knew wasn't there. Or rather, she was in there behind that blank stare, but she wasn't alone.

'Hi, Karen,' I said. 'It's me, Richard.'

'Richard,' she repeated, in a voice that seemed to struggle to find words. 'Do you want to watch me fly?'

'No,' I said. 'You can't fly. Repeat after me, I AM ME.'

'I AM . . .' Karen began. Then she stopped. She gritted her teeth. Her jaw muscles clenched as she stared at me with a desperate look on her face. I could see her mouth form the shape of ME, but it was as if an invisible hand twisted it to form YOU instead. I took a small step closer but stopped abruptly when she responded by taking a matching step backwards, even closer to the edge of the roof. Only now did I notice that she was barefoot, the mud and blood on her feet made it look like she was wearing shoes.

'I AM ME,' I repeated.

She nodded as if she understood. Her body was shaking as if she was tensing all her muscles.

'Come on,' I whispered. 'Come on, Karen, you can do it.'

'I AM . . .' she began, and the veins on her neck stood out as she chanted: 'YOUUUU . . .'

'He's dead!' I cried. 'He burned up, he's gone!'

But it didn't help, he was inside her, like a parasite, and I could see the despair in her face, the tears that welled up in her eyes and began to fall, and realised that she simply couldn't do it. She took another step, the heels of her bloody feet were sticking out over the edge now.

'Karen,' I said, 'I don't want to lose you. Do you hear me?'

She looked at me with sad eyes, as if she was asking for permission for what she was about to do. I blinked two tears out of my eyes and whispered the three words I had read and heard, but never said, and certainly never believed. Not until now, when I said them slowly, clearly and loudly:

'I love you.'

It was a farewell message. The last words she would hear. But she hadn't fallen yet. And something happened to her face, it was as if something broke. She looked at me with a look of disbelief.

'I,' she said, leaning towards me, 'AM . . . ME . . .'

It sounded like someone was whispering 'hush!', but at the same moment I realised it was the sound of her bloody feet slipping on the tin covering on the edge of the roof. I only managed to take a half a step forward before Karen was gone, swallowed by the darkness.

She fell without a sound.

I stared stiffly in front of me.

There was just a soft thud when she landed in the schoolyard.

I had a strange feeling of having been here before, of having experienced this very moment before. My eyes found the moon, which was hanging large and pale above the treetops to the east. I heard Agent Dale come out onto the roof behind me. Together we walked over to the edge, leaned over and looked down into the schoolyard. I could see the sweeping blue light of the fire truck that was parked down there. I saw the big, round firemen's canvas, held up by six men, including Frank. And, in the middle of the canvas, that still seemed to be swaying, I saw Karen lying on her back, looking up at the sky. Maybe she was looking for clouds, maybe she was looking for stars. But I thought – and still think – that she was looking for me.

# 23

WHEN I WAS ALLOWED INTO the room where Karen was lying, the nurse told me I could only have five minutes. She explained that the patient needed rest.

It was afternoon, and almost twenty-four hours had passed since the fire and Karen's fall from the school building.

'What lovely flowers,' she said when I put the bouquet – which I noted was much smaller than the others she had received – on the bedside table.

'I heard that you saved me,' she said.

'No, the men holding the firemen's canvas were the ones who saved you,' I said.

'But they say it was you who told them to be standing there.'

'Maybe.'

'Maybe? Yes or no?'

I just smiled.

'Tell me, you jerk!' Karen sat up in bed. I could see that she was already starting to get back to her old self. 'You see, I can't remember anything.'

'I heard about someone who had the same . . . er, illness, at Rorrim's, and jumped off the roof, so I was thinking that you might do the same thing.'

'But what I don't understand is how you knew that I'd be on the roof of the school.'

'It said in the book about white word magic that you would be hiding somewhere that only you knew about.'

'Only me.' She smiled. 'And you.'

We fell silent and looked out of the open window. The sound of crickets chirruping, bees buzzing, larks singing.

'Do you have to go back to Rorrim's?' she asked.

'No,' I said. 'Agent Dale has spoken to the Principal at Rorrim's, and with McClelland and the head teacher here. I'm starting back at school again on Monday.'

'That's great!'

We sat in silence again. There was no doubt about it, Karen was definitely the best person to be silent with, I wished that these five minutes could last forever.

'By the way, do you know what happened with that fire?' she asked.

'The house was almost burned down, but not entirely. Because of the rain,' I said.

'I hope there wasn't anyone inside?'

'I hope so too,' I said. Agent Dale had said they hadn't found any remains at the scene, and asked me to keep what I knew about the twins to myself until they knew more. As he put it, they wanted to avoid frightening the people of Ballantyne any more than was strictly necessary. The oak tree had also been killed by the damage it had received, and Agent Dale said they wanted to dig up the roots to see what they could find.

'You really don't remember anything?' I asked. 'None of the things I said to you on the roof, for instance?'

'Like what?' Karen smiled innocently.

'Nothing,' I said.

'I don't remember anything,' she said, picking up my bouquet and smelling it. 'But I . . . I think I dreamed something.'

'Like what?'

'Nothing,' she said. It was hard to tell if she was smiling or not behind the flowers.

I took a deep breath. It was now or never. 'When you get out of here . . .' I had to pause and take another deep breath.

'Yes?' Karen said.

'Would you like to go to the cinema with me?'

'The cinema?'

'A remake of *Night of the Living Dead*. They're showing it at the cinema in Hume in a week's time. Frank's going to teach me how to drive.'

'Hmm. Do you think it will be as good as the original?'

'No.'

She laughed. 'But scarier, maybe?'

'Maybe. I can hold your hand if it gets too scary.'

She looked at me thoughtfully. 'Can you?'

'Yes.'

'Can you show me how you'd do it, if we had to?'

'Hold your hand?'

'Yes.'

'Now?'

'Now,' she said.

# PART TWO

# 24

I HELD THE PHONE AWAY from me, at arm's length, made a real effort and screwed my eyes up to bring the text on the screen into focus.

The way you do when you've forgotten to bring your reading glasses with you.

I gave up and did what the plane's loudspeakers had just told me to do, and switched my mobile phone off. Not that I needed to read her text message again, because I already knew it by heart.

*Hi Richard. Yay, I heard you signed up too! It's going to be so great to see you again and find out what's been going on these past years. Quite a lot's happened to me, obviously! Hugs, Karen*

The plane broke through the clouds, and from my window seat

in business class I looked down on the pancake-flat, autumn-red forest landscape beneath us. It reminded me of the feeling when Karen and I stood on the roof of the school during lunch break, looking out across Ballantyne. Fifteen years had passed since then. What did she look like now? When I received the invitation to the reunion for our graduation class, that was my first thought. Obviously I could have tried to find the answer on social media, but I hadn't done that. Why not? Because I didn't want to risk seeing happy-family pictures, of her, Oscar and a couple of cute kids? Or because I could let myself think about her if I had to, but tapping those keys on my computer would be definite proof for the voice in my head that was always accusing me of not being able to forget Karen Taylor? Well, here I was, on a plane from the big city, and that was probably evidence enough in itself. Admittedly, there were a few other reasons why I had accepted the invitation. Such as seeing all the places that had inspired me to write the teenage horror novel that had changed my life, and that had recently been optioned as a film: *The Night House*. And seeing Frank and Jenny, who had been to visit me in the city so often. And then, of course, there was revenge. Seeing the respect, and hopefully envy, in the eyes of Oscar and the others when they said hello to celebrated children's author Richard Hansen. I really am that shallow. But perhaps this trip could actually help me grow a little. That – after seeing Karen – was the most important reason for going back. I wanted to apologise. Apologise for having been a bully, for trampling on those in our class who were even lower in the pecking order than I was.

The captain announced that we would soon be coming in to land at Hume Airport, and I fastened my safety belt. The last part of the flight was bumpy, but we were lucky – wind, rain and thunder were forecast for later in the day.

On the way through the arrivals hall I checked out a bookstand outside a kiosk, it had become a habit. When I couldn't see my book I quickly glanced round, then turned the stand. And there it was. The title, *The Night House,* was printed in jagged green lettering, in homage to the comic book *Swamp Thing*. The cover illustration was done in the same cartoon style, and showed a terrified boy trying to pull free from a telephone receiver that had already swallowed his arm all the way to the elbow. I took out a pen, opened the book at the first page, and read the first line.

*'Y-y-y-you're crazy,' Tom said, and I could tell he was scared, seeing as he stammered one more time than he usually does.*

Then I signed the book and put it back in the stand.

Frank was smiling as he stood in the doorway smoking his pipe when the taxi pulled up in front of the house. As I was paying I heard him call Jenny, and by the time I got out she was standing on the stone steps with her arms open while Frank was still standing in the doorway as if it needed someone to keep an eye on it. I walked into her deep, soft embrace, then into Frank's hard and more shallow but firmer version.

We went and sat down in the living room, Frank and Jenny on the sofa and me opposite them, in pride of place in the batwing chair. We drank tea while I asked about this and that, but they said there wasn't much new to report, they wanted to hear my news. So I talked. Mostly about the sort of thing I knew they liked hearing about, the latest successes on the book front, life in the big city. A famous film director I had had dinner with who wanted to make a film of *The Night House*.

'Who's that?' Frank asked.

I mentioned a couple of his films, and Frank grunted and

nodded with a smile, as if he'd seen them, while Jenny rolled her eyes at me.

'I bumped into Alfred yesterday,' she said. 'He asked how you were getting on.'

'*Everyone* always asks how you're getting on,' Frank added happily.

'Yes, we follow what you do,' Jenny said. 'You've really put Ballantyne on the map.'

I didn't bother to point out that that was probably a bit of an exaggeration, that you didn't have to be a lousy author to become famous, you just had to go on a reality television show. But that was a cheap shot, and one that I had used in too many interviews, and it really wouldn't have gone down well here.

'It's nice if people think about it that way,' I said. 'But I dare say there's a limit to the amount of success you might want your neighbour to have, here as much as anywhere else. Certainly if that neighbour was a bit of a jerk at school.'

Jenny looked at me uncomprehendingly, then looked at Frank, who shrugged. They probably hadn't realised – or hadn't wanted to realise – that their golden boy had been pretty much identical to the arsehole in *The Night House*.

'Yes, well,' Jenny said, as if to change the subject. 'Isn't it about time you met a nice girl, then?'

I shot her an apologetic smile and lifted my teacup to my mouth.

'Of course he meets girls,' Frank said, tapping his pipe. 'He's a celebrity, after all. Then you don't have to settle for the first one that comes along.'

Jenny slapped him on the shoulder. 'Like you, you mean?'

Frank laughed and put his arm round her. 'Not everyone strikes gold at the first attempt, you know.'

I smiled at them both, put my cup down and looked at the time. I pointed to indicate that I should probably go upstairs and change.

'Yes, of course, you need to get ready for the party,' Jenny said.

'Unless he's got to write,' Frank chuckled. 'He was always writing.'

'Yes, do you remember?' Jenny said, tilting her head to one side, dewy-eyed. 'Even on Saturday nights when we were sitting in front of the television with cakes and sweets and all sorts of goodies, you'd be sitting up there in your room writing and writing. We used to think what was on television could be a bit weird, but we had no idea of all the terrible things going on in your imagination up there.'

'I've thought about that,' Frank said, nodding as if agreeing in advance with his own conclusion. 'You came here from the big city back then, and you must have been properly bored. There was absolutely nothing going on here in Ballantyne, so you had to create a place where the most incredible, fantastical things could happen. Flesh-eating telephones and . . .' He paused for breath, and seemed to have run out of steam.

'Trees that reach out and grab you, and poor Jack who turned into a beetle,' Jenny quickly added. 'What does Jack say about that now? And you used *our* names too, come to that.'

'Yes, but not our surname,' Frank said, as if to prove that he hadn't dropped the ball. 'And you make me – a simple driving instructor – a fire chief. I liked that.'

'Speaking of which, there's one thing I've been wondering about,' Jenny said. 'Elauved. How did you come up with that particular surname?'

I took a deep breath. The moment had come, the moment I had been expecting, when I could finally tell them.

'Richard Elauved,' I said. '*Rich are the loved.* Rich are those who are loved. I did that for you. You took me in and loved me like I was your own child. You made me richer that any millionaire could have done.'

At any rate, that's what I thought I said, but when I saw the expectant looks on their faces I realised that I hadn't actually said it. Why was it so difficult?

'It just popped into my head,' I said instead, seeing as that wasn't a complete lie.

I looked around the living room. There was a picture next to the fireplace, a bird flying over a forest. It could well have been hanging there all the years I lived there, I just couldn't remember it. I don't know when these gaps in my memory had started to appear.

I stood up.

'I'll have dinner ready in half an hour,' Jenny said. 'Lasagne.' She winked at me, 'There's a towel on your bed if you want to have a shower.'

I thanked her and went upstairs. I stopped for a moment in front of the door to my room and listened. Both to the blissful silence in there, and to the comforting small talk and pottering from down in the kitchen. How could I manage to make declarations of love to people I didn't love, but not to those I really did love? I don't know. I honestly don't know. It's possible that I'm damaged in a more fundamental way than I'm actually aware of.

Then I pushed the door open. Nothing had changed, the room looked like a museum dedicated to Richard Hansen. Or possibly Richard Elauved. Either way, my eyes were drawn – as they always were – automatically to the floorboards below the window to see if a magicicada with Fatso's red eyes was staring up at me.

# 25

IT WAS TEN PAST SEVEN and the darkness of evening had settled outside when I walked into the classroom.

It was like stepping out of a time machine. All the faces at the desks turned towards me, as did Miss Birdsong, who was standing in front of the blackboard with the pointer in her hand. The only difference from fifteen years before was that someone had cast spiders' webs over their faces, moved some of the boys' hairlines back, and added a few kilos to their weight. It looked as if some pairs of glasses had changed owner, probably a combination of some people not caring about having to wear glasses now, while others no longer had to wear them because of laser eye surgery or contact lenses.

'You always were late, Richard,' Miss Birdsong said, with feigned strictness in her voice.

The class laughed with a ferocity that suggested a degree of overexcitement, but that's probably the way of things with school reunions. I looked around the desks as I cheerily replied that I was sorry, I realised on the way that I had left my maths homework at home, so had to go back and get it, and *then* my bicycle got a puncture. Naturally, this garnered even more laughter.

They all had glasses with some sort of fizz in. I saw a lot of faces I recognised, but also some I must have forgotten altogether. A mixture of my selective memory and the fact that some people can pass through others' lives without making any impression at all. Either way, I didn't see what I was looking for.

Karen.

Not until I reached the back of the room.

I saw Oscar first. He had put on weight, but had kept his hair. He was grinning with teeth as white as back then, and gave me the thumbs up.

Karen was sitting at the desk next to him. I didn't know what I had been hoping. Well, actually, I did know. I had been hoping she would have let herself go. That she would have lost her spark, her charm, that irresistible aura that might well have come from the very fact that she knew that she was irresistible, at least for a certain type of boy. I had been hoping that I would come here, make sense of everything, laugh it all off as a nostalgic memory now that *my* Karen Taylor was gone, torn down from her pedestal. And that I could have a bit of fun with effortless reminiscences, then go home a free man, liberated from this dream that had really been a bit of a nightmare, and had cost me so much time and energy.

But obviously that isn't what happened.

Karen was exactly the same, just with slightly more pronounced features and curves. And she smiled at me like I was the only person in the world, and gestured that the desk beside her was free with complete self-confidence. I felt my heart beat with unfeigned delight. Damn.

She leaned towards me the moment I sat down. 'Bastard!' she whispered, putting her hand on my arm. 'I was starting to worry you weren't going to show up!'

'Just staying in character,' I whispered back, then grabbed the already full glass in front of me and drank a toast with her. It felt like the champagne bubbles went straight to my head, and I remembered that I hadn't eaten much lasagne and ought to take things a bit carefully to stop myself getting drunk too quickly.

'Pay attention at the back, children!' Miss Birdsong scolded good-naturedly. Obviously her name wasn't Miss Birdsong, as I had called her in the book, but for the life of me I honestly couldn't remember what her real name was.

I happened to meet Oscar's gently curious gaze before he looked back at our teacher, who was running through the changes at the school since we were there. There was a lot about renovation and new buildings, changes of head teacher, reforms, other fairly boring facts.

After the 'lesson' we gathered in the gymnasium, which was decorated as if for a prom night. A girl from the party committee stood by a table with a sound system and balloons and gave a loud explanation of the plan for the rest of the evening. I saw Oscar and Karen in front of me. He had his arm round her shoulders, and now she was leaning her head sideways towards his neck.

'Congratulations on all your success, Richard,' a voice whispered. I turned round and saw a face I didn't remember, even though it belonged to a very handsome man. Broad-shouldered and slim. He actually reminded me of Agent Dale, the way I imagined him in the book.

'Thanks,' I said, looking more closely at him, because there was something about his voice. Something distinctive. Was it actually possible?

'Fatso?' I blurted out.

He laughed without the slightest sign of being offended. 'It's been a long time since I heard that, but yes, I'm Fatso.'

Not only the fat but the glasses were gone, and I could see that he had muscles under his well-fitting suit.

'Jack!' I said. 'Sorry, I was just so . . . What are you up to?'

'Dance,' he said. 'In the same city as you.'

'You're a dancer?'

'I was. Ballet school. Now I'm mostly a choreographer for other dancers. It's more comfortable and . . . well, much better paid. At least it is if you've made a bit of a name for yourself.'

'And you have?'

'Not as much as you, Richard. But I'm doing OK.'

'Family? Kids?'

'I have a husband. No kids yet. How about you?'

I shook my head. 'Neither of those.'

'That makes you the exception. People here are getting married and producing kids like a conveyor belt . . .' He nodded towards Karen and Oscar. 'Three kids. And the biggest house in Ballantyne. He bought it, tore it down and rebuilt it again from scratch. I guarantee that he'll invite everyone to an after-party there so he can show it off. And . . .'

The rest was drowned out when the music was suddenly turned up and the class cheered. An annoying hit that I hated when we were at school, but which now sounded great. A girl came over to us and, without a word, pulled Jack with her onto what had quickly become a dance floor, where everyone was twisting and jumping about. In the chaos I lost sight of Karen. Until she appeared next to me.

'Bloody hell, look at Jack dance,' she exclaimed over the music as we watched his acrobatic moves. 'What about Richard? Does he still not dance?'

I shook my head. I felt her boyish fringe tickle my cheek when she leaned closer so she didn't have to shout: 'Shall we get out of here?'

'What do you mean?' I asked without moving.

'Pretend it's lunch break. We can get lost for a while and let the idiots have their fun.'

She dangled an old, familiar key in front of my face and laughed that infectious, crazy laugh of hers.

The sharp autumn air hit my face as we stepped out onto the roof.

We walked over to the edge and looked down at the schoolyard.

Strong gusts of wind blew her fringe this way and that. To the south, towards Hume, lightning was flashing beneath the clouds.

'Hope he lands OK,' Karen said.

'He?'

'Tom. He should have been here by now, but his plane must be circling Hume because of the weather.'

I nodded. It looked like the storm was heading this way.

Karen raised her refilled champagne glass. 'Here we are again, then. How many confidences did we manage to share while we were sitting up here?'

*Me*, I thought. I was the one who came up with the confidences, you just asked and listened.

'Even so, I never shared my deepest secret with you,' I said, drinking another toast with her.

We drank, and Karen fell silent and looked out into the darkness. That was her trick, and she knew it.

'You mean the one about what happened to your parents?' she eventually said.

I didn't answer. I just noted that she had bypassed my ploy. And that this may have been best for both of us.

'You always said you didn't remember anything about them,' she said. 'Can you tell me what happened now?'

I thought about it. 'I don't know,' I said.

'Tell me what you do remember,' she said, laying the jacket she had brought with her on the roofing felt next to the pipe. She sat down and indicated that I should do the same. I slid down beside her and leaned back against the pipe. We were sitting so close together that my suit trousers were touching the fabric of her dress.

'They died in a fire,' I said.

'What sort of fire?'

'Arson. In the apartment where we lived.'

'Who started it?'

I swallowed hard. My mouth was so dry that I couldn't get a sound out. A barely audible rumble of thunder reached us.

Her voice sounded tentative, as if she were edging her way out onto thin ice: 'You?'

'No,' I said. 'My father.' I let the air out of my lungs.

'Why do you think he did that?'

'Because he was ill. And because my mum had thrown him out after he got violent.'

'So he set fire to the house after he got chucked out, but ended up getting killed himself in the fire?'

'Yes. He broke in while we were asleep to start the fire.'

'And this happened without warning?'

'No. Well, yes. He used to phone.'

'He phoned your mum?'

'Yes. Particularly at night. In the end she stopped answering the phone. So sometimes I would sneak out and answer.'

'What for?'

'Because . . . I don't know. Because I wanted it to stop ringing. Because I wanted him to stop frightening us. Because I . . . wanted to hear his voice.'

'Hear his voice?'

'He was my dad. He was in pain, too.'

'What did he say?'

I closed my eyes. It was a bit like when I sat and wrote, it just came to me, images, sounds, scenes – I could never be sure if they had actually happened or if they had just appeared in my mind, yet they still seemed just as real as Karen and me sitting there now.

'He said she was going to burn. That the woman I loved would burn, and that there was nothing I could do. Because I was small, weak and cowardly. Because I was like him, I was . . .' I gasped for breath. 'Garbage. And then he made me repeat that. "Say you're garbage or I'll kill her." '

'So you said it?'

I opened my mouth to say yes, but no sound came out. It felt like this was about someone else, not me, as if my body, my voice were just something a dispassionate writer had come up with, as if he was spitting out the first thing that came into his head. At the same time, I knew that every word was true, that this was exactly how it had happened. I nodded, then felt something warm trickle down my cheek and turned away. I had evidently drunk that champagne a bit too fast after all.

Karen put her hand on my shoulder. 'But he killed her anyway?'

I wiped the tears away. 'He had been diagnosed with schizophrenia. He was supposed to be in hospital. He *was* in hospital. A secure unit. I got to visit him once. The mental hospital was way out in the middle of a field, it had a tall fence around it. It was called Rorrim's. Then – without warning us – they let him out again. Three days later he started the fire.'

'How did you survive it?'

'I jumped.'

'You jumped?'

'I woke up, and my bedroom was on fire. I ran to the window. Our apartment was on the ninth floor, and there were fire engines down in the street. They held out a canvas and shouted up at me to jump. So I jumped. Without asking first if they had my mum. I could have saved her. I was thirteen years old, after all.'

'If your bedroom was on fire, you couldn't have done anything.'

'I'll never know.'

'Oh, Richard,' she said, and put her hand against my cheek.

Then I began to cry. I cried and cried, it was as if I had cramp in every muscle and my body didn't want to stop shaking. It was like in the book, when I was stuck on the electric fence. That, and a vague memory of something I couldn't quite get hold of.

Karen wrapped her arms round me. Now it no longer hurt. On

the contrary, it was like the plug in a drainpipe being removed and all the crap finally draining out. She didn't let go until I had stopped sobbing.

'Here,' she said. I looked up and took what she was offering. Then laughed.

'What is it?'

'Only a mother would make sure she had Kleenex with her even when she was wearing a party dress,' I sniffed as I wiped my nose.

'Mother?' she said.

'You and Oscar. I hear you've got three. In a ridiculously big house.'

Karen looked at me in disbelief. Then she started laughing too, and it was my turn to ask her what it was.

'It's true that Oscar has three kids,' she said. 'And yeah, a big house. But I have neither kids nor a house, I'm afraid.'

'No?'

'Oscar and I split up right after high school, right after . . . well, right after you left.'

'I see. Why did you split up?'

She shrugged. 'I was heading south to study medicine, he was going into his dad's business here. But regardless of that, I already knew that he and I weren't exactly meant for each other.'

'If you knew that, why were you together for so long?'

'You know what?' Karen said, looking at me, though she seemed to be looking inside herself. 'I've often wondered that. And I think it might have been because everyone thought Oscar Jr and I made such a good couple. Even my mother was astonished when I told her I wanted to break up.'

'What about Oscar, how did he take it?'

She shook her head. 'So-so.'

'It looks like he still has feelings for you.'

'And I do for him – Oscar's the sweetest boy in the world.'

'Do you still see each other?'

She shook her head. 'He gets in touch, but I just . . .' She swatted her hand as if to indicate that what she meant was obvious. I asked anyway.

'Just?'

She flashed a smile. 'Smooth everything over.'

I was about to ask who she was doing that for: Oscar, herself, or both, when we were interrupted by a cry from down in the schoolyard.

'Karen! Richard! We know you're up there!'

We peered over the edge. It was Oscar, of course.

'We're doing the circle now,' he called. 'Everyone has to join in!'

The circle meant everyone sitting on a chair in a big circle in the gymnasium while each of us took turns to say what we had been doing during the past fifteen years. We were each given three minutes. Some people got it done in thirty seconds, and no one stopped anyone who went over their allocated time. Most of them talked about their families and what they did in their free time rather than their careers. Apart from Oscar, who went into detail about how well business was going and only mentioned in passing that he was married and had three children. Jack made everyone laugh with a self-deprecating depiction of the boy who loved to dance in front of the mirror dressed up as the girl in *Dirty Dancing*, but had no idea he was gay until one of his aunts explained to him who Jack *really* was. Then it was Karen's turn. To my surprise – or possibly relief – she didn't reveal much except that she lived down south, where she had trained as a psychiatrist, that she worked far too much, didn't currently have a partner, and shared a beach house with two female colleagues.

I imagined I could hear a particularly expectant silence descend when it got to my turn as the last person in the circle. As if the story of the class celebrity was the dessert everyone had been looking forward to. Maybe not because they were interested in hearing yet another self-congratulatory success story – in this instance one they could even read about in the papers – but because they were curious about how I had *dealt* with it, the success, the few crumbs of acclaim. If I had become arrogant, if I thought they cared, if I was going to go over my three minutes to rub it in – all the things I had achieved that they hadn't.

I used just a few sentences to say that I wrote children's books, that some of the books had done well, some not so well, but one of the books had done well enough for me to make a living from it. That I was single and didn't have kids, and that even if I didn't have any plans to move back, I still thought a lot about the years I had spent in Ballantyne. Sometimes the good memories. Sometimes the bad ones.

'But not as bad for me as they must have been for some of you,' I said, and could already feel my throat tightening. Damn champagne. 'Because I wasn't a very nice boy. Let's say in my defence that I had been through some rough experiences that contributed to that, but all the same. I was a bully.'

I forced myself to look around at the faces in the circle, and it struck me how similar they looked in the dimly lit gymnasium, like white pearls on a string. As an outsider. Even so . . .

'I want to apologise, but I don't want to ask anyone's forgiveness,' I said. 'Because that's too much to ask for someone who has wrecked other people's childhoods. But I want you to know that I'm sorry . . .' My throat closed up completely and I had to stop. I hadn't expected my planned confession to feel so harrowing, I should have practised it before I came, should have said the words out loud to myself when I was on my own. I blew the air out of my bulging cheeks and blinked away the tears. '. . . And if this makes just one of you feel a little better, then this trip will have been worth it.' I let go of the last air I had in my lungs, leaned forward in my chair, rested my forehead on my hands and closed my eyes. The room was completely silent. For a long time.

'But . . .' a woman's voice eventually said, I couldn't place her, 'unless anyone else had a completely different experience, I don't remember you being a bully, Richard.'

'Nor me,' a man's voice said. 'Others were, but not you.'

Were they messing with me? I took my hands away from my face. But no, they were all looking at me with what appeared to be friendly seriousness.

'Do you know why you never bullied anyone?' Jack, Fatso, asked. 'You didn't have time, you were always in the library with Mrs Zimmer, reading the whole time.'

General laughter.

'Sorry, Richard,' Oscar said with a grin. 'You probably weren't as badass as you like to remember. But that's probably just how a writer's memory works.'

Even louder laughter. Relief. Well, at least that dissolved the awkward atmosphere I had evidently created. I swallowed. Smiled. And was about to say something when Jack jumped up on his chair and formed his hands into a megaphone in front of his mouth:

'Party time!'

Seconds later everyone was on their feet, the music came on, and we threw ourselves into dancing to the cheesy hits of our youth. Everyone changed partners with each song except Oscar, who I saw had laid claim to Karen. I danced like a lunatic, under the influence of champagne, moonshine, embarrassment at my badly judged confession, and sheer joy and relief that my guilty conscience all these years had turned out to be completely unfounded. To be honest, I wasn't sure who was misremembering the past, me or the rest of the class, but my behaviour evidently hadn't made any lasting impression on anyone, and that alone was worth celebrating!

I don't know how long I had been dancing, I was dripping with sweat and dancing with a girl I only vaguely recognised, but who was looking at me with a look that was so obviously full of lust that I suspected we must have known each other better that I remembered. And yet, back then I hadn't had eyes for anyone except Karen, had I? I don't know if she was reading my thoughts, but when the music stopped and we were standing facing each other in the sudden silence, she said loudly and clearly, with a cheeky smile:

'The barn.'

I smiled back with a vague nod.

'No!' She laughed incredulously. 'Bloody hell, you don't remember! The barn! You and me and . . . the hay?'

I carried on smiling.

'What's my name?' she asked aggressively.

My smile felt like it was glued on. I swallowed.

Her laughter sounded bitter now. 'You know what, Richard Hansen? You're a real –'

'Rita.'

She tilted her head and looked at me.

'Your name is Rita,' I said.

Her face relaxed, and I could tell from her smile that everything was forgiven.

The music came back on. It was the first slow song of the evening, a ballad, and Rita was advancing purposefully towards me when a figure cut between us. It was Karen.

'I think this one's mine,' she said, looking at me without even noticing Rita.

'I think she might be right about that,' I said to Rita, taking Karen's hand.

Soon we were gliding round the floor in a simple two-forward, one-back, while the syrupy ballad dripped from the speakers.

'It was brave of you to reveal how you felt,' Karen said. 'To tell everyone how you remember your schooldays.'

I flirted back: 'Even if no one else remembers them the way I do?'

'All experience is subjective. Bear in mind that you're sensitive, anything aimed at you had a strong impact. And you superimposed that sensitivity onto others, you assumed that they were as badly affected by whatever lesser things you aimed at them.'

I felt her soft hand in mine, the sway of her back, the warmth radiating from her body even though I was holding her at a decent distance. Could I come clean about the rest as well? Was I that brave?

The song faded away as Karen rested her forehead against my shoulder.

'I hope they play another slow one,' she whispered.

She got her wish.

Some way into the third ballad I pulled her closer to me. Not much, just a little, but she glanced up at me, smiled and looked like she was about to say something when it happened. The room was suddenly lit up by a huge flash. It came from the windows high up in the walls, a bluish light that seemed to shine through everything, so that for an instant I saw an X-ray image of Karen's head, the shape of her skull, empty eye sockets, teeth grinning horribly. Then it was gone, followed by a deep, almost groaning rumble of thunder. Karen moved closer to me and I shut my eyes, breathing in her scent. Another rumble, nearer this time. I felt Karen let go of me, and when I opened my eyes I realised that the music had stopped and the gymnasium was pitch-black.

'Short circuit,' someone declared.

The darkness lay like an invisibility cloak around us. This was our chance. But when I reached out my hand to Karen, she was gone. Someone lit a lighter and a couple of candles, then after a while a torch appeared in the doorway.

The caretaker.

Oscar, Harry Cooper – a bald guy I remembered because his hair was thinning even back then, and because he was an even bigger asshole than me – and I went with him down into the basement. There was a smell of scorched metal, and when the caretaker opened a large fuse box, sure enough, a cloud of smoke rose up in the light of the torch. I looked at the twisted, blackened fuses and switches in there. But it was the smell, not the sight, that there was something vaguely familiar about, like the girl with the amorous face, with whom something had happened that I ought to remember, but couldn't.

'There won't be any more lights on here tonight,' the caretaker said. 'And no more party.'

'We've got candles,' Oscar said.

'You can see there's been a fire here,' the caretaker said. 'I can't have anyone in the school if there's a chance some wires are smouldering somewhere, you understand that, right?'

We went back up to the gym, where Oscar stood on a chair and announced that he had both bad and good news. The bad news was that the party couldn't continue at the school.

'The good news is that my wife has taken the kids to see her mother this weekend,' he said, and I noticed that there was a hint of boastfulness in his voice. 'Which means I'm home alone, and we can . . .'

He was drowned out by the cheering.

It was getting close to midnight, and in the car park outside the school we were squeezing into the cars of the people who had driven to the party. The fact that none of the drivers was entirely sober didn't seem to bother anyone, everyone knew that Ballantyne's sheriff had better things to do on a Saturday night than hunt drunk drivers.

I got in an electric SUV that buzzed away, squeezed between Harry Cooper and Rita, and realised how exhausted I was. It had been a long day since I had woken up in the city, and I wondered if I shouldn't have thrown in the towel and gone home to my childhood bedroom. Instead I sat there with my eyes closed, thinking that Karen was going to be there too, and feeling nausea rise as the car slowed down when it hit the winding roads. I heard the crunch of gravel beneath the wheels, a subdued 'wow' from Harry Cooper, the squeal of a gate opening, then a more cautious crunching sound. Then we stopped completely.

'Here we are,' the driver said. 'Where's the drink?'

I felt the pressure of bodies relax and mild, stormy air flow in from the open doors on both sides. I opened my eyes and stumbled out, hoping that the fresh air would wake me up and soothe the beginnings of my headache. I straightened my back and stared at the building in front of me. I felt my blood freeze to ice in my veins. I should have realised. The house was completely new, rebuilt from scratch, or so it looked. But they must have used the original architect's plans or old photographs.

'Are you coming, Mr Author?' Rita called.

'Sure,' I said.

Admittedly, I couldn't see an oak tree, but the steps, the big windows, the wings, it was all like it had been before, even the devil's horns on the ridge of the roof. I was back at number 1, Mirror Forest Road. The Night House.

# 26

I STEPPED INTO THE GREAT hall. On a shiny white marble floor stood a gleaming black grand piano and a glass table with around twenty glasses of evidently ready-mixed drinks with slices of lemon in them. The furniture was arranged in groups, as if we were in a hotel lobby rather than a home. That impression was only reinforced by the crystal chandelier that hung above everything.

I grabbed a drink while I scanned the crowd for her. 'I have to say, young Oscar's done all right,' Harry Cooper said beside me. He put down a glass he had evidently already emptied and picked up a fresh one. 'Apart from the fact that it's completely wrong to put lemon in a gin and tonic, obviously, it should be lime.' He looked at me as if he was expecting me to engage in the classic debate. But I didn't respond, looked away from him and glanced round the room again. At last I found Karen, on her way into the corridor that led to the left wing. Or rather, Oscar was holding her hand, and it looked more like he was pulling her in that direction.

'Karen!' I called.

She turned round. 'Oscar's keen to show off the house,' she laughed with a resigned expression.

'Great!' I called.

It cost me less that it should have done to swallow my pride and the rest of my drink and hurry after them.

'Mind if I tag along?' I asked.

'Of course not,' Oscar said, not very convincingly, without turning to look at me.

We went into the corridor, which was hung with pictures of yachts and cars and portraits of what I assumed were Oscar's wife and children.

'Guest room,' Oscar said, opening a door.

'Great,' Karen said.

We walked on. Another door. Another guest room. And on.

'It's impressive, what you've done to the house,' I said, mostly for the sake of saying something. 'Because it burned down, didn't it?'

'I don't know about down,' Oscar said. 'It's true, it was hit by lightning and there was a bit of fire damage, but it was empty.'

'Richard's asking . . .' Karen said, turning towards me as if to ask for permission: '. . . because he wrote about a house that burned down in one of his books that was a bit like this.'

'Really?' Oscar said, without slowing down. 'I have to admit, I don't read fantasy stuff like that. Sorry, Richard.' He turned and put his hand on my arm. 'I don't mean to imply that it doesn't require a lot of an author. I mean, you've obviously hit on something that children like.'

'Young people,' Karen said 'I wouldn't read it to the kids, Oscar.'

Oscar smiled thinly, it looked like he didn't like being reminded of his marital status. 'This is the atrium, or conservatory,' he said, feeling along the wall inside the door. The room opened out in front of us, and there was a trickling sound like a fountain, but it was dark and I couldn't see much.

'This used to be the backyard, but I enclosed it with glass walls and a roof. But the house is obviously too big for us, because now I can't even find the light switch.'

At that moment there was another flash of lightning, and in the flash I saw the tree.

It was standing in the middle of the room, at the centre of a circle of water. I don't know if it was an oak, but it was certainly a young tree. A tree that hadn't had time to spread its roots particularly far. Even so, I felt uneasy just knowing that that was exactly what the roots were doing right now: spreading their white fingers in all directions beneath our feet, on a slow but remorseless search for food, sustenance. Prey.

Another flash of lightning. I saw Oscar standing there with his arm searching for the light switch, lit up the way Karen had been earlier that evening. But this X-ray wasn't like hers. The skull was small, and had tiny, sharp rodent's teeth. The arm didn't have the distinct bones of a human being, but a network of thin spines, like a bird's wing. I definitely shouldn't have downed that G&T so quickly.

'There,' Oscar said.

The lights in the room came on.

'Great!' Karen said.

'What do you think, Richard?'

'Unbelievable,' I replied.

'What's in there?' Karen was pointing to the door where the wing continued on the other side of the conservatory.

'The apartment where the couple who work here live. They were there when we moved in, so they kind of came with it. They look after the property, look after the kids, do the cooking. I called and got them to make the drinks when we were on our way, what do you think?'

'Great,' Karen said again. For a moment I considered saying that it should have been lime, not lemon, but just nodded as if I agreed with Karen.

Oscar looked happy. 'I've asked them to prepare a bite to eat, so I hope you're both hungry.'

'Great!' Karen repeated. I looked at her, but couldn't detect any trace of irony.

On the way back I lingered behind the other two in the corridor and saw Oscar take Karen's hand and lead her as if they were a couple again. I felt like hitting him in the back of the head with something hard.

The sound of music reached us from the hall, and when we arrived I saw that the dancing was in full swing again.

'Tom's landed!' Jack cried from the dance floor. 'He's just texted that he's on his way in a taxi.'

'Great!' Karen exclaimed, and I could feel the repetition beginning to annoy me.

'You wouldn't have a headache pill?' I asked Oscar, who still hadn't let go of Karen's hand.

'Of course,' he said. 'You'll find them in the cabinet in the bathroom. Upstairs, turn left, past the kitchen, third door on the right.' He looked at me with a grin that said something along the lines of nice-try-getting-me-to-leave-Karen-with-you-you-creep.

I left them, and felt so unsteady on my feet that I had to use the banister on one side of the broad staircase. I took a breather at the top and tried to collect myself. I could see Oscar, Karen and the others dancing round Jack, who was in charge in the middle of the floor, letting rip with a series of breathtaking moves and breakdance tricks. A backwards somersault garnered a roar of applause.

I stumbled on giddily, with a growing headache that was now throbbing like a bass drum against the inside of my temples. From behind the door I realised had to be the kitchen I could hear dragging footsteps and dull thuds, like a meat cleaver, then the clatter of pans. As I had been told, the bathroom was a couple of doors further along. It was big, modern and extremely clean, with a shower and jacuzzi and an open door that led into what was presumably Oscar and his wife's bedroom. The cabinet above one of the two basins was full of boxes and bottles of pills. I saw one pill bottle with the name Sarah Rossi on the label, but I couldn't see what they were for, because everything had begun to look a bit blurry. But I did at least recognise one of the boxes and swallowed two of the pills it contained. I sat down on the heated floor, leaned back against the wall, closed my eyes and hoped that the bathroom would stop pulsating and the world would stop spinning.

I don't know how long I had been sitting there when the door opened and Rita came in.

'There you are,' she grunted as she pulled her pants down beneath her skirt and sat down on the toilet. 'Are you ill?'

'Excuse me,' I said, getting to my feet and pulling myself

together as I looked at a face in the mirror on the cupboard doors that wasn't me, but which I realised had to be me all the same.

'It wasn't exactly anything to write home about,' Rita said as I heard her pee hit the water in the toilet. 'That time in the barn. I didn't ask at the time, I was trying to be kind, but I'm guessing it was your first time. Is that right?'

'Excuse me,' I repeated, and stumbled out into the corridor. Leaning against the wall, I made my way past the kitchen, where all I could hear were shuffling footsteps, as if the married couple were dancing a slow waltz in there. I stopped to listen. There was another sound too. Some sort of wet crackling. I pushed the door handle down to open it. But something – a vague premonition – stopped me. My heart was pounding and sweat was pouring off me. Everything had stopped behind the door, as if they were standing there waiting for me. I backed away, turned and carried on towards the gallery above the hall. The music had been turned off, and I could hear animated conversation from down below. I peered over the railing. People were standing, sitting on chairs or lolling on the sofas and eating. I caught sight of a tray of hamburgers that had replaced the drinks on the glass table. Perhaps that was what I needed, a bit of food.

I made my way down the stairs towards the tray but was too late, a guy I recognised as Henrik, the class's resident maths genius, was about to take the last one. When he saw me, he stepped back and indicated that I should take it.

'No, you were first,' I said, with a smile that probably looked rather forced.

'Great authors need food,' he smiled back amiably. 'I've already had one, and they're making more.'

'In that case, thank you,' I said, and snapped up the hamburger. I sank my teeth into it and felt my mouth fill with moisture from the freshly minced meat and thought to myself that is what we mammals are mostly made up of: water. I took another bite. God, it was good, just what I needed.

'My little boy was wondering if I'm Henrik the maths genius in your book.'

I looked at the man who was still standing there. He was one of the people who hadn't used up all their time when we talked about ourselves in the gymnasium. An accountant, wasn't that what he had said? Had he been aiming higher? An academic, perhaps? Did he think we expected more from him, is that why he hadn't said more? Or was he happy with his lot, just didn't think he had much exciting to say about his life so far?

'Yup,' I said with my mouth full of burger. 'That was you.'

'I was never a maths genius, but thanks,' he said.

'Yes, you were.'

He laughed. 'You should never trust your memory. It only ever gives you what it thinks you need. So . . . well, in that sense maybe it's just as well to trust it after all.' He laughed again.

I had taken another bite and was chewing slowly so I wouldn't have to reply. I just nodded again as thanks for the burger, walked across the floor and sat down on one of the sofas next to Karen. I let out the sort of groan of relief that can only come after a period of serious discomfort.

'You're feeling better,' she concluded with a smile, squeezing my neck between her thumb and forefinger.

'Yup,' I said, swallowing the hamburger. 'How long was I gone?'

'Quite a while. I was starting to get worried.'

'I'm fine. How about you? I see you've found yourself a sofa where you thought you'd be able to sit on your own for a while. Isn't it horrible to be so popular?'

'Terrible,' she laughed, opening her notebook. 'But no, I came and sat here because Tom was sitting here.'

'Tom? Has he arrived?' I looked round. 'Where is he?'

'He went off to the kitchen to help out,' she said as she wrote in her notebook.

'I see you kept the bookmark,' I said, nodding towards the pink hair clip fixed to the cover of the book.

'Yes.'

'Still planning to be a writer? If you use anything I say, I'll claim copyright and royalties.'

'Deal,' she said. 'Tom asked after you, by the way.'

'Really? What was he going to do in the kitchen?'

'Help out, like I said.'

'What for?'

She shrugged. 'Tom's the sort of guy who likes to give of himself.'

'He is?'

'That's what he said.'

'Said what?'

'That he wanted to go to the kitchen and give of himself. It obviously worked, you certainly seem to be enjoying that hamburger.'

'Did Tom make these?' I looked down at the last bit of meat and bread in my hand.

'The couple who served them called them burgers à la Tom, at any rate. And here they come with more . . .'

I heard shuffling footsteps on the stairs. I swallowed. An idea was starting to take shape. Then, very slowly, I turned round. I felt my mouth go dry and my tongue shrivel.

A crab. That was the first thing that struck me. They were moving sideways down the stairs on four legs, seeing as they were joined at the hip. In their right hand – raised like crab's claws – they were each holding a tray of steaming hamburgers. They looked like twins, limping, dressed in white.

I met her gaze. Vanessa's.

And then – as she turned so that her partner could step down – Victor's.

It felt like my head was going to explode. The pills. It must be the pills. What other explanation could there be for what was playing out in front of my eyes?

'Mmm, those look good!' Karen declared.

'Don't touch those hamburgers,' I said, putting down what was left of mine and getting to my feet.

'Is something wrong, Richard?'

'Yes,' I whispered. 'Something's wrong. Come with me.'

I took Karen's hand and pulled her with me, and when the grotesque human crab had reached the bottom of the stairs and was heading towards the glass table, we ran upstairs.

The kitchen door was slightly ajar, and as we got closer I heard the same sound I imagined when I wrote the scene where Tom gets eaten by the telephone receiver, a wet slurping sound, like maggots devouring the dead. I kicked the door open.

'B-b-but, if it isn't Richard?' The face of the man standing at the kitchen counter turning the handle of the large meat grinder lit up. He was fifteen years older, he'd put on some weight and grown a moustache, but there was no doubt about it: it was Tom.

'D-d-do you like me?' he asked.

I stared. Swallowed. His shirtsleeve was rolled up to the shoulder of the arm that wasn't turning the handle, and it was stuck so deep into the grinder that there wasn't much of it left. The wet slurping sound came from the lower part of the grinder, where strands of meat oozed out of the holes and hung for a moment before falling into a frying pan that was placed on a chair immediately beneath it.

'What are you doing?' I whispered in a thick voice, feeling that I was about to throw up.

'I'm doing what we should all d-d-do,' he said. 'I'm giving of myself. C-c-come, Richard, you should try it.'

'No thanks,' I managed to say as I started to back out through the door.

Tom let go of the grinder, and his hand shot out. I was standing more that two metres away from him, but he still managed to reach me. Thin, white fingers locked around my wrist and began to pull me towards him.

'I insist,' he said.

I resisted, tried to dig my heels into the floor, but he was just too strong.

'Come on, the shoal needs f-f-feeding.'

I was dragged closer and closer. He pulled what was left of his arm from the opening at the top of the meat grinder, its mouth. The end of the stump was jagged, red flesh with a white bone sticking out, but there was no blood pouring out. I looked at the large lettering on the side of the grinder. PIRANHA. Tom pulled my hand down into the mouth of the meat grinder.

'Karen!' I yelled, turning round.

Karen was standing in the doorway, just watching like a passive observer. Horrified, yes, but there was something else about the look on her face, as if she was – how can I put it? – half fascinated?

I felt my hand touch something sharp down there in the jaws. The blades of the grinder.

'Karen, dear,' Tom said. 'I haven't got any free hands, as you can see, so would you mind t-t-turning the handle for us?'

To my horror, I saw Karen nod and walk in.

'No, no, no!' I screamed as she took hold of the handle of the grinder. I looked around the kitchen counter and saw the meat cleaver. I grabbed it with my free hand and swung it as hard as I could towards the arm holding me. I felt the steel slide surprisingly easily through flesh and bone and into the worktop. A warm spout of blood hit my hand.

'Goodness!' Karen exclaimed with a smile, looking down at her now red-spattered dress.

'Goodness!' Tom mimicked, also smiling, as he looked down at his severed arm on the worktop. I stared in disbelief at what was left of him, a living, bleeding torso on two legs. Then I realised that Karen had begun to turn the handle. I felt the grinder blades against my skin before I quickly snatched my hand out.

Our eyes met. What did I see in hers? Curiosity? Compassion? I don't know, the whole situation was extremely confusing.

So I ran.

Out into the corridor, towards the hall.

I was so unsteady that it was like moving on the deck of a boat during a storm. When I reached the gallery I grabbed hold of the railings with both hands and threw up. I noted that some of the vomit hit the marble floor down below. I got my breath back. And heard a low buzzing sound, like the noise of a beehive. I raised my head. Down in the hall they were all standing in a circle, and right now they were all staring up at me. And I was staring at the man in the middle of the circle. It was Jack. He was naked now, standing in a classical ballet pose with his eyes fixed on me. His arms were stretched out above his head, hands curved in towards each other, one foot crossed in front of the other. The fifth position. How did I know that? Had I read about it, seen pictures in one of the books in the library where they had said I had spent all my time? Had I actually done that?

The buzzing was coming from his wings. They were sticking out from his back, thin, transparent, and beating so fast that they were only visible as a vibration in the air.

He straightened his feet out so that only the tips of his toes had contact with the marble floor. Until not even they did either . . .

He was floating in thin air.

I stopped breathing again. The humming of those wings was the only sound. Jack's body, which seemed frozen in position, rose upwards. I looked at the upturned faces of the others. They didn't really look that surprised, more devout, as if this were a prophesied miracle, or something they had seen before. Oscar was smiling beatifically. Rita looked enchanted, her lips moving as if saying a prayer. Vanessa/Victor were standing with two pairs of clasped hands.

Jack had reached the same height as the gallery and was moving towards me. I could feel the current of the air from his wings. The irises of his eyes had changed, they had turned red. I almost started to laugh, these hallucinations were so real I had a feeling that if I reached out my hand and touched him, I would have felt his skin beneath my fingertips. Was it the pills? Were they what was controlling the hallucinations, or was it me? I had no way of knowing, but it felt like I had some degree of control, that I was directing things. That I both could and couldn't decide what was happening, as if the narrative had its own will, an internal logic. If that was the case, could I stop it? Or was this just an ordinary nightmare, a performance you put on for yourself as a helpless onlooker who has no choice but to see and hear everything? In that case, I wanted to wake up now. I cleared my throat.

'Very impressive, Jack.' I tried to keep my voice steady. 'You really have managed to transform yourself into Tinker Bell.'

'While you are the same person you have always been,' Jack said. 'Imu.'

'What?'

'See for yourself,' Jack said, pointing to the big window.

I turned round, but could see nothing except for the black darkness outside.

'What do you mean . . . ?' I began, as a flash of lightning lit up the outside and I saw my own face reflected in the glass. Or rather, it wasn't my face, but the face I had seen in the mirror in the bathroom. Which was a face I had seen in a school photograph when I was little. That was the face I had in mind when I wrote *The Night House* and the main character – Richard – is standing outside the Principal's office at Rorrim's. I not only felt like my head was going to explode – I actually *hoped* it would. It was Imu Jonasson's face.

'Do you see now?' Jack asked. 'Do you get it, Richard?'

'No,' I said. 'All I get is that you've planned this.'

Jack smiled in response.

'How long . . . ?'

'Oh, since before we sent you the invitation to this reunion.'

'But . . . why?'

'Why? Oh, Richard, you know why.'

I shook my head slowly.

Jack sighed and tilted his head. 'You said it yourself.'

'The b-bullying thing?'

'You were a one-man gang bullying a group of lonely souls, Richard. But bullying is too weak a word for it, don't you think?'

'Erm . . .'

'Think about it. "Evil" would be more accurate. Look!' He gestured with one hand towards the classmates beneath him. 'Look and remember. Tom, me, Vanessa, Victor, Oscar. Even Karen. Everyone here. You took us, one by one, broke us down, terrorised us, you made our lives a living hell.'

I looked. And tried to remember. It came back to me now. Face by face. Victim by victim. I remembered the mantra I used to use. *You're garbage.* Because no one can convince you that you're garbage like someone who knows what it's like to be garbage.

I swallowed. 'So you were lying when you said my memories were wrong?'

'Sorry about that, but we had to get you to relax. To get you here.'

'OK. So, what now?'

Jack shrugged. 'Now we're going to eat you.'

There was movement in the crowd down below.

'I can't just let you do that,' I said, staring at them as they streamed up the stairs like a human river.

'Oh, we didn't expect you to,' Jack said. 'We'd actually prefer it if you tried to escape. It's a well-known fact that adrenalin gives meat a bit of extra flavour.'

The crowd had reached the top of the stairs and were moving towards me, led by the crablike twins. They only paused when I swung the meat cleaver at them. I clambered up onto the railing, stood up, balancing with my arms out, and yelled:

'Want to see me fly?'

As they stared at me, I plunged down towards the hall.

I fell.

Straight down towards the shiny marble floor.

I hit the equally shiny grand piano, felt the lid shatter, heard the strings snap and the piano break in two.

I lay on my back staring up at the crystal chandelier, at Jack hovering above me, at all the faces up on the gallery. I fumbled for the meat cleaver, found it, and got to my feet.

The crowd were already on their way back downstairs again, and I ran to the front door and pulled it open. Or rather, tried to pull it open. It was locked, and I could see no way to unlock it. I tugged again. Same result.

'Now do you see how it feels to reach a locked door?' Jack said. He was hovering right above my head, but too far away for me to reach him with the cleaver. 'And it's the people you thought loved you who locked it. What do you do then?'

I beat on the door frantically with my fists.

'Exactly!' Jack laughed. 'You bang on it! You hope someone will open it. But when they don't, what then?'

I turned round. The crowd had reached the foot of the stairs, and this time Oscar, Harry Cooper and Henrik were at the front. Their faces didn't express hatred, they didn't really express anything, just indifference, an odd ambivalence, as if their bodies were obeying commands that were out of their control.

'That's right, you make a call,' Jack said. He had raised one hand to his head, his thumb spread towards his ear, his little finger towards his mouth, like a telephone. 'You call, and hope that someone will pick up. You hope that the only person you still have any power over will take your call. And let you in.'

I let go of the door handle and swerved past the others, right across the hall into the corridor Oscar had led Karen and me down earlier. I kept running as I heard the echo of their footsteps bounce off the walls behind me. I reached the door to the conservatory and slammed it shut behind me, and saw that it had a lock. I turned it gratefully and leaned my back against the door. I heard a crush of bodies and felt the door shake. They shouted and pounded at the door. I looked up. Flashes of lightning were coming thick and fast outside the glass walls now, lighting up the conservatory.

The tree.

There was someone hanging from it.

The head was lolling down towards the chest, revealing the knotted rope behind the woman's neck. She was wearing a nightdress, and her bare feet seemed to be reaching out towards the ground that they couldn't quite touch.

I moved away from the door towards her, the cries getting weaker behind me.

The fair, boyish fringe was hanging down, obscuring her face.

As I got closer, it struck me that the tree must have grown since I last saw it, as if it had eaten. Maybe that's why the figure hanging there made me think of an empty shell, like an insect hanging in a spider's web after the spider has sucked out the innards.

I stopped beneath the tree and looked up at her. Her freckled face was so pale. So beautiful and pale. She – who was all that I had held dear – had been taken from me. I wasn't thinking, the word just slipped out of me:

'Mum.'

In response there was a great flash of lightning outside,

followed by a deafening bang, and the figure above me shook as if in a spastic dance. The next moment flames were shooting from the nightdress and glass was raining down around me. When I opened my eyes again, I could feel the night air on my face, and saw that the glass roof and walls had completely collapsed, meaning that I could now walk straight out into the garden. I could see the gate at the end of a shimmering white gravel path.

At that moment I heard the door open behind me. Oscar had evidently found the key.

OK, I thought. I can't take any more of this. It can end here, like this.

I closed my eyes again and felt my breathing calm down as a strange peace settled over me. A moment later I opened my eyes again. Because it wasn't true. I could take more. We can always take more. So I ran.

# 27

I RAN ALONG THE GRAVEL, out through the open gate and down the narrow cul-de-sac towards the forest. There were no street lights, but the lightning was coming so frequently that I could follow the road. The night and the mild air were like I had imagined when I wrote the end of *The Night House*, charged with electricity and ready for a biblical downpour. I was running as fast as I could, but it still sounded like my pursuers were gaining on me. Who would have thought they had such stamina? My own lungs were aching, my thighs were so stiff with lactic acid that they were starting to feel like lumps of wood, and I knew it wouldn't be long before they stopped obeying my brain. The road got even narrower, and if I remembered right it came to end up ahead. But just before that I ought to reach the path. It ran through part of the forest, across the bridge and down to the main road. That was quite a long way, but if I could just make it to the path, the crowd following me would have to get organised, seeing as the path wasn't wide enough for more than two, maybe three people at most, and hopefully that would slow them down. If I could reach the main road, that was lit up and usually busy – at least it was during the day.

But they were gaining on me fast, the panting and light, quick steps were right behind me now. I tried to speed up, but it was no good. I wasn't going to get to the path before them. I hardly had time to think that before my legs were kicked out from under me and I fell to the ground. I groped in the dark for the meat cleaver, but it was too late, they were on me. Hands yanked and pulled at me, I was hit in the temple, kicked in the stomach. I curled up into a ball and put my hands over my head.

'Turn him over!' a voice snarled. 'Let him look at us when we kill him!'

Hands grabbed me and rolled me over onto my back, and someone sat astride my chest. In the next flash of lightning I saw that it was Rita. I tried to tip her off me, but she was strong. Quite impossibly strong. She leaned down towards me and breathed alcoholic breath in my face.

'Richard Hansen,' she said. 'I hate you.'

Then she straightened up and raised both hands above her head. They were holding a croquet hoop with the sharp steel ends pointing down towards me. I flailed with my arms and legs as I lay there on my back like a helpless beetle, and realised that I was soon going to be a croquet court.

At that moment Rita's face was bathed in blinding light and she froze.

'In the name of the law, don't move!'

Everything became completely still, as everyone turned towards the light. I couldn't see anything, but realised the metallic voice that had shouted at us must have come from a megaphone. Something moved in the light. A silhouette came towards us, slowly, on the crunching gravel. I knew who it was before he got close enough for me to see his tall, broad-shouldered frame and blue-black hair. He was holding – of course – a pistol in his hand.

# 28

'BACK AWAY,' AGENT DALE SAID, and the crowd did as he said.

'You too, my girl,' he said to Rita, who was still sitting on top of me.

She hissed at both of us, but stood up and moved back to where the others were standing, shielding their eyes as they looked on.

Agent Dale helped me to my feet and supported me as we walked towards the light.

'W-what are you doing here?' I groaned.

'Me? I'm always here.'

'Here? In Mirror Forest?' I looked at him as I felt the first heavy raindrops.

'Yup. After all, we never completely solved that mystery. So I'm here in case he comes back.'

'Imu Jonasson?'

'Yes.'

The light was coming from a Pontiac LeMans. Obviously. Not red, not green, but pale blue. As we were getting in it, the skies finally opened and within a matter of seconds the rain was hammering on the roof.

'Just like that night,' Agent Dale said, pressing a button that locked all the doors with a click. 'Do you remember?' He smiled as if it was a cherished memory: the rain, the fire, the escape, Karen jumping from the roof.

'I don't remember anything,' I said quietly, trying to see anything through the water streaming down the windscreen.

'Of course you do,' Agent Dale said. 'You wrote a whole book about it, after all.'

'Until this evening, I thought I'd just made all that up,' I whispered, and realised I was still clutching the meat cleaver. 'You included.'

'Me?'

I rubbed my temple. 'Can we go now, Agent Dale?'

'Yes, we can.' Agent Dale grabbed a lever next to the steering wheel and the windscreen wipers came on. The water was swept away in a couple of seconds, and we could see. Their faces were pale, almost white in the light. They didn't seem bothered by the rain. Or the blinding light. They were moving slowly, almost robotically, towards us. As if they had all the time in the world and we had none. Something glinted. The meat cleaver. It was hanging from Jack's hand as he led the pack.

'Drive!' I cried. 'Run them down!'

'That won't do any good,' Agent Dale said. 'Look.'

And I looked. Behind them an electric SUV had arrived without a sound and parked across the road, blocking our escape.

'Wait here,' Dale said, drawing the pistol from his shoulder holster, opening the door and getting out in the rain. He leaned back in. 'Give me the megaphone.' I picked it up from the central console and handed it to him. The wide grey cone hit the lever next to the steering wheel and the windscreen wipers switched off again. Dale shut the door and I heard the metallic, amplified sound of his voice over the drumming of the rain:

'Stop, in the name of the law!'

Pause.

'Stop, I said! Or I'll shoot!'

I pushed the lever to switch the wipers on so I could see what was happening outside, but all that happened was that the headlights went from full to low beam. I heard a shot, it sounded like a small pop outside the car. Then another. Then a loud crash, but that was just a clap of thunder, and in the rumble that followed I couldn't hear anything. I realised I needed to twist the lever instead of pushing it, and the windscreen wipers finally came back on. As they swept the water away there was another crash. A body had landed on the hood of the car. It was Agent Dale. His face was pressed flat against the windscreen, lit up by the instruments on the dashboard. His black hair was splayed out around his face as he stared blankly back at me. The blood hadn't yet started to pour from where the meat cleaver was half buried in his forehead. There was a mixture of fear and resignation on his face as he was dragged backwards. He clawed desperately at the bonnet with the hand that wasn't holding the pistol, and when that didn't help he grabbed the windscreen wiper and snapped it off. Then he was gone.

I slid over to the left and pushed the button on the driver's door to lock the doors just as I heard someone tug at the handle. I slipped in behind the steering wheel and put my foot down on the accelerator. The engine gave a warning roar, like a water buffalo to an attacking pack of lions. I slipped the gearstick into drive, and the car slid on the gravel before it got a grip and lurched forward. I registered soft thuds as I drove over bodies that came and went from my field of vision. The Pontiac hit the SUV towards its rear – I was counting on it being lighter there, enough to turn it so I could push past. But the approach wasn't long enough for the Pontiac to build up sufficient speed, with the result that the SUV only moved slightly, whereas my car skidded and the two vehicles ended up side by side. There were longer gaps between the lightning now, and my headlights were pointing straight into the forest, but I could see movement in the darkness. And I could also see the path, it was right in front of the nose of the car. Could I manage to get to it before they reached me? I got the answer when something hit the side window. In a flash of lightning I saw that it was Henrik. His jaw was moving up and down as if he was chewing on something, and blood was dribbling from the corners of his mouth as he raised a club-like object to strike again. I realised that it was an arm. A severed arm, still wearing a black suit sleeve. He struck again, and the window shattered. Hands reached in towards me, fingernails scratched my face. Everything is simple when you've run out of options. I hit the gas.

I was thrown forward when the front of the Pontiac landed on the other side of the ditch, which wasn't wide enough to stop the car from carrying on along the path. The path was a metre and a half wide, far too narrow for the car, but as long as I could keep one front wheel and one rear one on the path, I might manage to build up some sort of head start. It actually worked better than I expected. I mowed down the vegetation, the bushes, scrub and small trees that hit the front right of the car, soon smashing the right headlight. But I was managing to steer and stay on the path with the help of the one headlight and single windscreen wiper. The path sloped down steeply towards the river, and I was aiming for the bridge. But then there was a sudden bang, the car stopped abruptly, and I hit my forehead on the windscreen. The Pontiac was no longer moving, and I saw that the front right side had hit a tree. I slammed the gearstick in reverse and hit the gas. But the tyres couldn't get any grip, the rain had made the path too muddy, and I could feel the wheels digging themselves deeper in.

I kicked the door open and began to run down the path towards the bridge and the river I could see through the trees. I heard branches breaking behind me. They were on their way, but if I could just cross the river, I would be able to get to the main road before them.

I had reached the edge of the forest when another flash of lightning lit up the last, uncovered hundred metres before the bridge. I stopped abruptly. Three figures, standing in the middle of the bridge. I was fairly sure that they hadn't seen me, so I ducked behind a tree and peered out. Another flash of lightning. They each had a bicycle. They looked like Apache bikes. The largest of the figures was wearing a lumberjack jacket. It looked like they were keeping watch. Why else would they be standing there? I needed to make a quick decision.

And then it was made for me.

In another series of lightning flashes, I saw a figure appear from above and land on the bridge. The other three didn't seem remotely surprised that a naked, flying man was suddenly standing among them – on the contrary, they immediately threw themselves into a discussion, pointing and shaking their heads. The three of them were clearly involved, and were reporting that they hadn't seen me.

I could forget about trying to get across the bridge.

I looked to my left, I was only ten metres from where the river emerged from the forest. And it was only six, maybe eight metres wide, but looked like a muscular boa constrictor as it twisted and coiled darkly towards the bridge, just like that time many years before. Fifty metres or so beyond the bridge the river turned, where it would be possible to get across without being seen from the bridge. And from there it was about a hundred, maybe a hundred and fifty metres to the main road. To a friendly local out for an evening drive, or a trucker driving a load of timber. To safety.

I heard voices behind me, and the light of a pocket torch danced between the trees. I crept towards the riverbank. Steeling myself against the cold, I slid into the water, which actually felt warmer that I was expecting, possibly because of all the running. I lay back and tried to float, regretting that I hadn't taken off my suit jacket, it felt like it was pulling me down. But at least I managed to keep my face above water and breathe. The eye automatically registers movement, but if I lay still like that, without moving, hopefully they wouldn't notice me.

I stared up at the sky, the lightning was so frequent now that it was like an unstable fluorescent light behind the clouds. The voices from the bridge were rapidly coming closer. I didn't move my head, I just lay there, stiff and motionless like a statue or a random lump of wood. Then the bridge and the four figures came into my field of vision. Jack and the man in the lumberjack jacket were deep in discussion, while the other two were leaning against the railing, looking down at the river. There was something familiar about their faces, about the whole situation, like a mirror image of a memory. For a fraction of a second I met the gaze of one of them. It was like looking in a mirror. As I passed under the bridge I heard footsteps running across the planks, and when I emerged on the other side, I caught a glimpse of the same face. I waited, but there was no cry. Then he was out of sight, and once more I was looking up at the black sky with its pulsating lights. Perhaps he thought he had seen something, but concluded that it must have been a lump of wood.

The voices from the bridge faded into the distance. The river turned. I rolled over onto my stomach and took five or six powerful strokes to reach the bank. But I couldn't find anything to grab hold of, only grass that came away in my hands, and suddenly I was out in the river again, being carried quickly downstream. I tried to pull my jacket off, but instead my right arm got stuck in the sleeve, trapped behind my back. I swallowed water and put my feet down, my shoe got caught beneath a root or something down there and I was dragged under. A crazy, almost comical thought struck me. That I was going to drown. That I was going to disappear and never be found again. But then I remembered the old saying: a man who is destined to hang doesn't drown. I pulled my foot from my shoe, managed to get my arm out of my jacket and made it to the surface. I swam to the bank, kicked up and just got my arm round a thin tree trunk that was leaning out over the river. For a moment I hung there, just feeling how exhausted I was. Then I pushed my tiredness aside and used the last of my strength to pull myself up onto land. I lay there on my back, panting for breath. And listening.

Nothing. No voices. But no traffic from the main road either.

The thunder sounded more distant, and the rain was no longer pouring down. The trees were just whispering and rustling above me. I got to my feet.

From a small rising by the bank I could see the telephone box, it was still there. And there was the main road. Lit up and empty. My heart sank. But then, at the end of the long, straight road, I saw a pair of headlights approaching. I stumbled towards the road on legs I could feel soon wouldn't carry me much further. The lights were getting closer, glinting off the wet tarmac. I forced myself to run. And fell just as I got close to the road. I got to my knees and started waving my arms as I closed my eyes against the blinding light. The vehicle made a series of groaning sounds as it braked and changed down through the gears, then a loud blast of the horn echoed across the landscape.

I had heard that horn before.

I opened my eyes. It was the fire truck.

It had stopped in the road some fifty metres ahead of me.

I got to my feet again.

The doors on both sides opened and they jumped out. I recognised them immediately. Frank in his full, red fireman's uniform. Sheriff McClelland in his uniform. And Jenny.

'Hi!' I called out. 'God, you have no idea how happy I am to see you! There's –'

I stopped abruptly when I saw that there were more of them.

Mrs Zimmer from the library. The Principal and Mrs Monroe from Rorrim? And Lucas, the caretaker.

I felt a lump in my stomach.

'Where did you come from?' I called out.

No answer. Their impassive expressions and the robotic way they moved . . . The last person to get out of the fire engine was

Feihta Rice; he waved his walking stick and started to walk towards me with stiff strides, like an old, blind dog that had found a bit of strength.

I turned round, and there, on the hill behind the telephone box, stood the others, motionless and menacing, like Indian braves in an old Western movie. My throat tightened, I felt like lying down and crying. So perhaps it was only the remnants of my survival instinct that made me stumble more than run towards the phone box, get inside and shut the heavy door behind me. I closed my eyes, but went on clutching the handle. Footsteps and the murmur of voices came closer. Someone tugged at the door, but I managed to keep it closed. There was snarling and growling, like a starving pack of wolves. Someone pulled at the door, harder this time. I opened my eyes. Their faces were pressed against the glass on every side of the phone box, like a gallery of people I had known. The only two who were missing were Karen and Imu.

'Mum,' I whispered. 'Where are you? Dad . . .'

The telephone started to ring.

I set my heels into the floor of the phone box and leaned back, pulling as hard as I could on the door, but it was being forced open, centimetre by centimetre. The phone seemed to be ringing louder and louder.

'D-d-don't eat everything,' a voice outside cried. 'I w-w-want some too.'

I picked up the receiver. I held it to my ear with one hand while I tried to hold the door shut with the other.

'Yes?' I whispered.

'Let go,' a soft, female voice whispered. 'Let go, Richard, and come to me.'

'But . . .'

At that moment I felt the receiver bite me gently, almost playfully, on my earlobe. I tried to pull away, but it was stuck. I opened my mouth to say something, but felt something grab hold of my tongue and pull it out. I looked down at the perforated microphone in the end of the receiver where my tongue was caught, apparently being eaten through the tiny holes. It was happening quickly. My head would soon be gone. It was remarkably painless, and I no longer felt any fear. Then I let go of the door. Let go of everything.

# PART THREE

# 29

LIGHT.

Not much, but it was there, on the outside of my eyelids.

'He's coming round.' The voice came from a long way away.

I opened my eyes.

The face of an older woman framed in light blue was looking down at me. She was smiling.

'How are you feeling?'

I tried to say something, but my tongue felt like it was rolled up.

'A bit confused?' she asked. She was wearing a pale blue plastic cap over a pale blue all-in-one outfit.

I nodded.

'Water.' She handed me a glass. 'It would be a good idea to drink a little now.'

I took a sip. It tasted bitter, as if it was dissolving my own congealed spit. The next sip tasted better.

'Do you remember anything?' she asked, taking the glass.

'I remember getting eaten by a telephone,' I said. 'From two different places on my head.'

She smiled. 'It was probably this.' She picked something up from a table behind her. They looked like wired earpods, only with metal diodes instead of earplugs. 'These were attached to your temples and forehead,' she said. 'Do you remember now?'

I shook my head.

'It's entirely normal to have gaps in your memory when you've had ECT treatment.'

'E . . . C . . . ?'

'Electroconvulsive therapy.' A few white hairs were sticking out from beneath her cap.

'I've been given . . . electric shocks?'

'Yes, but you won't have noticed anything, you were fully anaesthetised.'

'Where am I?'

'In Ballantyne Hospital.'

'There isn't a hospital in Ballantyne.'

'I don't know of any *place* called Ballantyne, Richard. As you know, our hospital is named after Robert Willingstad Ballantyne. Do you remember that, or has that gone too for the time being?' She patted my hand. 'It will soon come back.'

I blinked. Confusion lay like morning fog over my memory, but it was as if I could feel the sun, which would soon burn through part of the veil.

'Do I know this Robert?'

'No, he died a long time ago.'

'So why would I remember his name?'

'Well, because you've been here . . . quite some time.'

'Oh? How long?'

She took her time answering as she stifled a sneeze. When she smiled again, there was something sad about the smile. 'Fifteen years.'

I showered and got changed in my room. It was very basic. A bed, a desk, a wardrobe, a bathroom. Like a hotel, really. The gaps in my memory began to fill in. Among other things, I now remembered that I was given electroconvulsive therapy to *help* me forget. Not everything, just something very specific, a traumatic memory, as it's known. The treatment seemed to be working. Although I could now remember everything around me, what I was doing yesterday, what I was supposed to do later today, I couldn't remember anything about this supposed traumatic memory. I looked out of the window. The sun was shining from a blue sky down on an open, gently undulating landscape of green lawns that stretched between the brick buildings all the way to a forest of deciduous trees. From here, the whole place looked more like a university campus than a hospital. It was familiar, of course it was familiar. I had lived here for fifteen years, after all. So what was all the other stuff I also seemed to remember? The telephone that ate a classmate I had never had. The break times I spent sitting with a girl on the roof of a school I never attended. The old house in a forest I had never seen. The man at a dump I had never been to. Had all that just been a dream? Or the remnants of delusional psychosis? Maybe I had been there, maybe these were the memories they were trying to erase.

On the way down to the canteen to eat lunch I bumped into the caretaker, who was busy changing a light bulb above the lift.

'Looking good, Mr Jonasson,' he said. The caretaker in the residential part of the hospital had been addressing me as 'Mr' ever since I arrived as a teenager. I had always taken it as a mixture of light-hearted banter and old-fashioned professionalism, and had never asked him to use my first name.

'Thanks, Lucas,' I said. 'What are you reading at the moment?'

'*Infinite Jest* by Foster Wallace,' he said. He was always reading something, and sometimes I would borrow the books afterwards.

'Recommended?'

Lucas looked thoughtfully at the burned-out light bulb. 'Both yes and no. I might find something else for you, Mr Jonasson.'

In the canteen I helped myself to fried rice.

'It's good today, but be careful,' the otherwise taciturn chef said in his thick Czech accent from behind the counter. I assumed he had noted I had taken more than normal, presumably because I had had to fast before my anaesthetic.

I smiled. 'Thanks for the warning, Victor.'

Many of the patients who are on antipsychotic medication put weight on. Their brain and body tell them they want more long after they have had enough. Like Jack, whose weight goes up and down according to what medication he's on. Fortunately I've never had that problem, possibly because I eat in a mathematical way. I take what I know my body needs, not what it tries to convince me that it needs. Not that I still hear voices, unlike many of my fellow patients with a diagnosis of schizophrenia. But I also know that I need to keep control of my body and mind, that was one of the first things I learned when I started CBT, cognitive behavioural therapy.

I took my tray and went over to an empty table that Vanessa was wiping down.

'There you go,' she said, in the same tone and accent as Victor. I always assumed that was why Victor employed her two years ago, to have someone to talk to in his own language.

I ate slowly, thinking about my therapy appointment at one o'clock as I gazed out at the manicured lawns and forest.

'F-f-free?'

I look up. 'By all means.'

Tom put his tray down opposite mine and pulled out a chair. 'Sh-sh-shock treatment?'

'Yes. How do you . . . ?'

He pointed to his temples. 'I can see. They shave away the hair where they attach the electrodes.'

I nodded. Tom was said to be the person in the ward with the most ECT procedures behind him. That wasn't something they did unless you were psychotic and other things – medication and therapy – didn't work. Tom had supposedly had an electric current passed through his brain one time without anaesthetic, and had described it in such detail that I had nightmares about it on the nights leading up to my own ECT treatment.

'I didn't think you were psychotic these days,' Tom said. 'Wasn't there even talk about you being discharged?'

I nodded again. It was true, I had got better. Much better. People think that schizophrenics can't get better. In fact most people who get treatment do get better. Some of them an awful lot better, a few even completely free of symptoms. That's not to say that the symptoms can't rear their ugly heads again, but as my therapist says: 'Every good day is a gift, whether you're a patient or the president.'

'It's for PTSD, not psychosis,' I said.

'PTSD,' he said. 'I've got that too.'

Tom said this quickly, almost proudly, as if it were a badge of honour. In an odd way, it probably was. In a place where daily life focuses on symptoms, you often end up competing to come up with the most interesting, rare and worst possible diagnosis. If you have to be fucked up, you might as well be properly fucked up. Not that PTSD – post-traumatic stress disorder – was particularly rare among schizophrenics. Research shows that people who have experienced a trauma such as war, violence or abuse with subsequent PTSD have a greater tendency to develop schizophrenia. I've read a GWAS study which shows that the genes associated with PTSD overlap with the genes that increase the risk of schizophrenia as defined in the *DSM*-5 diagnostic manual. In short: I concluded that if you experience serious trauma and have a history of schizophrenia in the family, you're in a dodgy position. And that conclusion is based upon more than just what I've read.

'They've started using electric shocks to get rid of traumatic memories.'

'You're k-k-kidding,' Tom said.

'Nope, he isn't,' Jack said – currently in his relatively thin and moderately medicated incarnation – as he sat down at our table. 'They've been doing that for almost ten years now. First rats, now humans. We're basically the same, you know. How many treatments have you had?'

'Four,' I said.

'Is it working?'

'I can't remember.'

The other two laughed.

'No, I don't suppose you can remember what you've forgotten,' Jack said, shovelling down fried rice.

'I'm kidding,' I said. 'I can. But it's sort of breaking up, disappearing, like . . .' I poked at my food.

I saw Jack shuffle on his chair. 'Like?' he said. Because just as Jack couldn't handle half-finished games of chess or things that weren't symmetrical, he couldn't cope with unfinished sentences.

'Morning mist,' I said, and saw him calm down.

Jack claimed that he wasn't schizophrenic, but schizotypal, which is the milder version. And that he therefore didn't suffer from hallucinations, delusions, paranoia, voices in his head, becoming aggressive, and wasn't – like Harry – a silent, motionless statue who just stared into space. On the contrary, Jack was grateful for just the right amount of madness he had been given, which he claimed would one day make him a world-famous painter, author or choreographer, and make all the women in the world throw themselves at his feet. Because research showed – and here he could actually provide documentation – that schizotypal disorder was not only strongly correlated to creativity and artistic ability, but also to attractiveness and sex appeal.

After lunch I put my trainers on and went for a run. My usual route took me behind the main building, to the old, wrought-iron gate with the initials B.A., which visitors were told stood for Ballantyne, but which those of us who had lived here for a while knew stood for Ballantyne Asylum. I ran for ten, twelve minutes along the road before turning off into the woods and looping round so that I came out of the forest on the edge of the lawn that led to the front of the main building. Somewhere in the forest it dawned on me that I didn't actually recognise myself. I wasn't worried, I knew that the gaps that appeared in my memory after

ECT treatment usually filled in again after a few days. At least, the parts we didn't *want* to erase. But when I emerged from the forest and saw the main building, I thought for one horrible moment that I had suffered a relapse, that it was all a hallucination.

But then I remembered, and my pulse slowed down again.

The building was so-called collegiate Gothic style, with a four-storey central section and lower wings on either side. The ridge of the roof in the taller part had two horns. Some people called it the Night House because a lot of patients – like me – would wake up here and feel like the years that had passed since they arrived here had all been a dream. It was an attractive, friendly building, and the sun was shining right now, but even so, for some reason it made me shiver. Something I had dreamed while I was under the anaesthetic, perhaps. I ran back, showered and got ready for my therapy session. I felt my heart rate speed up slightly. It always did that when I was going to see my therapist.

'How are you feeling today, Richard?'

'Fine.'

'I heard that the ECT went well.'

'Yes.'

The therapist looked up from her notebook and brushed her short, boyish fringe away from her forehead and reading glasses. There were just the two of us. As usual, we were sitting in the therapy space, a large, airy room furnished like a cosy living room. She fiddled with the pink hair clip she used as a bookmark, then fixed her blue eyes on me. She smiled that smile that spreads sunlight and makes you feel not only that she sees you, but that she sees *only* you. But you don't have to be schizophrenic to harbour that sort of delusion. The idea of falling in love with your therapist when they're the opposite sex, the right age and not exactly unattractive is evidently so common that you'd wonder what was wrong if the patient *didn't* end up doing it. Karen Taylor fulfilled all the criteria, and there was sadly nothing wrong with me. I was hopelessly in love. And so hopelessly stupid that I sometimes allowed myself to imagine that the feeling was reciprocated, that it was only her integrity as a therapist that was holding her back. This, in spite of the fact that she had been my therapist for almost four years and knew the filthiest, most revolting recesses in the basement of my mind. The only thing I can say in my defence is that the fact that I was so susceptible was her doing, because she's the one who gave me the belief that I can be loved for who I am. Either way, I'm still clinging on to that, whether I've imagined it or not, because experience suggests that the framed embroidery on the wall behind her has got it more or less right, 'Rich Are The Loved'. Richer, happier, healthier.

'Consider how far you've come,' she said. 'Do you remember when we started?'

I nodded. There had obviously been a few setbacks along the way, but the progress was indisputable. Even if I would probably have to be on medication for the rest of my life, I was now managing on such small doses that the side effects were negligible. In consultation with the senior consultant, Karen had concluded that if they successfully erased the traumatic memory forming the basis of the PTSD diagnosis, that would reduce the risk of my becoming psychotic again. In short: I could be discharged.

Was that what I wanted?

The dilemma was obvious. I had been living here since I was a teenager, I had never had a job, I had no qualifications, I had never had a girlfriend or learned the rules of social interactions on the outside. I had inherited some money from my dad's side of the family, and together with the income from an apartment I rented out, that meant I could stay in a private hospital like Ballantyne. So what use was I actually going to be out there? I had begun to see the role of patient as my job, my contribution to society. I provided jobs, and I made myself available for the testing of new methods in the fight against the more unpleasant aspects of schizophrenia. Besides: when they say that the quality of any society can be measured by how it treats its weakest members, surely somebody – in order for this to be measured – has to volunteer to be the weakest?

Yes, obviously that was a rationalisation, constructing a reality in which it made sense for me to be alive, to get up in the morning, to stuff myself with the food that was put in front of me, to go on living one more day. All the same. When I saw what good I could realistically be out there, wasn't it better that I stayed here to be used for something like this: teaching psychiatry more about how a combination of therapy and ECT treatment could be used to erase psychosis-induced traumatic memories? Grossly simplified, the practice involved me giving a detailed account of the trauma, then shortly afterwards being anaesthetised and administered a few electric shocks. It's true that the technique was already ten years old, but there was still a lot they didn't know or understand.

'We were sitting here this morning before you had the ECT,' Karen said. 'Do you remember?'

'No,' I said. 'But I saw it on the calendar in my room, so I know it happened. But I remember everything from yesterday, from last week and last year. At least I think I do.'

'Do you remember anything at all about today before you woke up from the anaesthetic?'

'Yes,' I said. 'A lot.'

'A lot? Such as?'

'I was at a class reunion at the school I attended after the fire.'

'You remember being in a class after the fire?'

'No, I just dreamed it.'

'Are you saying that so I won't think the delusions are back?'

'The fact that you're schizophrenic doesn't mean that you don't dream, just like everybody else.'

Karen laughed softly. 'OK, go on.' I knew she trusted me now, seeing as over time I had shown that I wasn't lying, that I had invited her in and exposed myself. She said that self-deception was a way to protect yourself from pain, and that my honesty was a sign that I had become stronger, healthier, that I could handle more.

'First I dream that I'm living in a small town where I've been sent after my parents died in a fire. Then one of my classmates gets eaten by a telephone, and another one turns into an insect. And everyone – except the girl I'm in love with – thinks I'm responsible. And . . .' I swallowed. 'They're right. It *is* my fault. But then, in the end, I save the girl.'

I saw Karen noting something down. I guessed it was the words 'my fault'.

'And that's the whole dream?' she asked.

'No. Suddenly fifteen years pass, and I'm an author who just made up all that stuff about the phone and people disappearing, and it's now a hugely successful teen horror novel. It's like I'm dreaming that I've been dreaming, if you get what I mean?'

'*A dream within a dream*. Edgar Allan Poe.'

I smiled. She liked books, that was one of the things we had in common.

'Exactly. Either way, fifteen years have passed, and I come back for a class reunion. The evening starts normally, but gradually weird things start to happen, and I realise that the stuff I made up was actually true after all. Or that I'm experiencing it as true, anyway. And the others, all of them, are after me. They want to eat me.'

'Is it a dream within a dream, or are you dreaming a psychosis, do you think?'

'I don't know, because I'm seeing it from the inside, and it all seems real. You once said that dreaming can teach other people what it's like to suffer from delusions.'

'In part, yes. In dreams, just like in delusions, we accept the breaking of the laws of physics, impossible paradoxes, internal contradictions.'

'That's exactly what it was like. Only it still held together somehow. There was some sort of sense to it, if you get what I mean?'

'What sort of sense?'

'That . . .' I stopped. It was as if I had thought it through this far, but no further. But then I went on. 'That it was my fault anyway. That they were all after me because it's my fault.'

'What's your fault, Richard?'

'Everything.' I put my face in my hands. 'I know that whole business of them all being after me is classic paranoia, but isn't it OK to be a *bit* paranoid when you're dreaming?'

I'm fairly certain that somewhere in that notebook of hers she had written the words *paranoid schizophrenic,* which was my original diagnosis.

'Sure,' Karen said. 'Most of us have paranoid dreams from time to time.'

'You too?'

She smiled briefly, took off her reading glasses and polished them. 'Shall we take a look at your trauma memories, Richard?'

'OK.'

'We're not going to dig into them very deeply, we don't want to revive them, but just to check if the last ECT today has washed away a bit more.'

'Fine.'

'So what do you remember about the fire? Only in very brief terms.'

The fire. I had to think about that. Obviously I remembered that it was about a fire, but oddly enough, everything was completely blank for a moment. Then it came to me.

'We set fire to the house,' I said.

'We?'

'Me and the twins. Then we fled. The roots of the oak tree tried to catch us. I was saved by the fact that the gate was electrified, that meant I managed to hold on. But then I lost contact with the ground and got dragged back towards the tree. Luckily Frank and Agent Dale appeared and saved me.'

'Frank and Dale?' Karen asked as she took notes.

'Yes.'

'That's all?'

'You said you wanted the short version.'

'Yes, OK, that's fine,' she said, but I could see the concern she thought she was so good at hiding. 'Only that isn't the fire I was thinking of.'

'No? Oh, you mean the fire in the field I started, the one next to the dump where I lived with Frank and Jenny?'

'Frank and Jenny,' she repeated calmly, and only an almost imperceptible shrug of the shoulders revealed that she had been slightly unsettled by my last statement.

'Relax, Karen,' I said. 'It's nothing delusional, I'm just telling you about my dreams. That's the only thing I can remember that has anything to do with fires.'

There was a little thud as her pen hit the parquet floor, but she didn't seem to notice.

'Is that true, Richard?'

'Why would I lie?' The answer to that was as obvious as it was true. To please you, Karen Taylor. Because I'll do whatever it takes to see you smile.

I bent down and picked up her pen and handed it to her. Her shoulders slowly relaxed as a smile of . . . well, a smile almost of happiness spread across her face.

'Do you know what, Richard? I think this is looking good. I think this is looking *really* good. Do you mind waiting while I go and get some of the others?'

I nodded. 'The others' were the team of therapists, psychiatrists and psychologists who worked closely with the patients. Because the human mind was – as they put it – too complex for one person alone to be expected to draw all the correct conclusions.

As her footsteps faded away down the corridor behind the door, I looked at the notebook she had left on her chair. She had never left it behind before. Well, she had never left *me* before in any of our sessions throughout the course of these four years. That alone told me that this was a special day. Naturally, I was wondering what was going to happen now, but even more than that, I was wondering what Karen had written in that notebook over the years. Because it was the same book, I recognised every furrow and every nuance in the brown leather cover. How many times had I fantasised about what she had written about me in it? The journals she typed up on her computer and submitted after each session were one thing, they were obviously purely professional. But this notebook was something else, it probably contained her immediate, personal, private thoughts and reflections about the patient. Wouldn't it? Would she have revealed anything about herself in her writing?

I hesitated for a moment.

Then I leaned forward, picked the book up off the chair, pulled out the pink hair clip and started to leaf through it. Not that I was expecting to find anything that jumped out at me, like a young girl's pencil case, *I love Kurt Cobain*, that sort of thing. But I knew from experience that when you sit and scribble, the half-thought-out ideas that end up on the paper are often more revealing than the carefully formulated ones. Which is why I was disappointed when I quickly realised that the notes maintained the same professional style as the finished journals that she always let me read if I asked to see them.

*Current state: R.J. is well-turned-out, makes good formal and informal contact. He is aware of time, place and situation. No signs of reality deficit or hallucinations. Normal mood spectrum. Good verbal skills.*

I read a few more pages. It was familiar stuff, like looking at pictures of yourself.

*11 April, 11.15: R.J. is relaxed, funny and charming when he talks about his running. When we pick up the threads from yesterday and talk about his childhood again, R.J. repeats that he had a harmonious and loving relationship with both father and mother before his father's illness. R.J.'s body language and mood are neutral and restrained, but as usual change when we get to the fire. This is, however, an improvement from when therapy started (i.e. sudden sideways glances, long periods of silence, clear signs of hallucinations). Body language and voice still show signs of stress, more so in descriptions of what happened to his parents than the danger he himself was in. I have no doubt that this incident triggered many of R.J.'s problems, and that there remains a lot of work to do to deal with this trauma. ECT an option? I would like to recommend to the team that we consider rethinking this. Perhaps R.J. can talk about the incident in a new, more profound way, because at the moment he just seems to be repeating what he has said before, with the same pain, but without any fresh insight.*

When I loosened the hair clip that was holding several pages together, two folded sheets of A4 fell out. I straightened them out and saw that they were covered in writing. The heading read: 'The Fire'. I read the first few sentences and was surprised that I neither recognised the contents nor had any recollection of having written them. But there was no question that it was my handwriting. I hesitated. I realised the risk I was taking. The CBT therapy, the electric shock treatment, all of that could be ruined if I read this now. On the other hand, I could only actually get proof that it had worked, if it really had erased unwanted memories, if I read this.

I closed my eyes. Took a deep breath. And opened them again.

*The Fire*

*When I was thirteen years old, Dad got so ill that I started to get worried about him. He had had periods when he behaved strangely, but now he started to have delusions. Among other things, he accused Mum of having orgies when he wasn't home, of picking up strangers – women as well as men – in the street. And of selling his things to them. As proof of this, he mentioned suits, watches, musical instruments, radios, even cars he had never owned, all of which he now claimed were gone. On other days he could sit motionless just staring at the wall for hours without saying a word or eating anything, and that was almost worse. On those occasions I was afraid that I had lost my dad. Mum tried to get Dad sectioned, but his family put a stop to that, they said other family members with the same 'eccentric' tendencies had managed fine, they just needed rest. And they said that getting committed to a lunatic asylum would bring dishonour on their family when there was no need to for it.*

*One night Dad woke me up and said that the voices had told him that he and I were Siamese twins, that we had been born joined at the hip and had been separated. The reason I seemed younger than him was because the ageing gene was in his part of the body, which meant I was ageing much more slowly. He showed me a scar on his hip as proof, and when I said I didn't have a scar, he didn't believe me and made me take my pyjama bottoms off to check. Mum, who had been woken up by the noise, came in and misunderstood what she saw. And even when I explained what was going on, and said that Dad had never, ever laid a finger on me, and definitely not in that way, I could see that she wasn't convinced.*

*A few days later Mum told me that Dad had hit her and threatened her with a knife. The police had come and taken him away, but they were going to let him go unless she made an official complaint. My grandmother – Dad's mother – had advised her, basically as good as threatened her, not to do that. They agreed that Dad would move back home to Grandma and Grandad's and stay away from us until he was better. Mum changed the locks on the door of our apartment, and when I asked why, she said Dad was never going to get better, you only had to look at his two uncles. When I asked what had happened to them, she said it was best if I didn't know.*

*The next day Dad came to our apartment. He got past the door down on the street, but when he reached our apartment on the ninth floor and discovered that the locks had been changed, he was furious and started hammering on the door.*

*'I know you're in there!' he roared. 'Let me in! Richard, do you hear me?'*

*Mum and I were standing in the kitchen, next to the front door, she had her arms round me, and now she put her hand over my mouth. 'Don't answer,' she whispered, her voice choked with tears.*

*He went on banging. 'I know your mother won't let me in, Richard, but you, Richard, you will! You're my flesh and blood! This is my home, I made it for you!'*

*I wanted to pull free, but Mum was holding me tight. After another ten minutes of banging, kicking and shouting, a sob crept into his voice:*

*'Garbage!' he yelled. 'Richard, you're garbage! Your mother's going to burn in hell, and there's nothing you can do about it. Because you're small and weak and a coward. You're garbage. Do you hear? You're garbage. And you're going to let me in.'*

*Almost half an hour passed before we heard Dad's shouting and cursing as he made his way along the corridor.*

*Mum called Grandma and told her what had just happened, and she said she'd get some medication from the family doctor, she said she knew what was wrong with Dad, and knew how to take care of her boy.*

*But just two days later Dad was back outside our door again.*

*'You're both going to burn! This is my apartment, and the boy is my flesh and blood! My flesh and blood!'*

*In the end some of the neighbours came out of their apartments, we heard their voices in the corridor. They managed to calm Dad down and eventually got him out of the building, I saw him cross the street out of the window. He looked so small and lonely down there.*

*That night I had a nightmare. In the dream I didn't exist as a separate person, I was just a growth on his back. The weird thing was that when we were standing there banging on the door and shouting at Mum, I joined in. I felt his despair, his rage, his fear. Maybe it was because I loved and admired Dad more than anything else on the planet, even if I loved Mum too. Exactly what I admired so much is hard to put my finger on, Dad was an ordinary man, a hard-working insurance salesman with no special talents, except that he could stick two fingers in his mouth and whistle louder than anyone I knew. Sure, Dad came from a wealthy family, but I think he was actually a bit of a disappointment to them. But to me Dad was still the most important person in the world to be seen and acknowledged by. Presumably that's why I always did whatever he said without the slightest objection. Like a well-trained dog, as Mum used to say. But there might have been another reason why I – at least in the dream – took Dad's side, even though it was obviously wrong. Because Mum had been unfaithful, I knew that. She had had an affair with her boss the year before; they worked together in the library next to the school. One of the boys in my class told me he'd seen them kissing between the bookshelves, that my mum was a whore. I punched him and got sent to the scary red door, the Principal's office. But that wasn't so bad, I just sat there and pretended to listen while he lectured me, and said nothing myself. I didn't say anything to Dad either when I got home. But I told Mum what they were saying at school, and she cried and admitted that she and her boss had had an affair, but said it was over now. As if to prove this, at dinner she announced that she had handed in her notice at work, which surprised Dad. He said she had seemed happy there. Then he added, as if to console her, that the important thing was to do a job that made her happy. She smiled at him while I looked down and carried on chewing my food, resisting the impulse to throw my arms round him.*

*The evening before Dad set fire to the apartment I was lying in bed listening to the sounds of the city. Especially the police sirens, I loved that noise, the rising and falling, almost plaintive sound always made me shiver, because those sirens meant something dramatic had happened. At the same time, it was the sound of security, because they were on the case, things were going to be OK, someone was keeping watch. That was what I wanted to do, keep watch. I wanted to be a policeman, ideally an FBI agent, with a police car, blue lights on the roof, and a siren that sang a bedtime lullaby to the city's inhabitants.*

*When I woke up, at first I thought it was a siren, but then I realised it was the phone in the hall.*

*I lay there for a while before realising that Mum wasn't going to answer it. Maybe it was the sleeping pills the doctor had given her after she threw Dad out. The ringing stopped, but just as I was getting back to sleep it started again. My heart was pounding. Because of course I knew who it was. I got up and crept into the hall, trying not to let the whole of my feet touch the ice-cold floor. I picked up the phone.*

*'Hello?' I said quietly.*

*I heard someone breathing down the phone. 'Richard, my boy.' It was Dad's high, almost feminine voice. 'You want to unlock the door.'*

*'Unlock it?'*

*'I want to get in. And you want to let me.'*

*'Dad . . .'*

*'Hush. You're my boy. You're my flesh and blood, and you'll do as I say.'*

*'But –'*

*'Not "buts". I'm better now, but your mum doesn't understand, she doesn't want to hear. But I have to talk to her, so she realises that the three of us should be together. We're a family, aren't we?'*

*'Yes, Dad.'*

*'Yes, Dad, what?'*

*'Yes, Dad, we're a family.'*

*'Good. So unlock the door and go back to bed. When you wake up tomorrow morning, Mum and I will have sorted things out and we'll have breakfast together, and everything will be like it was before.'*

*'But you –'*

*'I've got medicine, my head has calmed down, I'm better. Unlock the door and go back to bed, Richard, you've got school tomorrow.'*

*I closed my eyes. Imagined that breakfast. From my chair at the kitchen table I could see the building on the other side of the street, the sun was still hidden behind it, but it gave the building a halo that gradually rose higher as Mum and Dad talked in short sentences about practical things, organising the day. Family. Love. Security. Belonging. Meaning.*

*The next thing I remember is lying in bed. I'd just woken up from a dream. Mum, Dad and I were driving in a car through a flat forest landscape, we were on our way to a prison where we were going to visit one of Dad's uncles, the road was dusty, the windscreen was dirty, there was a smell of windscreen-wiper fluid. I lay in bed, listening. I could still smell windscreen-wiper fluid, and I could hear something, maybe a chair, as it toppled and fell. I slipped out of bed and went out into the passageway. The smell of spirits hit my nose, and the parquet floor felt wet and sticky beneath my bare feet. The door to Mum's bedroom was open, and there was light coming from it. I crept towards it and peered in.*

*Sure enough, there was a chair lying on the floor. And above it hung Mum. Or rather, she was slowly spinning round as her bare feet looked like they were reaching towards the floor, trying to find the ground. Her transparent, white nightdress was dripping, tick, tock, tick, tock. Because of the way her body was turning, at first I saw her back, and the fact that her hands were tied together. Then her front turned towards me, and I looked up. Her hair was stuck to her face as if it had been raining. Her mouth was covered with silver-coloured tape. Her eyes were open, but I knew they couldn't see anything as they stared out blankly. The rope around her neck was attached to the ceiling, to the same hook the lamp was hanging from. I had never seen a dead body before, but I knew just as surely as I knew that I was alive: Mum was dead. My throat tightened, but I still managed to squeeze out the words as I saw the little yellow flame.*

*'No. Dad, don't do it.'*

*Dad turned round slowly as he stood there next to Mum and looked at me with the eyes of a sleepwalker. A gentle smile spread across his face.*

*'But, my boy, I've already told you. If you really want to kill them, you have to do it twice. If you don't, they come back.'*

*He raised the lighter and the flame caught hold of the edge of Mum's nightdress. There was a soft thump, and it felt as if all the air was sucked out of the room. Then Mum was on fire. I could only just see her through the flames. Curtains of flame fell to the floor, which caught light as well. I backed away, staring at the flames that crept towards me along the trails of spirits, like long yellow and blue fingers. I didn't want to back away, I wanted to go in, grab the quilt and wrap it round Mum, smother the fire and put it out. But my body wouldn't obey me. Because Dad was – as usual – right. I was a coward. Weak. Garbage. So I backed away. Away from the door, back along the passageway, all the while with those hungry flames creeping after me, until I could open the door to my own room, get inside and shut everything out. Then I pressed my hands over my ears, screwed my eyes shut and screamed.*

*I don't know how long I stood like that, but when I felt the wave of heat against my face and body, I opened my eyes and saw Dad filling the doorway, the entire hallway in flames behind him. I stopped screaming, but the scream carried on anyway, and it took me a moment to realise that it wasn't a scream but the fire alarm. Dad came in and closed the door behind him, then crouched down in front of me and put his hands on my shoulders. Outside the alarm switched from a continuous wail to an intermittent howl. Between the howls I could hear the flames, a growing crackle, like thousands of corpse-maggots eating.*

*'It had to happen this way,' Dad said in his soft voice, the one he used when he told me I had to let the school doctor give me an injection, or why he couldn't take me to film club to watch* Night of the Living Dead *because Mum wouldn't let him. 'The voices said so, and they know best. You understand that, don't you?'*

*I nodded. Not because I understood, but because I didn't want him to think that I didn't understand him, that I wasn't on his side. Dad pulled me close to him.*

*'Do you hear the voices too?' he whispered in my ear.*

*I didn't know if I should nod or shake my head. I could hear something in the distance between each howl of the fire alarm. Not voices, but sirens.*

*'Do you?' he repeated, shaking me gently.*

*'What are they saying?' I asked.*

*'Don't you hear? They're saying we're going to fly away. You and me, we're going to fly away, like . . . like two fireflies.'*

*'Where to?' I asked, trying to stifle the sobs that were caught between my stomach and my throat.*

*Dad coughed. Then he stood up and went over to the window. He pushed the curtains back, then opened the windows on either side of the central strut. At once I felt a rush of cold night air on my face, as if the apartment had been holding its breath. He peered out, up at the sky.*

*'You can't see them because we're in a city,' he said. 'But do you know what, Richard? Up there, there are millions like us. Fireflies, frozen in time. Stars. They shine, showing the way. But no one can catch them. Come.'*

*He had climbed up onto the windowsill and was crouching in the window. Now he was holding out his hand to me. I remained standing by the door.*

*'Come!' he said, and when I heard his voice change character and get that sharp, flinty edge, I obeyed at once.*

*He took my hand and pulled me up onto the windowsill next to him. We crouched there together on either side of the central strut of the frame, our heads outside, he with a firm grip of my hand. If either of us leaned out a bit further and fell, the other would fall too. The sirens had come closer, and down in the street I could see that people had begun to gather, and that more were joining them from the door to our building. When I looked up, I really did think I could see the stars, stars dancing in the sky. His hand felt warm around mine. It felt unreal, as if it was all just a dream.*

*'Isn't it beautiful?' Dad said.*

*I didn't answer.*

*'I'll count to three, then we fly,' he said. 'OK? One . . .'*

*'Dad,' I whispered. 'Please, don't hold my hand so tight.'*

*'Why not? We have to hold hands.'*

*'I can't fly unless you hold me less tightly.'*

*'Says who?' he said, and instead of loosening his grip, he tightened it instead.*

*'The voices,' I said. 'The voices say so. And the voices know best, don't they?'*

*He looked at me for a long time. 'Two,' he said in a toneless voice, his body already starting to move forward. This isn't a dream, I thought. This is happening. We're falling.*

*'Three,' he said, and I felt his big, warm hand loosen its grip slightly. I snatched my hand back, grabbed hold of the central strut and saw Dad half turn his head towards me. There was a look of surprise on his face. Then it was gone.*

*For a few seconds I followed his body as it fell silently down the side of the building. It disappeared into the darkness before reappearing outside the windows where the lights were on. The fire alarm had stopped, and the only sound I could hear was the siren song of the fire engines: 'We're on our way, we're on our way.' I didn't hear Dad's body hit the tarmac below, just the screams from the crowd. And then their cries when they saw me in the window on the ninth floor. I don't know how long I sat there waiting on the window-sill, but by the time the fire engine had arrived, the firemen's canvas was stretched out beneath me and they were shouting at me to jump, my bed was burning behind me. Everyone down in the street was shouting now, it was like a chorus.*

*'Jump, jump, jump!'*

*So I jumped.*

That's where it stopped.

I read the first few sentences again, looking for something I couldn't find. The *person* I couldn't find, the stranger who had evidently been through all this. Or had made it all up. But it still didn't bring any memories back to life. Did that mean I was cured, better? Well, better in the sense that someone can get better after an amputation.

Yes, that was actually what it felt like. But how could I be sure?

I heard footsteps, slipped the hair clip back in, closed the book and put it back on the chair.

'Richard!' Dr Rossi, the senior consultant, said with a smile as he shook my hand with both of his, as if we were good friends. That wasn't unreasonable, considering that he had now been at Ballantyne for eight of my fifteen years here, but I preferred a certain distance. Rossi, on the other hand, believed in dismantling the barriers between doctor and patient. 'If the people are good, there's no danger in being personal,' he used to say. I assumed that was easier to say and do if you worked somewhere with the amount of resources per patient that they had at Ballantyne.

Behind him stood Karen and Dale. Dale was a psychologist and a researcher at the university. He was investigating ECT therapy for the removal of trauma memories in PTSD patients, and was following me and two other patients who were receiving the same treatment at Ballantyne. As usual, Dale was – unlike Rossi – impeccably dressed in a black suit that matched his thick, almost blue-black mane of hair.

'I hear we're doing such a good job that we risk losing you,' Rossi said as he sat down on one of the three chairs opposite me, leaning back and crossing the legs dressed in comfortably worn jeans and vintage Nikes. Rossi was the sort who wore university sweaters and decorated his office with relics from his youth. He probably hoped it would make him appear boyish, accessible, charming. Like the original Luke Skywalker figure or the framed first edition of *Swamp Thing*, the one with the big, snarling bat on the cover. One day when Rossi left me alone in his office I even considered stealing one of his relics, just for the hell of it.

'That remains to be seen,' I said, looking over at Dale, who had also sat down. He was sitting straight-backed, and nodded.

'It looks promising,' he said. 'But even if you are discharged, I'd like to continue to follow your progress.'

'It's looking good, Richard, but we shouldn't count any chickens,' Rossi said. 'You arrived here right after a family tragedy, and have been here ever since. You haven't participated in life outside, and we can't expect the transition to be entirely problem-free.'

'Institutionalised,' I said.

'Erm, exactly. We're thinking of suggesting that we start with you spending two days a week on the outside, then we'll increase that when we can see that things are going well. What do you say to that, Richard?'

I had been relatively well for so long that I was considered capable of giving my consent on all matters now.

'I'm sure that'll be fine . . .' I said, and hoped he hadn't noticed that I had almost said 'Oscar' at the end of the sentence. Rossi liked us to use his first name, and I don't know why I could never bring myself to do it. It wasn't just that business of distance, but something I had noticed about the way he looked at Karen.

'Great,' Rossi said, clapping his hands together. 'Now, let's take a look at the results and see what progress you've made, and discuss your medication and therapy going forward.'

Obviously there wasn't going to be any discussion, but it made the patients more willing to cooperate if they felt they were part of the decision-making process.

'We're going to miss you,' Karen said as she and I were walking along the path towards the edge of the forest. Once Dale and Rossi were finished and had left, Karen had said she had a little surprise, a sort of leaving gift.

'I'm only going to be gone two days a week,' I said.

'So I'll miss you two days a week,' she said, smiling.

Obviously I heard that she said *I* rather than *we* in that last sentence. That could just have been a slip of the tongue, of course. Whether it was Freudian or not didn't really matter. She was the therapist and I was the patient, and those two – according to the psychiatric association's ethical guidelines – could never become one. Except in my imagination. And if there was one thing I was good at, it was using my imagination.

'Are you scared?' she asked.

'Of life outside?' I realised that I was unconsciously mimicking Oscar Rossi's voice and upper-class intonation. 'Well, I tried it out before. And that went OK. For a while. The problem is . . .'

'Yes?'

I shrugged. 'I haven't got anything constructive to do. I haven't got a context to fit into. As a patient, at least you're part of a larger machine.'

'I've thought of that,' she said.

'Oh?'

'We all need something to do, so we can feel that we're contributing.' She waved to the old gardener, Feihta, who was sitting like a king on the Japanese lawnmower that was gliding back and forth across the grass, but he didn't see us. 'And I know that you can make a contribution as something other than a patient.'

'As what then, if I may ask?'

We followed the path into the forest. The sunlight filtered down on us through the foliage.

'Do you remember back before we started the ECT therapy, when I asked you to write down your trauma memory, in as much detail as you could remember?'

'No. Should I?'

'It's just as well if you don't remember. I did it so that we – when we went through the memory ahead of each session – would have a record of everything, and weren't leaving any threads that could lead your memory back to this specific incident later on. But when I read what you had written, I discovered something else.'

'Oh? What?'

'You like writing.'

'What do you mean?'

'You didn't just write a report of what happened. I don't know if it was something you planned or if it just turned out that way, but you became a storyteller. You tried to bring what had happened to life for the reader, you tried to turn it into literature.'

'OK,' I said, with feigned scepticism, while at the same time I felt something. Excitement. As if this was something I had been waiting for. 'Did I succeed?'

'Yes,' she said simply. 'You did with me, anyway. And I showed it to a couple of other people, and they agreed.'

It was as if my lungs and heart expanded, like when I do a lot of exercise and the space between my ribs and my back feels too constricted. But this was caused by happiness. And pride. Pride in a text I couldn't remember writing, but had read a little while ago. *A couple of other people*, I thought. That meant a huge deal to me.

We crossed a wooden bridge over the stream in the forest. We were surrounded by intense birdsong, like outside my window just before dawn. We reached a hill crowned by a small summerhouse that I usually ran past when I was out jogging.

'Come,' Karen said, and her hand brushed mine as she took me by the elbow.

The summerhouse had six sides, with glass walls, almost like a greenhouse, and it was built round the trunk of an old oak tree that provided shade. Karen opened the door and we went inside. There was a table and chair in there that hadn't been there before. On the table were a typewriter, a pile of paper and a jar of pens.

'I don't know if you want to use a computer or a typewriter,' she said. 'Or write by hand. Or if you even want to write at all.'

I looked at her. She was smiling broadly, but she was blinking rapidly and had a few deep red patches on her neck.

'Oh,' I said, swallowing and looking out at the view of the hills around us. 'I want to write. And I want to try using a typewriter.'

'Great,' she said, and I could hear the relief in her voice. 'I think this could be an inspiring place. Somewhere to get started, at least.'

I nodded. 'Somewhere to get started.'

'Well, then,' Karen said, folding her hands and standing on tiptoe the way she did when she was happy or excited. 'I'll leave you to it. You can spend as much time as you want here.'

'Thanks,' I said. 'This was your idea, wasn't it?'

'I suppose so, yes.'

'What I can do in return?'

'Oh. When you eventually get discharged and are no longer my patient, how about a cinema ticket?'

She tried to make it sound casual and nonchalant rather than flirtatious, but it was clearly a sentence she had practised saying in a light-hearted way.

'Maybe,' I said. 'Any special requests for the film?'

She shrugged. 'Some romantic nonsense,' she said.

'Deal.'

She walked out, closing the door behind her. Through the glass walls I saw her disappear into the forest. I walked round the table a couple of times. Moved the chair. Tried sitting on it. The floor wasn't completely flat and it rocked. I put a sheet of paper in the typewriter. Tapped one of the keys to test it out. It took more effort than I expected. But that was probably just a matter of practice. I straightened my back and pulled the chair closer . It was still rocking. Then I wrote, painstakingly and with two fingers:

*THE NIGHT HOUSE*

*'Y-y-y-you're crazy,' Tom said, and I could tell he was scared, seeing as he stammered one more time than he usually does.*

# The new thriller in the *Sunday Times* bestselling Detective Harry Hole series

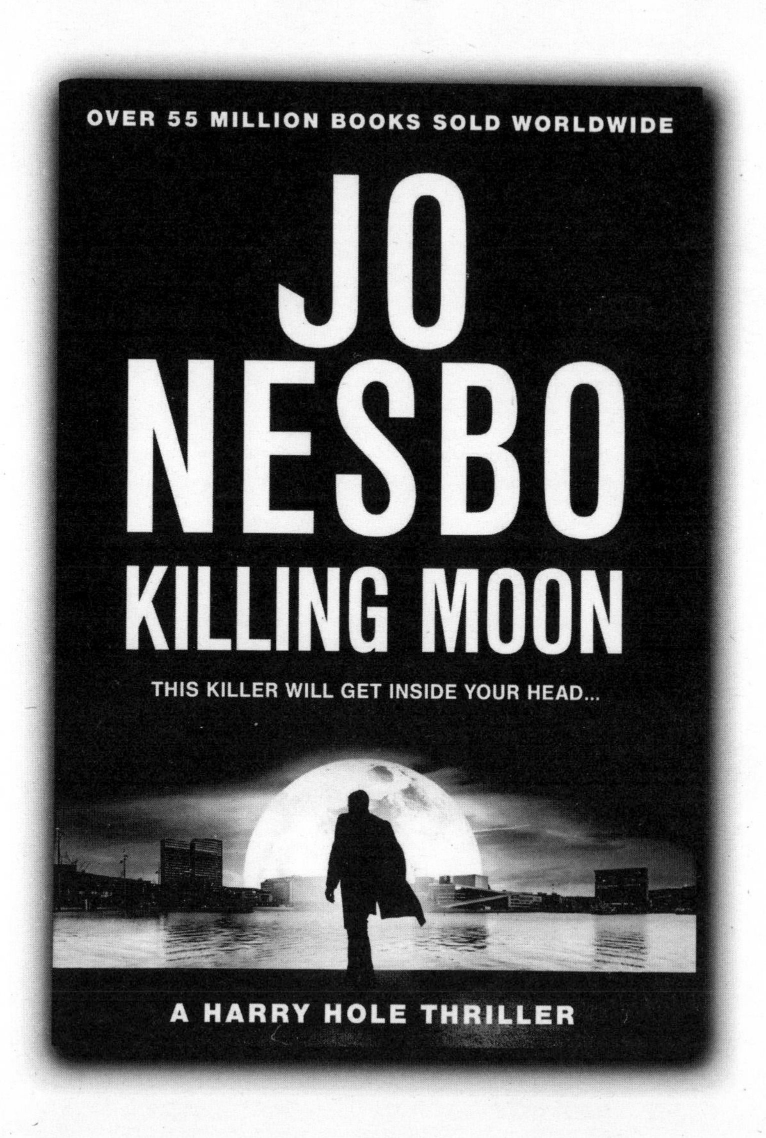


## EAD ON FOR AN EXCLUSIVE EXTRACT

# 1

# FRIDAY

EIGHT O'CLOCK. HALF AN HOUR since the September sun had gone down over Oslo, and past bedtime for three-year-olds.

Katrine Bratt sighed and whispered into the phone: 'Can't you sleep, darling?'

'Gwanny is singing wong,' the child's voice answered, sniffling. 'Whe ah you?'

'I had to go to work, darling, but I'll be home soon. Would you like Mummy to sing a little?'

'Yeah.'

'Well, then you have to close your eyes.'

'Yeah.'

' "Blueman"?'

'Yeah.'

Katrine began singing the melancholy song in a low, deep voice. *Blueman, Blueman, my buck, think of your small boy.*

She had no idea why children had, for over a century, felt happy to be lulled to sleep by the story of an angst-ridden boy who wonders why

Blueman, his favourite goat, hasn't returned home from grazing, and who fears it's been taken by a bear and now lies mutilated and dead somewhere in the mountains.

Still, after just one verse she could hear Gert's breathing become more regular and deep, and after the next verse she heard her mother-in-law's whispered voice on the phone.

'He's asleep now.'

'Thanks,' said Katrine, who had been squatting on her haunches so long she had to put her hand on the ground. 'I'll be back as soon as I can.'

'Take all the time you need, dear. And I'm the one who should be thanking you for wanting us here. You know, he looks so much like Bjørn when he's asleep.'

Katrine swallowed. Unable, as usual, to respond when she said that. Not because she didn't miss Bjørn, not because she wasn't happy that Bjørn's parents saw him in Gert. But because it simply wasn't true.

She concentrated on what lay in front of her.

'Intense lullaby,' said Sung-min Larsen, who had come and crouched down next to her. '"*Maybe now you lay dead*"?'

'I know, but it's the only one he wants to hear,' Katrine said.

'Well, then that's what he gets.' Her colleague smiled.

Katrine nodded. 'Have you ever thought about how as children we expect unconditional love from our parents, without giving anything in return? That we are actually parasites? But then we grow up and things change completely. When exactly do you think we stop believing that we can be loved unconditionally just for being who we are?'

'When did *she* stop, you mean?'

'Yeah.'

They looked down at the body of the young woman lying on the forest floor. Her trousers and knickers were pulled down to her ankles, but the zip on the thin down jacket was pulled up. Her face – which was turned to the starry skies above – appeared chalk-white in the glare of the Crime Scene Unit's floodlights, which were positioned among the trees. Her make-up was streaked, and looked like it had run and dried out several times. Her hair – bombed blonde by chemicals – was sticking to one side of her face. Her lips were stuffed with silicon, and false eyelashes protruded like the eaves of a roof over one eye, which was sunken down in its socket, staring glassily up and past them, and also over the other eye, which was not there, only an empty socket. Perhaps all the barely degradable synthetic materials were the reason the body had remained in as good condition as it had.

'I'm guessing this is Susanne Andersen?' Sung-min said.

'I'm guessing the same,' Katrine replied.

The detectives were from two different departments, she was with Crime Squad at the Oslo Police and he was with Kripos. Susanne Andersen, twenty-six years old, had been missing for seventeen days and was last spotted on a security camera at Skullerud metro station around a twenty-minute walk from where they were now. The only lead on the other missing woman, Bertine Bertilsen, twenty-seven years old, was her car, which was found abandoned in a car park in Grefsenkollen, a hiking area in another part of the city. The hair colour of the woman in front of them tallied with the security camera footage of Susanne, while Bertine was, according to family and friends, currently a brunette. Besides, the body had no tattoos on the naked lower body, while Bertine was supposed to have one – a Louis Vuitton logo – on her ankle.

So far, it had been a relatively cool and dry September, and the discoloration on the corpse's skin – blue, purple, yellow, brown – might be consistent with it lying outdoors for close to three weeks. The same went for the smell, owing to the body's production of gas, which gradually seeped out from all orifices. Katrine had also noted the white area of thin hair-like filaments below the nostrils: fungus. In the large wound on the throat, yellowish-white, blind maggots crawled. Katrine had seen it so often she no longer had any particular reaction. After all, blowflies were – in Harry's words – as loyal as Liverpool fans. Turning up at a moment's notice no matter the time or place, rain or shine, attracted by the smell of dimethyl trisulfide which the body begins to excrete from the moment of expiration. The females lay their eggs, and a few days later the larvae hatch and begin gorging on the rotting flesh. They pupate, turning into flies, which look for bodies to lay their own eggs in, and after a month they have lived their life to the end and die. That's their life cycle. Not so different to ours, Katrine thought. Or rather, not so different to mine.

Katrine looked around. White-clad members of Krimteknisk, the Forensics Unit, moved like soundless ghosts among the trees, casting eerie shadows every time the flashes on their cameras lit up. The forest was large. Østmarka continued on, for mile after mile, virtually all the way to Sweden. A jogger had found the body. Or rather, the jogger's dog, which had been allowed off the lead and had disappeared from the narrow gravel road and into the woods. It was already getting dark. The jogger – running with a headlamp – had followed after while calling out to the dog and had eventually found it, next to the body, wagging its tail. Well, no wagging had been mentioned, it was something Katrine had pictured.

'Susanne Andersen,' she whispered, not knowing quite to whom. Perhaps to the deceased, as comfort and assurance that she had finally been found and identified.

The cause of death appeared obvious. The cut that had been made across her throat, running like a smile over Susanne Andersen's narrow neck. The fly larvae, various forms of insects and perhaps other animals had probably helped themselves to most of the blood; however, Katrine still saw traces of blood spatter in the heather and on the trunk of one tree.

'Killed here *in situ*,' she said.

'Looks that way,' Sung-min replied. 'Do you think she was raped? Or just sexually assaulted after he killed her?'

'After,' Katrine said, shining the torch on Susanne's hands. 'No broken nails, no signs of a struggle. But I'll try and have them undertake a forensic post-mortem over the weekend and we'll see what they think.'

'And a clinical autopsy?'

'We won't get that until Monday at the earliest.'

Sung-min sighed. 'Well, I guess it's only a question of time before we find Bertine Bertilsen raped and with her throat slit somewhere in Grefsenkollen.'

Katrine nodded. She and Sung-min had become better acquainted over the past year, and he had confirmed his reputation as one of Kripos's best detectives. There were many who believed he would take over as Senior Inspector the day Ole Winter stepped down, and that from then on the department would have a far better boss. Possibly. But there were also those who voiced reservations about the country's foremost investigative body being led by an adopted South Korean and homosexual who dressed like a member of the British aristocracy. His classic tweed hunting jacket and suede-and-leather country boots stood in stark contrast to Katrine's thin Patagonia down jacket and Gore-Tex trainers. When Bjørn was alive, he had called her style 'gorpcore', which, she had been given to understand, was an international term for people who went to the pub dressed as though they were headed up the mountains. She had called it adapting to life as the mother of a small child. But she had to admit that this more subdued, practical style of dress was also owing to the fact that she was no longer a young, rebellious investigative talent but the head of Crime Squad.

'What do you think this is?' Sung-min said.

She knew he was thinking the same as her. And that neither of them intended to say those words out loud. Not yet. Katrine cleared her throat.

'The first thing we do is stick to what we've got here and find out what happened.'

'Agreed.'

Katrine hoped 'agreed' was a word she would hear often from Kripos in future. But she did, of course, welcome all the help they could get. Kripos had let it be known they were ready to step up from the point Bertine Bertilsen was reported missing exactly a week after Susanne, and under strikingly similar circumstances. Both women had gone out on a Tuesday evening without telling any of those the police had spoken to where they were going or what they were doing, and had not been seen since. Besides, there were other circumstances linking the two women. When these came to light, the police shelved their theory of Susanne having been in an accident or having taken her own life.

'All right, then,' Katrine said and stood up. 'I'd better notify the boss.'

Katrine had to remain standing for a moment before regaining the feeling in her legs. She used the light on her mobile phone to ensure she trod on more or less the same footprints they had made on their way into the crime scene. Once beyond the cordon tape, which was strung between trees, she tapped in the first letters of the name of the Chief Superintendent. Bodil Melling picked up after the third ring.

'Bratt here. Sorry for calling so late, but it looks like we might have found one of the missing women. Murdered, her throat is cut, probable arterial spatter, likely raped or sexually assaulted. Fairly certain it's Susanne Andersen.'

'That's too bad,' Melling said, in a voice lacking any tone. And at the same time Katrine pictured the lack of expression in Bodil Melling's face, the lack of colour in her attire, lack of emotion in her body language, guaranteed lack of conflict in her home life and lack of excitement in her sex life. The only thing that triggered a reaction in the newly appointed Chief Superintendent, she had discovered, was the soon-to-be vacated office of Chief of Police. It wasn't that Melling wasn't qualified, Katrine just found her unbearably boring. Defensive. Gutless.

'Will you call a press conference?' Melling asked.

'OK. Do you want to . . . ?'

'No, as long as we don't have a positive ID on the body, you take it.'

'Together with Kripos, then? They have people at the scene.'

'All right, fine. If there's nothing else, we have guests.'

In the pause that followed Katrine heard low chat in the background. It sounded like a genial exchange of views, the kind, that is, where one person confirms and elaborates on what the other has said. Social bonding. That was how Bodil Melling preferred it. She would almost certainly be annoyed if Katrine brought up the subject again. Katrine had suggested it as soon as Bertine Bertilsen was reported missing and suspicion arose that the two women might have been killed by the same man. She wouldn't get anywhere either, Melling had made that very clear, had, in effect, put an end to the discussion. Katrine ought to just let it go.

'Just one thing,' she said, letting the words hang in the air as she drew a breath.

Her boss beat her to it.

'The answer is no, Bratt.'

'But he's the only specialist on this we have. And he's the best.'

'And the worst. Besides, we don't *have* him any longer. Thank God.'

'The media are bound to look for him, ask why we're not—'

'Then you just tell them the truth, which is we don't know his whereabouts. Moreover, considering what happened to his wife, coupled with his unstable nature and substance abuse, I can't imagine him functioning in a murder investigation.'

'I think I know where to find him.'

'Drop it, Bratt. Resorting to old heroes as soon as you're under pressure comes across as an implicit disparagement of the people actually at your disposal in Crime Squad. What will it do to their self-esteem and motivation if you say you want to bring in a wreck without a badge? That's what we call poor leadership, Bratt.'

'OK,' Katrine said and swallowed hard.

'All right, I appreciate that you think it's OK. Was there anything else?'

Katrine thought for a moment. So Melling could actually be antagonised and bare her teeth after all. Good. She looked at the crescent moon hanging above the treetops. Last night, Arne, the young man she had been dating for almost month, told her that in two weeks there would be a total lunar eclipse, a so-called blood moon, and they should mark the occasion. Katrine had no clue what a blood moon was, but apparently it occurred every second or third year, and Arne was so eager that she hadn't had the heart to say maybe they shouldn't plan something as far in the future as two weeks, seeing as they barely knew each other. Katrine had never been afraid of conflict or of being direct, something she had probably inherited from her father, a policeman from Bergen who'd had more enemies than that city had rainy days, but she had learned to choose her battles and the timing of them. But now, having thought about it, she understood that unlike a confrontation with a man she didn't know whether she had any future with, this was one she had to face. Now rather than later.

'Yes, actually,' Katrine said. 'Would it also be OK to say that at the press conference if anyone asks? Or to the parents of the next girl who is killed?'

'Say what?'

'That the Oslo Police District is declining the assistance of a man who has cleared up three serial killer cases in the city and apprehended the three culprits? On the grounds we think it may impact on the self-esteem of some colleagues?'

A long silence arose, and Katrine could not hear any chat in the background now either. Finally, Bodil Melling cleared her throat.

'You know what, Katrine? You've been working hard on this case. Go ahead and hold that press conference, get some sleep at the weekend, and we'll talk on Monday.'

After they hung up, Katrine called the Forensic Medical Institute. Rather than go through the proper channels, she called the direct line of Alexandra Sturdza, the young forensic medical officer, who had neither partner nor child, and wasn't too averse to long working hours. And sure enough, Sturdza replied that she and a colleague would take a look at the body the following day.

Afterwards, Katrine stood looking down at the dead woman. Maybe it was the fact that in a man's world she had got where she was on her own that would not allow her to set aside her contempt for women who willingly depended on men. That Susanne and Bertine lived off men was not the only circumstance that bound them, but also that they had shared the same man, one more than thirty years their senior, the property mogul Markus Røed. Their lives and existences relied on other people, men with the money and the jobs they themselves did not have, providing for them. In exchange, they offered their bodies, youth and beauty. And – insofar as their relationship was exposed – their selected host could enjoy the envy of other men. But, unlike children, women like Susanne and Bertine lived with the knowledge that love was not unconditional. Sooner or later their host would ditch them, and they would have to seek out a new man to feed upon. Or allow themselves to be fed upon, depending on how you viewed it.

Was that love? Why not, simply because it was too depressing to think about?

Between the trees, in the direction of the gravel road, Katrine saw the blue light of the ambulance, which had arrived noiselessly. She thought about Harry Hole. Yes, she had received a sign of life in April, a postcard – of all things – with a picture of Venice Beach, postmarked Los Angeles. Like a sonar pip from a submarine in the depths. The message had been short. '*Send money.*' A joke, she wasn't sure. Since then there had been silence.

Complete silence.

The final verse of the lullaby, which she had not reached, played in her head.

*Blueman, Blueman, answer me, bleat with your familiar sound. Not yet, my Blueman, can you die on your boy.*

# 2

# FRIDAY

## Value

THE PRESS CONFERENCE TOOK PLACE as usual in the Parole Hall at Police HQ. The clock on the wall showed three minutes to ten, and while Mona Daa, *VG*'s crime reporter, and the others waited for the police representatives to take to the podium, Mona could conclude that the attendance was good. Over twenty journalists, and on a Friday evening. She'd had a brief discussion with her photographer on why double murders sold twice as well as single ones, or if it was a case of diminishing returns. The photographer believed that quality was more important than quantity, that as the victim was a young, ethnic Norwegian, of above-average attractiveness, she would generate more clicks than – for example – a drug-addicted couple in their forties with previous convictions. Or two – yes, even three – immigrant boys from a gang.

Mona Daa didn't disagree. So far only one of the missing girls was confirmed killed, but realistically it was only a matter of time before it turned out the other had suffered the same fate, and both were young, ethnic

Norwegians and pretty. It didn't get any better. She wasn't sure what to make of that. If it was an expression of extra concern for the young, innocent and defenceless individual. Or if other factors played a part, factors pertaining to the usual things that got clicks: sex, money and a life the readers wished they themselves had.

Speaking of wanting what others had. She looked at the guy in his thirties in the row in front. He was wearing the flannel shirt all the hipsters were supposed to be wearing this year and a porkpie hat à la Gene Hackman in *The French Connection*. It was Terry Våge from *Dagbladet*, and she wished she had his sources. Ever since the story broke, he'd had his nose in front of the others. It was Våge, for instance, who had first written about Susanne Andersen and Bertine Bertilsen having been at the same party. And Våge who had quoted a source as saying both girls had had Røed as a sugar daddy. It was annoying, and for more reasons than simply that he was competition. His very presence here was annoying. As though he had heard her thoughts, he turned and looked right at her. Smiling broadly, he touched a finger to the brim of his idiotic hat.

'He likes you,' the photographer said.

'I know,' she said.

Våge's interest in Mona had begun when he made his improbable comeback to newspaper journalism as a crime reporter, and she had made the mistake of being relatively friendly towards him at a seminar on – of all things – press ethics. Since the other journalists avoided him like the plague, her attitude must have come across as inviting. He subsequently got in touch with Mona for 'tips and advice', as he termed it. As if she had any interest in acting as a mentor for a competitor – indeed, had any desire to have anything to do with someone like Terry Våge; after all, everybody knew there had to be *something* in the rumours doing the rounds on him. But the more stand-offish she was, the more intense he became. On the phone, social media channels, even popping up in bars and cafes, as though from nowhere. It had, as usual, taken a little time before she understood it was *her* he was interested in. Mona had never been the boys' first pick, stocky and broad-faced as she was, with what her mother had called 'sad hair' and a congenital hip defect which gave her a crablike gait. God knows if it was an attempt to compensate, but she had begun training with weights, grown even more stocky, but had taken one hundred and twenty kilos in the deadlift and a third place in the national bodybuilding championships. And because she'd had to learn that a person – or at least she – didn't get anything for free, she had developed a pushy charm, a sense of humour, and a toughness which the Barbie dolls of this world could just forget about, and which had won her the unofficial throne of crime queen – and Anders. Out of the two, she valued Anders higher. Well, just about. No matter: even though the type of attention from other men which Våge displayed was unfamiliar and flattering, it was out of the question for Mona to explore it any further. And she was of the opinion that she – if not in so many words, then in tone and body language – must have made this clear to Våge. But it was as though he saw and heard what he wanted. Sometimes when she looked into those wide-open, staring eyes of his, she wondered whether he was on something or if he was all there. One night he had shown up at a bar, and when Anders went to use the men's room, he had said something to her, in a voice so low it couldn't be heard above the music, but still not quite low enough. 'You're mine.' She had pretended not to hear, but he just stood there, calm and confident, wearing a sly smile, as if it were now a secret they shared. Fuck him. She couldn't stand drama, so she hadn't mentioned it to Anders. Not that Anders wouldn't have handled it just fine, she knew he would, but still she hadn't said anything. What was it Våge imagined? That her interest in him, the new alpha male in their little pond, would grow in proportion with his position as a crime reporter who was always one step ahead of the others? Because he was, that wasn't open to discussion any longer. So yes, if she wanted something someone else had, it was to be leading the race again, not downgraded to one of the pack chasing behind Terry Våge.

'Where does he get it from, do you think?' she whispered to the photographer.

He shrugged. 'Maybe he's making it up again.'

Mona shook her head. 'No, there're good grounds to believe what he's writing now.'

Markus Røed and Johan Krohn, his lawyer, had not even attempted to refute any of what Våge had written, and that was confirmation enough.

But Våge had not always been the king of crime. The story lingered about him, always would. The girl's stage name was Genie, a retro glam act à la Suzi Quatro, for those who remembered her. The matter had occurred about five or six years prior, and the worst part of it was not that Våge had manufactured pure lies about Genie and had them put in print, but the rumour he had dropped Rohypnol into her drink at an after-party in order to have sex with the teenager. At the time, he had been a music journalist for a free newspaper and had obviously become infatuated with her, but had – in spite of his eulogising her in review after review – been turned down repeatedly. Nevertheless he had continued showing up at gigs and after-parties. Right up to the night when – if the rumours were to be believed – he had spiked her drink and carried her off to his room, which he had booked at the same hotel as the band were staying at. When the boys in the band realised what was happening, they barged into the hotel room where Genie lay unconscious and in a state of half-undress on Terry Våge's bed. They had given Terry such a beating that he suffered a skull fracture and was hospitalised for a couple of months. Genie and the band must have figured Våge had had punishment enough, or may not have wanted to risk prosecution themselves; in any case, the matter was not reported to the police by any of the parties involved. But it was the end of the glowing reviews. In addition to panning her every new release, Terry Våge wrote about Genie's infidelity, drug abuse, plagiarism, underpayment of band members, and false information on applications for grants for tour support. When a dozen or so stories were referred to the Press Complaints Commission, and it turned out that Våge had simply made half of them up, he was sacked and became *persona non grata* in the Norwegian media for the next five years. How he had managed to make it back in was a mystery. Or maybe not. He had realised he was finished as a music journalist, but had been behind a crime blog that gathered more and more readers, and eventually *Dagbladet* said that one could not exclude a young journalist from their field just because he had made some mistakes early in his career, and had taken him on as a freelancer – a freelancer who currently got more column inches than any of the newspaper's permanent reporters.

Våge finally turned away from Mona when the police made their entrance and took their places on the podium. Two from Oslo Police, Katrine Bratt – the inspector from Crime Squad – and Head of Information Kedzierski, a man with a Dylanesque mane of curly hair; and two from Kripos, the terrier-like Ole Winter and the always well-dressed Sung-min Larsen, sporting a fresh haircut. So Mona assumed they had already decided that the investigation would be a joint effort on behalf of the Crime Squad, in this case the Volvo, and Kripos, the Ferrari.

Most of the journalists held their mobiles up in the air to record sound and pictures, but Mona Daa took notes by hand and left the photographs to her colleague.

As expected, they didn't learn much other than a body had been found in Østmarka, in the hiking area around Skullerud, and that the deceased had been identified as the missing woman Susanne Andersen. The case would be treated as a possible murder, but they had, as yet, no details to make public about the cause of death, sequence of events, suspects and so on.

The usual dance ensued, with the journalists peppering those on the podium with questions while they, Katrine Bratt in the main, repeated 'no comment' and 'we can't answer that'.

Mona Daa yawned. She and Anders were supposed to have a late dinner as a pleasant start to the weekend, but that wasn't going to happen. She noted down what was said, but had the distinct feeling of writing a summary she had written before. Maybe Terry Våge felt the same. He was neither taking notes nor recording anything. Just sitting back in his chair, observing it all with a slight, almost triumphant, smile. Not asking any questions, as though he already had the answers he was interested in. It seemed the others had also run dry, and when Head of Information

Kedzierski looked like he was drawing breath to bring things to a close, Mona raised her biro in the air.

'Yes, *VG*?' The head of Information had an expression that said this better be short, it's the weekend.

'Do you feel that you have the requisite competence should this turn out to be the type of person who kills again, that is to say if he's—'

Katrine Bratt leaned forward in her chair and interrupted her: 'As we said, we don't have any sound basis to allow us to state that there's any connection between this death and any other possible criminal acts. With regard to the combined expertise of the Crime Squad and Kripos, I dare say it's adequate given what we know about the case so far.'

Mona noted the inspector's caveat of *what we know*. And that Sung-min Larsen seated in the chair next to her had neither nodded at what Bratt said nor given any indication of his view on this expertise.

The press conference drew to a close, and Mona and the others made their way out into a mild autumn night.

'What do you think?' the photographer asked.

'I think they're happy they have a body,' Mona said.

'Did you say *happy*?'

'Yeah. Susanne Andersen and Bertine Bertilsen have both been dead for weeks, the police know that, but they haven't had a single lead to go on apart from that party at Røed's. So, yeah, I think they're happy they're starting the weekend with at least one corpse that might give them something.'

'Bloody hell, you're a cold fish, Daa.'

Mona looked up at him in surprise. Considered it for a moment.

'Thanks,' she said.

It was a quarter past eleven by the time Johan Krohn had finally found a parking spot for his Lexus UX 300e in Thomas Heftyes gate, then located the number of the building where his client Markus Røed had asked him to come. The fifty-year-old defence lawyer was regarded among colleagues as one of the top three or four best defence lawyers in Oslo. Due to his high media profile, the man in the street regarded Krohn as unquestionably the best. Since he was, with a few exceptions, a bigger star than his clients, he did not make house visits, the client came to him, preferably to the offices of the law firm of Krohn and Simonsen in Rosenkrantz' gate during normal working hours. Still, there were house calls and there were house calls. This address was not Røed's primary residence; he officially resided at a 260-square-metre penthouse on the top of one of the new buildings in Oslobukta.

As he had been instructed on the phone half an hour ago, Krohn pressed the call button bearing the name of Røed's company, Barbell Properties.

'Johan?' Markus Røed's out-of-breath voice sounded. 'Fifth floor.'

There was a buzz from the top of the door, and Krohn pushed it open.

The lift looked sufficiently suspect for Krohn to take the stairs. Wide oak steps and cast-iron banisters with a form more reminiscent of Gaudí than a venerable, exclusive Norwegian town house. The door on the fifth floor was ajar. It sounded like a war was taking place within, which he understood to be the case when he stepped inside, saw bluish light coming from the living room and peered in. In front of a large TV screen – it had to be at least a hundred inches – three men were standing with their backs to him. The biggest of them, the man in the middle, was wearing VR goggles and had a game controller in each hand. The other two, young men in perhaps their twenties, were apparently spectators, using the TV as a monitor to look at what the man in the VR goggles was seeing. The war scene on the TV was from a trench, in the First World War, if Krohn was to judge by the helmets on the German soldiers rushing towards them, and whom the large man with the game controllers was blasting away at.

'Yeah!' one of the younger men shouted, as the head of the last German exploded inside his helmet and he fell to the ground.

The larger man removed the VR goggles and turned to Krohn.

'That's *that* taken care of, at least,' he said with a grin of satisfaction. Markus Røed was a handsome man, his age taken into consideration. He had a broad face, a playful look, his permanently tanned complexion was smooth, and his swept-back, shiny black hair as thick as a twenty-year-old's. Granted, some weight had spread to his waist, but he was tall, so tall that the stomach could pass as dignified. But it was the intense liveliness in his eyes that first caught your attention, a liveliness indicating the energy which meant most people were initially charmed, then flattened, and eventually exhausted by Markus Røed. Within that time he had probably got what he wanted, and you were left to your own devices. But Røed's energy levels could fluctuate, as could his mood. Krohn assumed both had something to do with the white powder he now saw traces of under one of Røed's nostrils. Johan Krohn was aware of all this, but he put up with it. Not just because Røed had insisted on paying half of Krohn's hourly rate up front to – as he had put it – guarantee Krohn's undivided attention, loyalty and desire to achieve a result. But mostly because Røed was Krohn's dream client: a man with a high profile, a millionaire with such an odious image that Krohn, paradoxically, appeared as more courageous and principled than opportunistic by taking him on as a client. So he would – as long as the case went on – just have to accept being summoned on a Friday night.

The two younger men left the room at a signal from Røed.

'Have you seen *War Remains*, Johan? No? Fucking great VR game, but you can't shoot anyone in it. This here is a sort of copy the developer wants me to invest in . . .' Røed nodded in the direction of the TV screen while he lifted a carafe and poured whiskey into two crystal rocks glasses. 'They're trying to retain the magic of *War Remains*, but make it so you can – what would you say? – influence the course of history. After all, that's what we want, right?'

'I'm driving,' Krohn said, raising a palm to the glass Røed was holding out to him.

Røed looked at Krohn for a moment as if he didn't understand the objection. Then he sneezed powerfully, sank down onto a leather Barcelona chair, and placed both glasses on the table in front of him.

'Whose apartment is this?' Krohn asked, as he settled into one of the other chairs. And immediately regretted the question. As a lawyer it was often safest not knowing more than you needed to.

'Mine,' Røed replied. 'I use it as . . . you know, a retreat.'

Markus Røed's shrug and scampish smile told Krohn the rest. He'd had other clients with similar apartments. And during an extramarital liaison, which had fortunately come to an end when he realised what he was in danger of losing, he had himself considered buying what a colleague called a bachelor pad for non-bachelors.

'So what happens now?' Røed asked.

'Now Susanne has been identified, and murder has been established as the cause, the investigation will enter a new phase. You need to be prepared to be called in for fresh interviews.'

'In other words, there'll be even more focus on me.'

'Unless the police find something at the crime scene that rules you out. We can always hope for that.'

'I thought you might say something like that. But I can't just sit here hoping any longer, Johan. You do know Barbell Properties has lost three big contracts in the last fortnight? They offered some flimsy excuses, about waiting for higher bids and so on – no one dares say right out that it's down to these articles in *Dagbladet* about me and the girls, that they don't want to be associated with a possible murder, or are afraid I'll be put away and Barbell Properties will go under. If I sit idly by hoping that a gang of public-sector, underpaid knucklehead cops will get the job done, then Barbell Properties might go bust long before they've turned up something that gets me off the hook. We need to be proactive, Johan. We need to show the public that I'm innocent. Or at least that I believe it serves my interest for the truth to come out.'

'So?'

'We need to hire our own investigators. First-rate ones. In the best-case scenario they find the killer. But failing that, it still shows the public that I'm actually trying to uncover the truth.'

Johan Krohn nodded. 'Let me play devil's advocate here, no pun intended.'

'Go on,' Røed said, and sneezed.

'Firstly, the best detectives are already working for Kripos, as they pay better than the Crime Squad. And even if they were to say yes to quitting a secure career to take on a short-term assignment like this, they'd still have to give three months' notice, plus they'd have an obligation of confidentiality covering what they know about these missing persons cases. Which in effect renders them useless to us. Secondly, the optics would be pretty bad. An investigation being bankrolled by a millionaire? You'd be doing yourself a disservice. Should your investigators uncover so-called facts that clear you, this information would automatically be questioned, something which would not have happened if the police had uncovered the same facts.'

'Ah.' Røed smiled, wiping his nose with a tissue. 'I love value for money. You're good, you've pointed out the problems. And now you're going to show me that you're the best and tell me how we solve those problems.'

Johan Krohn straightened up in his chair. 'Thank you for the vote of confidence, but there's the rub.'

'Meaning?'

'You mentioned finding the best, and there is one person who is perhaps the best. His previous results certainly point to it.'

'But?'

'But he's no longer on the force.'

'From what you've told me that ought to be an advantage.'

'What I mean is that he's no longer in the police for the wrong reasons.'

'Which are?'

'Where do I begin? Disloyalty. Gross negligence in the line of duty. Intoxicated on the job, clearly an alcoholic. Several cases of violence. Substance abuse. He's responsible, although not convicted, for the death of at least one colleague. In short, he's probably got more crimes on his conscience than most of the criminals he's hauled in. Plus, he's supposed to be a nightmare to work with.'

'That's a lot. So why are you bringing him up if he's so impossible?'

'Because he's the best. And because he could be useful with regard to the second part of what you were saying, about showing the public you're trying to unearth the truth.'

'OK . . . ?'

'The cases he's solved have made him one of the few detectives with a public profile of sorts. And an image as uncompromising, someone with don't-give-a-damn integrity. Overblown, of course, but people like those kind of myths. And for our purposes that image could allay suspicions of his investigation being bought and paid for.'

'You're worth every penny, Johan Krohn.' Røed grinned. 'He's the man we want!'

'The problem—'

'No! Just up the offer until he says yes.'

'—is that no one seems to know exactly where he is.'

Røed raised his whiskey glass without drinking, just frowned down at it. 'What do you mean by "exactly"?'

'Sometimes in an official capacity I run into Katrine Bratt, the head of Crime Squad where he worked, and when I asked, she said the last time he gave a sign of life was from a big city, but she didn't know where he was in that city or what he was doing there. She didn't sound too optimistic on his behalf, let's put it that way.'

'Hey! Don't back out now that you've sold me on the guy, Johan! It's him we want, I can feel it. So find him.'

Krohn sighed. Again regretted opening his mouth. Being the show-off he was he had of course walked right into the classic prove-you're-the-best trap that Markus Røed probably used every single day. But with his leg stuck in the trap it was too late to turn. Some calls would need to be made. He worked out the time difference. OK, he may as well get right on it.

# 3

# SATURDAY

ALEXANDRA STURDZA STUDIED HER FACE in the mirror above the sink while routinely and thoroughly washing her hands, as though it were a living person and not a corpse she would soon touch. Her face was hard, pockmarked. Her hair – pulled back and tied in a tight bun – was jet black, but she knew the first grey hairs were in store – her Romanian mother had already got them in her early thirties. Norwegian men said her brown eyes 'flashed', especially when any of them tried to imitate her almost imperceptible accent. Or when they joked about her homeland, a place some of them clearly thought was a big joke, and she told them she came from Timişoara, the first city in Europe to install electric street lighting, in 1884, two generations before Oslo. When she came to Norway as a twenty-year-old, she had learned Norwegian in six months while working three jobs, which she had reduced to two while studying chemistry at NTNU, and now just one, at the Forensic Medical Institute while also concentrating on what would be her doctoral thesis on DNA analysis. She had at times – although not that often – wondered what it was that made her so obviously attractive to men. It couldn't be her face and direct – at times harsh – manner. Nor her intellect and CV, which men seemed to perceive as more threatening than stimulating. She sighed. A man had once told her that her body was a cross between a tiger and a Lamborghini. Odd how so cheesy a comment could sound totally wrong or completely acceptable, yes, wonderful even, depending on who said it. She turned off the tap and went into the autopsy room.

Helge was already there. The technician, two years her junior, was quick-minded and laughed easily, both qualities Alexandra viewed as assets when one worked with the dead and was tasked with extracting secrets from a corpse about how death occurred. Helge was a bioengineer and Alexandra a chemical engineer, and both were qualified to carry out forensic post-mortems, if not full clinical autopsies. Nevertheless, certain pathologists attempted to pull rank by calling post-mortem technicians *Diener* – servants – a hangover from German pathologists of the old school. Helge didn't care but Alexandra had to admit it got to her now and again. And especially on days like today, when she came in and did everything a pathologist would do in a preliminary post-mortem – and equally well. Helge was her favourite at the institute, he always showed up when she asked, not something every Norwegian would on a Saturday. Or after four o'clock on a weekday. Sometimes she wondered where on the index of living standards this work-shy country would have been placed if the Americans hadn't discovered oil on their continental shelf.

She turned up the light on the lamp hanging above the naked body of the young woman on the table. The smell of a corpse was dependent on many factors: age, cause of death, if medication was being taken, what food had been eaten and – of course – how far along the process of decay had come. Alexandra had no problems with the stench of rotting flesh, of excrement, or urine. She could even tackle the gases created by the process of decomposition that the body expelled in long hisses. It was the stomach fluids that got her. The smell of vomit, bile and the various acids. In that sense, Susanne Andersen was not too bad, even after three weeks outdoors.

'No larvae?' Alexandra asked.

'I removed them,' Helge said, holding up the vinegar bottle they used.

'But kept them?'

'Yeah,' he said, pointing to a glass box containing a dozen white maggots. They were saved because their length could be indicative of how long they had fed on the corpse, in other words, how long it had been since they hatched, and therefore, something about the time of death. Not in hours, but in days and weeks.

'This won't take long,' Alexandra said. 'Crime Squad just want the probable cause of death and an external examination. Blood test, urine, bodily fluid. The pathologist will perform a complete post-mortem on Monday. Any plans for tonight? Here . . .'

Helge took a photograph of where she was pointing.

'Thought I might watch a movie,' he said.

'What about joining me at a gay club for a dance?' She made notes on the form and pointed again. 'Here.'

'I can't dance.'

'Rubbish. All gays can dance. See this cut on the throat? Starts on the left side, gets deeper further along, then shallower towards the right. It indicates a right-handed killer who was standing behind and holding her head back. One of the pathologists was telling me about a similar wound that they thought was murder, and it turned out the man had cut his own throat. Pretty determined, in other words. What do you say, want to go dance with some gays tonight?'

'What if I'm not gay?'

'In that case . . .' Alexandra said, taking notes, '. . . I wouldn't actually want to go out anywhere with you again, Helge.'

He laughed out loud and snapped a picture. 'Because?'

'Because then you'll block other men. A good wingman needs to be gay.'

'I can pretend to be gay.'

'Doesn't work. Men notice the smell of testosterone and back off. What do you think this is?'

She held a magnifying glass just below one of Susanne Andersen's nipples.

Helge leaned closer. 'Dried saliva, maybe. Or snot. Not semen, in any case.'

'Take a photo, then I'll take a scrape sample and check it at the lab on Monday. If we're lucky, it's DNA material.'

Helge took a picture while Alexandra examined the mouth, ears, nostrils and eyes.

'What do you think has happened here?' She raised a penlight and shone it in the empty eye socket.

'Animals?'

'No, I don't think so.' Alexandra shone the light around the edges of the eye socket. 'There's nothing remaining of the eyeball inside and no wounds around the eye from the claws of birds or rodents. And if it was an animal, why not take the other eye as well? Take a photo here . . .' She illuminated the eye socket. 'See how the nerve fibres look like they've been cut at one place, as though with a knife?'

'Jesus,' Helge said. 'Who does something like that?'

'Angry men,' Alexandra said, shaking her head. 'Very angry and very damaged men. And they're on the loose out there. Maybe I should stay in and watch a movie tonight as well.'

'Yeah, right.'

'OK. Let's see if he's assaulted her sexually too.'

They took a cigarette break on the roof after determining there were no obvious signs of injury to the exterior or interior of the genitalia nor any traces of semen on the outside of the vagina. If semen had been present within the vagina, it would have been drawn into the rest of the body long ago. The pathologist would go over the same ground as them on Monday but she was pretty certain they would not arrive at a different conclusion.

Alexandra was not a regular smoker, but had a vague belief in cigarettes smoking out any potential demons from the dead that had taken up residence within. She inhaled and looked out over Oslo. Over the fjord, glittering like silver beneath a pale, cloudless sky. Over the low hills, where the colours of autumn burned in red and yellow.

'Fuck, it's nice here,' she said with a sigh.

'You make it sound like you wish it wasn't,' Helge said, taking over the cigarette from her.

'I hate getting attached to things.'

'Things?'

'Places. People.'

'Men?'

'Especially men. They take away your freedom. Or rather, they don't take it, you bloody well give it away like a wuss, as if you're programmed to. And freedom is worth more than men.'

'You sure?'

She snatched the cigarette back and took a long, angry drag. Blew the smoke out just as hard and gave a harsh, rasping laugh.

'Worth more than the men I fall for anyway.'

'What about that cop you mentioned?'

'Oh, him.' She chuckled. 'Yeah, I liked him. But he was a mess. His wife had kicked him out and he drank all the time.'

'Where is he now?'

'His wife died and he skipped the country. Tragic business.' Alexandra stood up abruptly. 'Right, we better finish up and get the body back in the refrigerator. I want to party!'

They returned to the autopsy room, collected the last samples, filled out the rest of the fields on the form and tidied up.

'Speaking of parties,' Alexandra said. 'You know the party this girl and the other one were at? That was the same party I was invited to, the one I then invited you to.'

'You're kidding?'

'Don't you remember? A friend of one of Røed's neighbours asked me. She said the party was taking place on *the* best rooftop terrace in Oslobukta. Told me it would be crawling with the well-heeled, with celebrities and party people. Said they'd prefer women came in skirts. *Short* skirts.'

'Ugh,' Helge said. 'Don't blame you for not going.'

'Fuck that, course I would've gone! If I hadn't had so much work on here that day. And you would have come with.'

'Would I?' Helge smiled.

'Of course.' Alexandra laughed. 'I'm your fag hag. Can't you picture it, you, me and the beautiful people?'

'Yes.'

'You see, you are gay.'

'What? Because?'

'Tell me truthfully, Helge. Have you ever slept with a man?'

'Let me see . . .' Helge wheeled the table with the corpse towards one of the cold lockers. 'Yes.'

'More than once?'

'Doesn't mean I'm gay,' he said, opening the large metal drawer.

'No, that's only circumstantial evidence. The proof, Watson, is that you tie your sweater over one shoulder and under the other arm.'

Helge chuckled, grabbed one of the white cloths on the instrument table and flicked it at her. Alexandra smiled as she ducked down behind the top end of the table. She remained like that, stooped over, her eyes fixed on the body.

'Helge,' she said in a low voice.

'Yeah.'

'I think we've missed something.'

'What?'

Alexandra reached out towards Susanne Andersen's head, lifted the hair and pulled it to the side.

'What is it?' Helge asked.

'Stitches,' Alexandra replied. 'Fresh stitches.'

He came round the other side of the trolley. 'Hm. Guess she must have hurt herself then?'

Alexandra lifted away more hair, followed the stitches. 'These weren't carried out by a trained doctor, Helge, no one uses thread this thick or stitches this loosely. This was just done in a hurry. And look, the stitches continue all the way round the head.'

'As though she's . . .'

'As though she's been scalped,' Alexandra said, feeling a cold shudder go through her. 'And then the scalp has been sewn back on.'

She looked up at Helge, saw his Adam's apple rise and fall. 'Will we . . .' he began. 'Will we check what's . . . underneath?'

'No,' Alexandra said firmly, straightening up. She had taken home enough nightmares from this job, and the pathologists earned two hundred thousand kroner a year more than her, they could earn it.

'This is outside our field of competence,' she said. 'So it's the kind of thing *Diener*s like you and me leave to the grown-ups.'

'OK. And OK to partying tonight too, by the way.'

'Good,' Alexandra said. 'But we need to finish the report and send it along with the photos to Bratt at Crime Squad. Oh fuck!'

'What is it?'

'I just realised that Bratt is bound to ask me to run an express DNA analysis when she reads about that saliva or whatever it is. In which case I won't make it out on the town tonight.'

'Come on, you can say no, everyone needs time off, even you.'

Alexandra put her hands on her hips, tilted her head to one side and looked sternly at Helge.

'Right.' He sighed. 'Where would we be if everyone just took time off?'

# 4

# SATURDAY

## Rabbit hole

HARRY HOLE WOKE UP. THE bungalow lay in semi-darkness, but a white strip of sunlight, coming from under the bamboo blind, stretched across the coarse wooden floor, via the stone slab serving as a coffee table, and over to the kitchen worktop.

A cat was sitting there. One of Lucille's cats; she had so many of them up in the main house that Harry couldn't tell one from the other. The cat looked like it was smiling. Its tail was waving slowly as it calmly observed a mouse scuttling along the wall, stopping now and then to stick its snout in the air to sniff, before continuing. Towards the cat. Was the mouse blind? Did it lack a sense of smell? Had it eaten some of Harry's marijuana? Or did it believe, like so many others seeking happiness in this city, that it was different, special? Or that this *cat* was different, that it meant well and wouldn't just eat him?

Harry reached for the joint on the nightstand while keeping his eyes on the mouse, who was headed straight towards the cat. The cat struck, sinking its teeth into the mouse and lifting it up. It writhed a few moments in the predator's jaws before going limp. The cat laid its prey on the floor, then viewed it with its head cocked slightly to one side, as though undecided on whether to eat the mouse or not.

Harry lit up the joint. He had come to the conclusion that joints didn't count with regard to the new drinking regimen he had embarked upon. Inhaled. Watched the smoke curl upward to the ceiling. He had dreamt about the man behind the wheel of the Camaro again. And the number plate that read Baja California Mexico. The dream was the same, he was chasing them. So not exactly hard to interpret. Three weeks had passed since Harry had stood in the parking lot outside Creatures with a Glock 17 aimed at him, fairly certain his imminent demise was a second or two away. Which had been just fine by him. So it was strange that the only thing that had been in his head after those two seconds had elapsed, and every day since, was *not* to die. It had begun with the hesitation on the part of the man in the polo shirt; perhaps he was considering the possibility that Harry was a mental case, a manageable obstacle to be overcome, who didn't need shooting. He would hardly have had more time to think before Harry's chisel punch struck him in the throat and put him down for the count. Harry had physically felt the man's larynx give way. He had lain squirming on the gravel like a worm, his hands to his throat and eyes bulging while he gasped desperately for air. Harry had picked the Glock up off the ground and stared at the man in the car. Due to the tinted windows he hadn't seen much, only the outline of a face, and that the man looked to be wearing a white shirt buttoned right up to the neck. And that he was smoking a cigarette or a cigarillo. The man made no move, just looked calmly out at Harry, as though evaluating him, committing him to memory. Harry heard someone shout 'Get in!' and noticed Lucille had started her own car and pushed open the door on the passenger side.

Then he had jumped in. Down the rabbit hole.

The first thing he asked as she turned down towards lower ground and Sunset Boulevard, was who she owed money to and how much.

The first answer – 'The Esposito family' – didn't mean much to him, but the next – 'Nine hundred and sixty thousand dollars' – confirmed what the Glock had already told him. That she wasn't in a little trouble but a lot. And that from now on that trouble included him.

He explained that under no circumstances could she go back home, and asked if there was anyone whose place she could lay low at. She said, yes, she had a lot of friends in Los Angeles. But after thinking about it for a minute, she said none of them would be willing to run the risk for her. They stopped at a petrol station, and Lucille called her first husband, whom she knew had a house he hadn't used in several years.

And that was how they had ended up on this property, with its dilapidated house, overgrown garden and guest bungalow. Harry had installed himself in the bungalow with his newly acquired Glock 17 because from there he had a view of both gates, and because it was fitted with an alarm that went off should anyone break into the main house. Any prospective intruders wouldn't hear that alarm, meaning hopefully he could take them from the rear, given that he would be coming from the outside. Up until now, he and Lucille had hardly left the property, just short trips for the absolute essentials: alcohol, food, clothes and cosmetics – in that order. Lucille had taken up residence on the first floor of the main house, which after just a week was full of cats.

'Aw, in this town they're all homeless,' Lucille told him. 'You put some food out on the stoop a few days in a row, leave the front door open, some more food in the kitchen, and before you know it you've got enough pet friends for an entire lifetime.'

Yet not quite enough it seemed, because three days previously Lucille decided she couldn't endure the isolation any longer. She had taken Harry to a former Savile Row tailor she knew, to an elderly hairdresser in Rosewood Avenue and then – most important of all – to John Lobb's shoe store in Beverly Hills. Yesterday, Harry had picked up the suit while Lucille got ready, and a few hours later they had gone to eat at Dan Tana's, the legendary Italian restaurant where the chairs were as worn out as the clientele, but where Lucille seemed to know everybody and had beamed all evening.

It was seven o'clock. Harry inhaled and stared at the ceiling. Listened for sounds that shouldn't be there. But all he heard was the first cars on Doheny Drive, which was not the widest street, but popular because it had fewer traffic lights than the roads running parallel. It reminded him of lying in bed in his apartment in Oslo, listening to the sounds of the city waking outside the open window. He missed it, even the ill-tempered ringing and the shrill screech of a braking tram. *Particularly* the shrill screech.

But Oslo was behind him now. Following Rakel's death he had sat at the airport, looked at the departure board, and rolled a dice that determined his destination would be Los Angeles. He had figured it was as good as anywhere. He had lived in Chicago for a year while attending the FBI's course for serial homicides, and thought he was familiar with American culture and their way of life. But not long after arrival, he realised that Chicago and LA were two different planets. One of Lucille's movie friends, a German director, had described Los Angeles with bluster in a broad accent at Dan Tana's the night before.

'You land at LAX, the sun is shining and you're picked up by a limousine which drives you to a place where you lie down by a swimming pool, get a cocktail, fall asleep and wake up to discover that twenty years of your life have gone by.'

That was the director's LA.

Harry's introduction to LA had been four nights at a dirty, cockroach-infested motel room without air con in La Cienega, prior to his renting an even cheaper room in Laurel Canyon, also without air con, but with larger cockroaches. But he had settled in somewhat after discovering Creatures, the neighbourhood bar, where the liquor was cheap enough for him to deem it possible to drink himself to death.

But after staring down the barrel of a Glock 17 this desire to die had ceased. As had the drinking. That type of drinking at any rate. If he was to be capable of keeping watch and looking out for Lucille, he would have to be somewhat sober. He had, therefore, decided to test out the drinking regimen his childhood friend and drinking partner Øystein Eikeland had recommended, although frankly it sounded like bullshit. The method was called Moderation Management, and was supposed to turn you into a substance user, meaning a substance abuser who exercises moderation. The first time he had told Harry about it, the two of them had been sitting in Øystein's taxi at a rank in Oslo. His enthusiasm had been such that he had hammered on the steering wheel while proclaiming its virtues.

'People have always derided the alcoholic who swears that from now on he's only going to have a drink in social settings, right? Because they don't think that's possible, they're sure it isn't, almost as if you'd be defying the law of gravity for, like, alcoholism, yeah? But you know what? It is possible to drink to just the right level of drunkenness even for a full-blown alkie like you. And me. It's possible to programme yourself to drink to a certain point and stop. All you have to do is decide beforehand where to draw the line, how many units. But, it goes without saying, you have to work at it.'

'You have to drink a lot before you get the hang of it, you mean?'

'Yeah. You're smirking, Harry, but I'm serious. It's about that sense of achievement, of knowing that you can. And then it's possible. I'm not kidding, I can offer the world's best substance abuser as living proof.'

'Hm. I presume we're talking about that overrated guitarist you like so much.'

'Hey, have some respect for Keith Richards! Read his biography. He gives you the formula right there. Survival is about two things. Only the purest, best dope, it's the stuff mixed in with it that kills you. And moderation, in both drugs and alcohol. You know exactly how much you need to get sufficiently drunk, which in your case means pain-free. More liquor after doesn't help soothe the pain more, now does it?'

'Suppose not.'

'Exactly. Being drunk isn't the same as being an idiot or weak-willed. After all, you manage not to drink when you're sober, so why shouldn't you manage to stop when you're at just the right level. It's all in your head, brother!'

The rules – in addition to setting a limit – were to count the number of units and decide on set days where you abstained completely. As well as take a naltrexone an hour before your first drink. Putting off drinking for an hour when the thirst suddenly hit actually helped. He had kept to the regimen for three weeks now and had yet to crack. That was something in itself.

Harry swung his legs out of bed and stood up. He didn't need to open the fridge, he knew it was empty of beer. The Moderation Management rules specified a maximum of three units per day. That meant a six-pack from the 7-Eleven down the street. He looked in the mirror. He had actually put a little more meat on his lean bones in the three weeks since the escape from Creatures. As well as a grey, almost white, beard. It hid his most conspicuous feature, the liver-coloured scar. Whether that would be enough for the man in the Camaro not to recognise him again was doubtful, however. Harry peered out of the window towards the garden and the main house while he pulled on a ragged pair of jeans and a T-shirt starting to tear at the neckline reading 'Let Me Do One More illuminati hotties' on it. Put the old, non-wireless earphones in his ears, his feet in a pair of flip-flops and noted that nail fungus had created a grotesque artwork of sorts on the big toe of his right foot. He walked out into a tangle of grass, bushes and jacaranda trees. Stopped by the gate and looked up and down Doheny Drive. Everything seemed fine. He turned on the music, 'Pool Hopping' by illuminati hotties, a song that had lifted his spirits ever since he had heard it for the first time live at Zebulon Café. But after walking a few metres down the pavement, he caught sight of a car pulling away from the kerb in the wing mirror of one of the parked cars. Harry continued on, turning his head ever so slightly to check. The car was moving slowly behind at the same speed about ten metres back. While living in Laurel Canyon, he had been stopped twice by police cars simply because he was on foot and therefore deemed a suspicious individual. But this wasn't a police cruiser. It was an old Lincoln, and as far as Harry could make out only one person was in the car. A broad bulldog face, double chin, small moustache. Fuck, he should have taken the Glock! But Harry couldn't envision the attack happening in the middle of the street in broad daylight, so he continued walking. Turned off the music discreetly. Crossed the street just before Santa Monica Boulevard and entered the 7-Eleven. Stood and waited while scanning the street. But he didn't see the Lincoln anywhere. Maybe it had been a prospective house buyer cruising slowly along while checking out the properties on Doheny.

He made his way between the aisles towards the refrigerators with beer at the back of the premises. Heard the door open. Remained standing with one hand on the handle of the glass door, but without opening, so he could see the reflection. And there he was. In a cheap, check suit and a body to match his bulldog face: small, compact and fat. But fat in the way that might mask speed, strength and – Harry felt his heart beat faster – danger. Harry could see the man behind him hadn't drawn any weapon, not yet. He kept the earphones in, figuring he might have a chance if the man believed he had the element of surprise on his side.

'Mister . . .'

Harry pretended not to hear and watched the man approach and stop directly behind him. He was almost two heads shorter than Harry, and was now reaching out, maybe to tap Harry on the shoulder, maybe for something else entirely. Harry wasn't planning on waiting to find out what it was. He turned halfway towards the man, quickly threw an arm around his neck at the same time as he opened the glass door with his other hand. He twisted back while simultaneously kicking the man's feet from under him, causing him to fall into the shelves of beer. Harry released his hold on the man's neck and drove his own bodyweight against the glass door, squeezing the man's head against the shelves. The bottles toppled over, and the man's arms were pinned between the door and the jamb. The eyes in his bulldog face widened and he called out something from behind the door, his breath misting the cold glass on the inside. Harry eased up slightly so the man's head slipped down to the shelves below, then he pushed again. The edge of the refrigerator door pressed right against the man's throat and his eyes bulged. The man had stopped shouting. His eyes had stopped bulging. And the glass was no longer misting in front of his mouth.

Harry gradually eased off the pressure on the door. The man slid lifelessly onto the floor. He clearly wasn't breathing. Harry had to quickly assess priorities. The man's health weighed against his own. He chose his own and put his hand into the inside pocket of the fat man's check suit. Fished out a wallet. Opened it and saw a photo of the man on an ID card: a Polish-sounding name and – of more interest and in large letters at the top of the card – *Private Investigator Licensed by the California Bureau of Security and Investigative Services.*

Harry looked down at the lifeless man. This wasn't right, this wasn't how debt collectors operated. They might use a private detective to find him, but not to make contact or rough him up.

Harry flinched and ducked his head when he noticed a man standing between the shelves in the aisle. He was wearing a 7-Eleven T-shirt, and his arms were raised and pointing towards Harry. His hands gripped a revolver. He could see the man's knees were trembling and the muscles in his face twitching uncontrollably. And he also saw what the 7-Eleven man saw. A bearded guy, dressed like a homeless person, holding the wallet of a guy in a suit who he's obviously just assaulted.

'Don't . . .' Harry said, putting the wallet down, lifting both hands in the air and getting to his knees. 'I'm a regular here. This man—'

'I saw what you did!' the man said in a shrill voice. 'I shoot! The police is coming!'

'OK,' Harry said, and nodded down at the fat man. 'But let me help this guy, OK?'

'Move and I shoot!'

'But . . .' Harry began, but held back when he saw the revolver being cocked.

In the silence that followed only the humming of the fridge and the sirens in the distance could be heard. Police. Police and the unavoidable consequences that brought, of interrogations and charges, were not good. Not good at all. Harry had outstayed his welcome long ago and had no papers to prevent them throwing him out of the country. After they had thrown him into prison, of course.

Harry took a deep breath. Looked at the man. In the vast majority of countries he would have made a defensive retreat, in other words, got to his feet with his hands above his head and calmly walked out of there, secure in the knowledge that the individual wouldn't put a bullet in him, even though he appeared to be a violent thief. But this was not one of those countries.

'I shoot!' the man repeated, as though in response to Harry's deliberations, and moved his legs further apart. His knees had stopped trembling. The sirens were getting closer.

'Please, I must help . . .' Harry began, but his voice was drowned out by a sudden fit of coughing.

They stared down at the man on the floor.

The detective's eyes were bulging again, and his whole body shook from a continued bout of coughing.

The 7-Eleven man's pistol swung this way and that, unsure if the hitherto presumed dead man now also represented a danger.

'Sorry . . .' the detective whispered as he gasped for breath, '. . . for sneaking up on you like that. But you are Harry Hole, right?'

'Well.' Harry hesitated while considering which of the evils was lesser. 'Yes, I am.'

'I have a client who needs to get in touch with you.' The man, groaning, rolled onto his side, took a phone from his trouser pocket, tapped a key and held the phone out to Harry. 'They are eagerly awaiting our call.'

Harry took the already ringing phone. Placed it against his ear.

'Hello?' a voice said. Strangely, it sounded familiar.

'Hello,' Harry answered, glancing at the 7-Eleven man, who had lowered the revolver. Was Harry mistaken or did he look slightly more disappointed than relieved? Maybe he was born and raised here after all.

'Harry!' the voice on the phone exclaimed. 'How are you? This is Johan Krohn.'

Harry blinked. How long had it been since he had heard Norwegian?

# Credits

Vintage would like to thank everyone who worked on the publication of *The Night House*

**Translator (*The Night House*)**
Neil Smith

**Translator (*Killing Moon* extract)**
Seán Kinsella

**Agent**
Niclas Salomonsson

**Editor**
Katie Ellis-Brown
Liz Foley

**Editorial**
Sania Riaz
Kate Fogg

**Copy-editor**
Katherine Fry

**Proofreader**
Sarah Barlow

**Managing Editor**
Graeme Hall

**Production**
Konrad Kirkham
Polly Dorner

**Inventory**
Georgia Sibbitt

**Contracts**
Laura Forker
Gemma Avery
Ceri Cooper
Rebecca Smith
Toby Clyde
Anne Porter

**Digital**
Anna Baggaley
Claire Dolan

**Publicity**
Bethan Jones
Mia Quibell-Smith

**Operations**
Sophie Ramage

**Design**
Dan Mogford

**Illustrator**
Stephen Andrade

**Finance**
Ed Grande
Jerome Davies

**Marketing**
Sophie Painter
Carmella Lowkis

**Sales**
Nathaniel Breakwell
Malissa Mistry
Caitlin Knight
Rohan Hope
Christina Usher
Neil Green
Jessica Paul
Amanda Dean
Andy Taylor
David Atkinson
David Devaney
Helen Evans
Martin Myers
Phoebe Edwards
Richard Screech
Justin Ward-Turner
Amy Carruthers
Charlotte Owens

**Rights**
Jane Kirby
Lucy Beresford-Knox
Rachael Sharples
Beth Wood
Maddie Stephenson
Lucie Deacon
Agnes Watters

**Jo Nesbo** is one of the world's bestselling crime writers. When commissioned to write a memoir about life on the road with his band, Di Derre, he instead came up with the plot for his first Harry Hole crime novel, *The Bat*. His books *The Leopard, Phantom, Police, The Son, The Thirst, Macbeth* and *Knife* have all since topped the *Sunday Times* charts. He's an international number one bestseller and his books are published in 50 languages, selling over 55 million copies around the world.

Sign up to the Jo Nesbo newsletter for all the latest news: jonesbo.com/newsletter.

**Neil Smith** has translated many acclaimed Norwegian and Swedish novels, including books by Fredrik Backman and Leif G. W. Persson's *The Dying Detective*, winner of the CWA International Dagger 2017. He lives in Norfolk.